Advance praise for *Come Back for Me*:

Evocative and heart-wrenchingly beautiful, Come Back for Me *is a must read for anyone with a moral conscience and a soul.*

—Leah Kaminsky, winner of the Voss Literary Prize for her debut novel, *The Waiting Room*

This wonderful debut novel, with great sensitivity and tenderness, captures the emotional contours of loss and renewal that haunt the post-Holocaust universe ... a joy to read.

—Thane Rosenbaum, author of *The Golems of Gotham, Second Hand Smoke,* and *Elijah Visible*

Sharon Hart-Green writes passionately and intelligently about trauma, history, and the true meaning of home. This novel is poignant and compassionate, vividly evoked and deeply satisfying.

—Molly Antopol, author of *The UnAmericans* and lecturer at Stanford University

A gripping tale told from a place in the heart that is both broken and alive. Anyone who has ever lost something precious and human will follow Artur on his heartbreaking and hopeful journey.

—Ruchama Feuerman, author of *In the Courtyard of the Kabbalist* and *Seven Blessings*

Sharon Hart-Green writes with great generosity of heart and a searing sense of what it means to be buffeted by history.

—Jonathan Wilson, author of *A Palestine Affair* and professor of English at Tufts University

...a deeply affecting novel that explores unbearable loss and the possibility of starting again.

—Tova Mirvis, author of *Visible City* and *The Ladies Auxiliary*

With tenderness and clarity, Sharon Hart-Green's novel tells the story of how one generation transforms inherited trauma into a hopeful future ... a lovely debut.

—Amy Gottlieb, author of *The Beautiful Possible*

COME BACK FOR ME

Happy Birthday

Rhonda

Love

B B

2017

COME BACK FOR ME

A NOVEL by Sharon Hart-Green

NEW JEWISH PRESS

This edition published in 2017 by
New Jewish Press
Anne Tanenbaum Centre for Jewish Studies
University of Toronto
170 St. George Street, Room 218
Toronto, Ontario M5R 2M8
www.newjewishpress.ca

Cover and book design by Mark Goldstein

LIBRARY AND ARCHIVES CANADA CATALOGUING IN PUBLICATION

Hart-Green, Sharon, 1954–, author
    Come back for me/a novel by Sharon Hart-Green.

Issued in print and electronic formats.
ISBN 978-1-988326-06-1 (softcover). — ISBN 978-1-988326-07-8 (HTML)

    I. Title.

PS8615.A773669C66 2017   C813'.6   C2017-901146-4
                                                 C2017-901147-2

MIX
Paper from
responsible sources
FSC® C004191

PRINTED IN CANADA

In memory of my beloved parents, Paul and Bess Mintz (z"l)
always with me
always coming back

even in the burned forest the bird
has come back to sing.

Abba Kovner, "What's Not in the Heart"

1

Suzy Kohn
Toronto, Ontario
August 1968

After Uncle Charles died, a deep chasm opened up in the family that threatened to swallow us whole. My mother, whose resolute cheerfulness had sustained us like a weight-bearing wall, was now oddly preoccupied, even glum. And my father, whose thirst for lively conversation once seemed insatiable, had become withdrawn, impatient, and short-tempered. But it was Aunt Bella who changed the most—to the point that I barely recognized her anymore. Bella had always been slightly moody and prone to emotional flare-ups. But when her husband Charles died, she retreated into a world of her own. As if she had entered a room with no exit.

Uncle Charles was only thirty-nine when he died. But as long as I can remember, I thought of him as old. Perhaps it was the way he pulled back his shoulders too far like he was standing at attention. Or maybe it was his European attire—polished onyx cufflinks, embroidered handkerchiefs, and cravats bound so tightly around his neck that they made his head look as though it were detached from his body. His death occurred in the middle of the summer, while my sisters and I were away at overnight camp in Quebec: I was working as a counsellor and they were there as campers. My parents didn't mention Charles' death in any of their letters to us. Perhaps they thought it would spoil our summer. Yet how could they not tell us? After all, Charles and Bella lived next door and were almost like second parents to me and my two younger sisters, Julia and Jan. I was particularly steamed about it. At seventeen, I was the oldest child in the family and surely should have been told.

When we returned to Toronto in late August, Father gathered us together around the dining room table that evening to make the announcement. Uncle Charles, he said, had suffered a massive heart attack and died shortly thereafter. It had been too late to save him. There was nothing anyone could have done.

Aunt Bella, who was visiting at the time, suddenly cut in. "It's all my fault," she cried as she paced around the room, weeping into her sleeve. Though Bella was my father's sister, it was Mother who rushed to console her.

"Don't be foolish, Bella. You can't blame yourself. You know that Charles had been ill for some time."

"You don't understand. It's still my doing."

"Bella. That's enough. There are children here. Let's leave this for another time." My jaw tightened. Why was Mother scolding Bella? Couldn't she see that she was still in shock? Bella was only thirty-eight, far too young to be a widow. I rushed to my aunt's side and put my arm around her hunched shoulders, rubbing my cheek against her damp brown hair. If Mother refused to comfort her, then I would.

Besides, I was still incensed that by not telling me about Charles' death until the end of the summer, my parents had excluded me from both the funeral and the *shiva*. Didn't anyone realize that losing Uncle Charles was a blow to me as well?

After her sobbing subsided, I helped Bella gather her belongings and escorted her next door. I offered to come in, but she murmured something about being able to take care of herself. Closing the wood-framed screen door, I crossed the lawn and returned to our house, which was almost a carbon copy of Bella's: a mock-Tudor built of russet-brown bricks with a steep dormer roof and a lone red maple set onto a narrow plot of patchy grass. Since it was a mild night, I sat down on the porch step and pulled a pack of cigarettes out of my pocket. My parents disapproved of my smoking so I knew not to go inside. I didn't care. I was in no mood to talk to them anyway. I lit up and exhaled into the cool night air. The combination of the tobacco and the late August breeze helped soothe my blazing head.

I couldn't believe that Uncle Charles was gone. He was still so vivid in my mind. As I recalled his bashful smile hidden beneath his finely groomed moustache, a rush of tears began streaming down my cheeks. Most people didn't realize how gentle he had been. I knew him in a way that was different from how others saw him. Like the way he persisted in calling me Zsu-Zsu, a childhood nickname that everyone else had dropped in favour of Suzy. And the way he liked to quiz me on what I'd learned in Hebrew school when I was younger, playfully trying to trick me by mispronouncing the words. I also remembered how he brought home gifts for my sisters and me after being away on business trips—paper-dolls, bat-a-ball sets, and later, coloured pencils and mystery novels. He never made a show of his gift-giving. He waved away our thanks as if it offended him to hear them. But you could see by the tiny glint in his cloud-grey eyes that it gave him pleasure. Since he and Bella were never able to have kids of their own, all their affection was poured onto us. And I secretly knew that, being the oldest, I was their favourite.

I spent a lot of time at their home when I was younger. During my visits, Bella did most of the talking. In her throaty voice that still bore traces of European diction, she regaled us with story after story, popping open new ones like bottles of champagne. She often recounted tales of her childhood in Budapest, where she and my father had spent their earliest years, before escaping with their parents to Canada in early '44, just as the Nazis were about to invade.

Unlike Bella, however, Uncle Charles never spoke about his European childhood. Except for once. I was twelve years old, standing in the kitchen pouring a glass of milk, my unruly hair pulled off my forehead by a thick plastic hairband. I was humming a tune I'd heard on the radio when Uncle Charles walked in, then stopped abruptly.

"Manya," he said, his voice choked.

"Who?" I asked.

Squeezing his eyes shut, Uncle Charles shook his head rapidly. "Nothing. It's nothing—just someone I used to know—when I was a child." His lips tightened and his eyes turned to stone; I knew not to ask anything further. Years earlier, I once heard Mother mention that Charles had arrived in Canada just after the war with no family, no money, and no belongings. It didn't make sense to me then. But at age twelve, I glimpsed it briefly in the hollows of his eyes: he was a man whose past had died, along with everyone else who'd been part of it.

———

All of a sudden, a voice bellowed, "Suzy, what's that smell out there? Is that smoke?" It was Father, hovering on the inside of the screen door like a shadow.

"It's nothing," I said, wiping my wet cheeks with the back of my wrist. I flung my cigarette on the ground. Who cared? I had just lit a third one and the nicotine tasted putrid anyhow.

"Why are you sitting alone in the dark?" Father asked.

"Can't I have any privacy? Why does everyone treat me like a child?"

Hearing my father's footsteps recede, I pulled another cigarette from the pack. But before I could flick the match to light it, the sudden shriek of an ambulance siren made me jump up and drop the pack on the ground. The sound grew so loud that I ran to the side of the road to see if it was coming this way. To my surprise, it was speeding down my street—sirens howling, lights flashing—and screeched to a stop directly in front of Bella's house. Two medics jumped out and dashed toward Bella's front door.

No. Dear God. Don't let this happen. I can't lose Bella too.

2

Artur Mandelkorn
Szegda, Hungary
May 1944

I was only fourteen when the Germans came to our town and started rounding up the Jews. It is hard to describe the terror it caused. Mama's ruddy cheeks turned ashen when she heard that all the Jews in a nearby village had been taken away. When I asked her about it, she clutched the sides of her head and cried, "The world has gone mad, Artur. I never thought it could happen here."

We lived in a German-speaking area not far from the city of Szombathley. Our town was just inside the Hungarian border with Austria, so we had been spared until 1944. But we knew about the atrocities being committed elsewhere. Such things could not be concealed for long. When they came to our town, we knew that this was the end for us.

My parents had a friend, an elderly Hungarian bachelor who made clocks for a living and had taught Papa to mend pocket-watches as a boy. He agreed to hide all six of us—my parents, my three siblings, and me—in his cellar. As I lay on the cold mud floor, I could hear the sound of his clocks ticking at different intervals all night long. It was horrible. Like fate ticking inside my ears. However, when the clock-maker's sister found out that he was hiding us, they had a terrible row and she threatened to inform the Germans—which meant we were forced to leave at nightfall the next day.

But I refused to go into hiding again. I was sure that I'd be trapped, that I would never get out. That I'd never get that ticking clock out of my brain. My sister Manya said she knew of an abandoned house with a broken chimney close to some farms. She and her friends called it the "sunken ship," imagining that it looked like an old pirate ship moored in the fields. Manya and I tried to convince Mama and Papa that hiding there was our best hope. From there, we argued, we could head eastward, away from the German offensive.

I couldn't tell what Mama was thinking. Her eyes started blinking rapidly and she shook her head from side to side like a madwoman. Lurching forward she clutched us by the shoulders and whispered in Yiddish, "You go, children. Run. Get away. As far as you can go. But you must escape without us—my lungs are weak and Papa's feet are bad. And we have a baby to tend to. We would only slow you down. You must run."

But my older brother, Karl, tried to talk us out of it, arguing that it was better to stay near the town, where there was a chance that someone would hide us. At least then we would be assured of food. With his practical turn of mind, he was sure that we would starve if we had no one to provide for us. Karl was like an old man in that way. He was only eleven months older than me, but his thinking was old.

In the end, Manya and I agreed to go off together, though I was only a boy of fourteen, and she was two years younger. Karl insisted on staying with my parents and my baby sister, Kati. They planned to seek shelter with a family they knew who owned a small goat farm not far from town.

When we said our hasty good-byes, Mama's face was blotched

and streaked with tears, while Papa tightened his lips in an effort to seem brave. Departing from them quickly, I tried to ignore the thick lump forming in my throat. After all, we promised that we'd see each other soon, perhaps in a few weeks, when all of this madness would surely have passed.

As Manya and I tried to make our way to the "sunken ship," it was pouring rain, sharp and fierce, like spears being hurled from the sky by an angry war-god. We didn't use the streets but stuck to the back alleyways. I couldn't help thinking that I had recently played in those alleys in such a carefree way, and here I was running down those same paths like a hunted animal. The alleys opened onto a huge field, which in the dark looked like a big black void. We ran and ran across it, not knowing where we were going. When we got to the edge of the field, however, we couldn't find the "sunken ship" or anything else that looked familiar. We realized that we must have run the wrong way.

After moving around for half the night, we at last found shelter in a barn and tried to warm ourselves under a pile of straw. Suddenly we overheard a voice outside. It sounded close and we realized that it must be the farmer talking to a farmhand, or perhaps to one of his sons. "Those bloody Germans," he rasped. "Stealing everything they can get their hands on. They're storing their loot in the shack down the road."

"Which one?"

"The empty one. With the broken chimney."

Shivers raced down my spine as I realized how lucky we were that we hadn't found the "sunken ship." We would have walked straight into the arms of the Germans.

I can't say how many barns we slept in after that night. We never stayed in any of them more than one night because we didn't want to risk being discovered in the light of day. Since the farmers got up at dawn, we developed a kind of sixth sense and trained ourselves to rise before the rooster crowed. It became like a game for us—how far could we get before we heard the rooster start his cock-a-doodle-doo. We stuck to the back roads, but mostly cut through fields, searching for bits of grain to eat. Sometimes we'd even "borrow" an egg from a hen's nest and eat it raw. To us, that was a feast.

Manya never complained, no matter how hungry or tired she was. She had never been much of a talker, but she loved music and could sing any tune that she heard even once. She had a lovely voice for a child—sweet and full at the same time. People in our town used to call her "the lark." She could sing songs in Hungarian, German, Polish, and Yiddish. I even think that she knew some songs in Czech.

When Manya and I were younger, we were constantly together—collecting chestnuts, playing *kendö*, and inventing our own board games using pebbles, twigs, and bark. In summer, we would trap insects in jars so that we could study them up close, and sometimes I sketched pictures of them in a special notebook that Papa had brought me back from Budapest. But Manya couldn't bear to see the insects banging up against the sides of the jar and always insisted on releasing them. I would be angry with her for a while, but it never lasted long.

A frightful incident occurred in the final winter before the Nazi invasion, which brought me even closer to Manya. The two of us were skating on a snow-covered pond when the ice cracked beneath me and I plunged into the freezing water. Screaming for help, I clutched at some chunks of ice on the surface, as my legs grew heavier and pulled me downward. If it hadn't been for Manya, I would have surely frozen to death. She threw me her muffler and somehow managed to drag me out. I have never understood how she found the strength to pull me from the icy water. When I asked her about it later, she just bit her bottom lip and shook her head slowly. "I had to save you," she said. "That's all I know."

After weeks of sleeping in one barn after another, my hopes began to sink. I started thinking that it was only a matter of time before we would be discovered. Just as I was about to give up all hope, we came upon a town nestled in the bottom of a valley. In the evening light, its darkened shops and empty sidewalks looked unreal, like a stage set. We had no idea if it was safe, but we were desperate for food and decided to take a chance and make our approach. Spotting a small inn that was set back from the centre of town, we advanced with caution. The inn was bordered by a field of barley, whose stalks seemed to beckon us toward them as they arched and tilted in the wind. Hiding ourselves among the stalks, we watched an apron-clad woman sitting on the front steps of the inn, peeling potatoes into a bowl; she seemed to take little notice of the random peels that fell onto the ground.

Those potato peels were like gold to us. As soon as the woman went inside, we dashed toward them. But before we could reach them, a thick hand reached down and grabbed me from behind by the collar. I shouted for Manya to run, but instead she tore at the dense fingers of the burly man who was holding me, trying to loosen his grip. But to no avail. Before we knew it, he was dragging both of us by our collars into the inn, telling us to quiet down or he'd beat us with a brush.

We were hauled into a kitchen that was so full of steam we could hardly see. Inside, the man pushed us down into rough wooden chairs, banged a loaf of bread onto the table, and roared, "Eat! Eat! Quickly, before the rats get it first!" At that, he threw back his broad chin, revealing a large pink mole buried in the fat of his neck, and laughed so hard that the whole room shook. While we shoved hunks of bread into our mouths, the man told us that his name was Ferko and that he was the owner of the inn. That took me by surprise. With his ox-like shoulders, turnip nose, and cheeks rutted with pockmarks, he looked more like a farmhand than the proprietor of an inn. He pointed a thick finger at the woman we'd seen peeling potatoes on the steps. "That's my wife, Ana. She's the boss. She can read and do arithmetic. Not like me," he chuckled, smacking his wide belly. "I'm as dumb as a tree stump!"

Ana could not have been more different from her husband. Diminutive in height and thin as a spindle, her bony shoulders seemed barely able to support the apron that sagged from her yellow-veined neck. She brought us cocoa from the stove and hardly raised her eyes as Ferko began his swift interrogation. Poking his chin close to our faces, he lowered his voice to a bare whisper. "So what are you two street-urchins doing in this town? Are you Jews? Don't answer that. I don't want to know. But if you ask me—and nobody *is* asking me right now—I would say that you are good Catholic children separated from your parents, who—what? Got wounded in some crossfire? Killed? Maimed? What do you think?"

I started to nod in agreement, not sure whether he was asking or telling. Meanwhile, Manya opened her bag and removed an object that, until that moment, I hadn't known she had with her. It was a toy hurdy-gurdy that had belonged to our brother, Karl; he had given it to Manya when he was too old to play with it. She set it down on the table and announced in her small deep voice, "No. We're not orphans. We're musicians. Our parents are waiting for us in Budapest, but we've lost our papers. Would you care to hear a song?" Manya cranked the handle of the hurdy-gurdy and began to sing an odd little folksong in Hungarian about a bird and a worm—one of those riddle songs that made no sense at the end. When the innkeeper's wife heard it, she put her hands over her mouth and stood transfixed. She looked at her husband and said, "It is an angel's song." Crossing herself, she rushed toward us as if we were the heavenly host coming to offer her comfort, hope, resurrection.

I wanted to run, to escape the woman's luminous eyes. At that moment I was more afraid for my soul than I was for my body. But

Manya, dear patient Manya, stood there calmly and held the woman's hands in hers. They didn't exchange any words, yet I knew at that moment that we were safe—and that we would be staying with them for quite some time.

Manya and I soon became the children of Ferko and Ana Papp. Not literally, of course, but in every other way. They told people that we were their family—the children of Ana's sister who died young. No one questioned it. And why should they? Ana and Ferko loved us like their own. We *were* their own.

We lived and worked at the inn, helping out with the chores. I hauled crates of brandy, chopped wood, learned to fish and shoot rabbits. Ferko even taught me how to drive a truck. I also became a good Catholic, and went to mass on Sundays like a dutiful son of the church. Manya helped Ana in the kitchen and sang in the church choir. Since Ana was unable to have children of her own, she seemed to believe that Jesus had sent us to her to help absolve her of her sins.

My mind, however, was in a constant state of turmoil. There were times when I truly felt that I was who I was pretending to be. But most of the time, I knew I was just play-acting. Sometimes I even got pleasure from how clever I was at it. Ferko and Ana never asked any further questions about us, and we never spoke of our past. I assumed they believed Manya's story that we had been on our way to our parents in Budapest. To me, the fact that Ferko and Ana never raised any questions about our past or about finding our parents, was merely a sign of how much they cared for us. Oftentimes Ferko would playfully grab my chin and declare, "You bring me luck, Artur—just like a son." I would be proud for a moment. But then the thought of my own father would cause a dull ache to form in my throat and travel to the pit of my stomach where it settled like a stone.

Manya seemed to possess the innate ability to survive more peaceably than me, perhaps because she had the imagination to do so. It was not that she had forgotten about our parents. On the contrary, almost every time we were alone she would tell me that she knew for certain they were safe, and that they were surely searching for us at that very moment. I was never so certain. Being older than Manya, or perhaps because of my own melancholic nature that I tried for years to overcome, I saw most things in their bleakest light.

It was an unexpected letter that brought an end to our days of relative tranquility with the Papps. One morning in late October, Ferko woke us early before the mist had risen from the fields. It was so dark in the room that I could barely make out his wide pockmarked face. But I could hear the urgency in his strained whisper—telling us to make haste and pack our things. "We must leave. Right now. All four of us. Quickly. Quickly. Time will not be kind to us."

Once we were on the road, Ferko explained that Ana had received a letter the day before from a friend who was arriving that day from Ana's hometown in Bohemia. "You see, Artur," he said, his face dripping with sweat, "her friend knows that Ana has no sisters or brothers."

I must have looked confused. "Donkey-head!" he cried. "She would know right away that you could not be Ana's niece and nephew." My head was spinning. Although the Germans had already liquidated the town of its Jews, they were still on the lookout for hidden Jews or those who secretly possessed Jewish blood. For the most part, they relied on local spies who traded information about suspected Jews in return for bushels of straw, wheat, or cabbage. Suddenly it all became clear: Ferko had known all along that we were Jews. Not only were our lives in danger, but theirs too if they were discovered sheltering Jewish children.

When we arrived at the train station at the edge of the town, it was empty except for a bald pointy-headed man selling tickets behind a screen. He seemed to be well acquainted with Ferko and jokingly asked him questions about where we were "fleeing" to so early in the morning. Ferko invented something about a distant relative in Debrecen, a will, and a lawyer's letter, hinting that he was about to receive a large inheritance. The ticket man bowed down to him in jest and the two men chortled over Ferko's impending fortune.

We boarded the train but we never made it to Debrecen. At one of the stops along the way, Ferko hustled us all off. We found ourselves in a small village where there were more cows and goats on the platform than people. Ana bought some black cherries from a young peddler and we sat on a bench and ate them from the basket. From there, we took a train travelling south. After we had gone some distance, the train came to a halt at a crossroad. Ferko peered out the window to see what was happening and his expression stiffened. Following the line of his gaze, I saw two German soldiers board the train. "Don't say a word," Ferko whispered. "Even if they question you directly. I will take care of everything."

When one of the soldiers reached our seats, Ferko hung his head, pushed out his bottom lip, and spoke in a strange broken German that I could only partly understand. He mumbled and rolled his eyes in such a peculiar way that I thought he was losing his mind until I realized he was pretending to be some kind of simpleton. "Take a look at that dumb lump," chortled the soldier. He started to pass us by, but the second soldier, who had a nose like a sow, stopped in front of us and snapped, "Papers. Now."

Ferko made a big show of rifling through his pockets, producing a set of keys, remnants of food, and assorted documents. The soldier grabbed some papers from the pile, squinted at them, and after a brief grunt of approval, snarled, "And the children? Where are their papers?" Shrugging his shoulders, Ferko stuck his tongue in his cheek, "Children? They lose everything. They even lose me sometimes," and guffawed at his own joke. The soldier's face hardened. Drawing in his breath, he snapped, "Off the train. The four of you. *Schnell.*"

We were herded into the back of an enormous truck along with a group of others who'd been pulled off the train. Manya clung to me as we found a spot to crouch in a corner. As soon as the truck began to move, a man began to howl uncontrollably, spittle gushing from his nose and mouth. He then soiled himself, causing a terrible stench to spread through the enclosed compartment. When the soldiers stopped the truck, they pulled him out and shot him on the spot, just like that, as if they were shooting a rat or a squirrel. Hearing the shots, Manya gripped my arm so tightly that it became numb. Despite my own trembling knees and the nausea rising in my throat, I knew I had to stay strong for her sake.

We finally arrived at our first destination: a tar-covered warehouse that had been turned into some kind of German holding station. There we slept on a damp concrete floor that smelled of urine. The next day we were forced to march to another tar–encrusted building near the city of Komló where a thousand others like us were being held with barely any food or water. Once a day we lined up for a cup of thin broth that tasted like quinine. But the nights were the hardest—the constant sounds of people moaning filled my ears from dusk to dawn. I tried to fall asleep by pretending I was hearing the familiar sound of mooing cows outside my window at Ferko's inn. Or the hooting of barn owls in the forest that bordered the town. But nothing helped.

Manya and I were separated and put into different sections. I had never felt so alone; it made my stomach ache in a way that was worse than hunger. What is more, Ferko had disappeared. I eventually heard rumours that he had been put in a unit reserved for suspected spies and was beaten daily by guards who made bets on who could draw the most blood.

Somehow Manya devised a way to secretly send me a note that was passed along through several hands. Although it was written in rounded juvenile script, her words were anything but childish. Ana was with her, she wrote, but was in a terrible state—a kind of delirium—and could not swallow any food or drink. She was afraid that the guards would kill her if they found her that way, so Manya was trying to conceal Ana's condition from them.

The following day we were ordered to line up outside with our possessions because, we were told, we were being transferred to a work facility. Those who were unable to do heavy labour would be left behind and sent to another holding station. From a distance, I saw Manya clasping Ana's elbow and carefully guiding her like a nurse leading a blind woman. All of a sudden, from out of the crowd, there came a piercing scream followed by cackling laughter. It was Ana shrieking, "The gates of heaven are closing! Open the gates!"

Instantly, there was a deafening round of gunfire and people were running in every direction. I hurled myself onto the ground and pitched my forehead into the gravel. Out of nowhere, I felt a small body trembling beside my own; when I opened my eyes I found Manya on the ground beside me, clutching the end of my shirt in her fist. How Manya had managed to find me in the midst of that chaos I couldn't fathom. She was shaking so badly that I had to use all my strength to hold her down until the shooting subsided. She kept rolling her head back and forth, mumbling, "She's dead, she's dead."

Finally the bullets stopped and we were ordered to get up. Manya had blood on her hair and neck.

"Manya," I whispered, anxiety gripping my throat, "Are you hurt?"

"No," she said, her voice quivering. "It's Ana's—" I understood right away. Ana had been shot and it was her blood that sprayed onto Manya.

The guards surrounded us, cursing and shouting at us to be quiet or they would shoot us all. Seconds later, a hulking commander caught sight of Manya and snapped, "Wounded—unfit." He ordered her to move out of the line.

"You can't take her!" I screamed. "It's not her blood!"

The commander laughed and snorted, "All 'Jew-blood' is the same." Dragging Manya from the line, he thrust her into a crowd of people who were also deemed unfit—old men, pregnant women, and swarms of wailing children. I started to run after her, but one of the guards threw me on the ground and kicked me in the legs like a dog. As the group began marching, the guard shoved me back into the line-up with the sharp end of his rifle.

Suddenly from a distance, I heard Manya calling, her voice pleading, "Come back for me!"

Her cheeks were flaming and streaked with tears, while her hands grasped the air as if it could save her.

"I'll come back," I cried, as we marched out of the gates. "I promise!" Struggling to look back, I could still see Manya's thin arms reaching out to me, flailing against the darkness of the autumn sky.

3

Suzy Kohn
Toronto, Ontario
September 1968

I think I missed Aunt Bella almost more than Uncle Charles. Ever since she'd been rushed to the hospital that night, imagining that she was having a heart attack, she was like a balloon with the air squeezed out of it.

I preferred to remember the old Bella. The way she used to be. Witty, vivacious, immaculately dressed. Far more worldly than most of the other adults I knew. With her flashing blue eyes, trim figure, and sleek mane of light-brown hair, she used to take pride in the fact that people would mistake her for my sister. But that was then. Looking at her now, it was hard to believe that she was still the same person. Whenever I visited, her eyes looked sunken, her blouse was half-undone, and her hair that was usually rolled and swept to the side "French style" now fell limply to her shoulders, its texture resembling the coarse beige wadding found in old upholstery.

To me, Bella had been more than just my aunt. She was the antidote to everything ordinary. Known for her skill as an embroiderer of fine fabrics based on her ingenious use of beads and pearls, Bella had acquired a following of clients who sought her ornamental beadwork for their evening clothes, linens, and tapestries. Once she was even hired by the National Ballet to embroider a costume for its prima ballerina. Whenever I visited, her dining room table was piled high with skeins of silk threads and bins of glittering ornaments. I loved to watch as she sewed her beads in patterns that were completely original and unexpected: a pear tree in a silver orchard; humming birds shimmering beneath the moon; a mermaid flourishing a peacock's tail.

When I was growing up, Bella often took me along on her monthly "excursions" to escape from the suburbs to downtown Toronto. We frequently started our days at the Isaacs Gallery on Yonge Street or the Hart House Theatre at the University of Toronto, and ended up at the Windsor Arms hotel where we'd sit among the potted palms and order root beer floats in tall iced glasses. On some of our trips downtown, we'd go nowhere in particular. We'd just stroll along Bloor Street or explore the jagged lanes between Cumberland and Scollard, peering into the iron-grated windows, imagining we were in Paris or Rome. Bella didn't have to imagine too hard. With her penchant for long silk scarves tossed over one shoulder, she was already attired for the mist-enchanted Europe of our dreams.

After Bella was released from the hospital with an official diagnosis of dysautonomia, or "nervous collapse," I went to see her every day after school. On my first visit, I thought that if I were cheerful and upbeat, my mood would rub off on her. As soon as I walked into her house, I pasted a wide smile on my lips.

"What are you so happy about?" she muttered.

"Nothing."

"Well, stop it then. It's aggravating."

I should have known that Bella would see right through me. Despite her condition, she was still as sharp as a tack. After a few failed attempts at conversation, I asked Bella if she needed anything.

"All I need is sleep," she said as she stumbled toward the stairs leading up to the bedroom.

"What if some of your clients call? What should I say?"

"Tell them to stop bothering me. I want to be left alone."

I took that as my cue to leave. I figured that when I returned the next afternoon, I had better be prepared for the same treatment. The Bella I'd known was far away. And I doubted that she'd return any time soon.

My final year of high school felt different from the years that preceded it. It wasn't just the departmental exams and the prospect of university applications. It was something else entirely. There was a heady sense of rebellion in the air. And a hankering for change that seemed to affect everyone, even the most socially inept students. Despite being Canadian, we were all feeling outraged by the senseless war in Vietnam and the assassination of civil rights heroes such as John F. Kennedy and Martin Luther King. Not to mention the latest blow—the murder of Bobby Kennedy. When the news hit the school that day in June, several girls ran through the halls weeping and tearing at their clothing as if he were one of our own.

Everything that mattered to the graduating class only a year or two earlier was now hardly discussed—prom dates, football playoffs, Varsity letters, making the Honour Roll. If they were mentioned at all, it was said with a sneer, as if only the most pathetic among us could take them seriously. At best, we regarded them as a joke. What really mattered to us was what our young history teacher with scraggly sideburns called "social consciousness"—opposing racial inequality, capitalist exploitation, and the bourgeois rules of privilege and power.

The most admired student advocate of social change at my school was Ned Finberg, known to everyone as Fin. With long black curls and eyes like sapphires, he looked like a cross between Bob Dylan and Rasputin. More than anything, it was his voice that won everyone over—especially the girls. Accompanying himself on guitar, he could sing anything—folk, jazz, ballad, rock and roll—and make it sound as if he'd invented it. During lunch hour, a bunch of us began to gather around him at a park not far from the school. Sitting cross-legged on the grass with our eyes half-closed, we swayed to the sweet sound of his voice singing earnest renderings of protest songs, spirituals, and freight-train blues. It was mesmerizing. As far as I was concerned, there was no one who embodied justice and equality more than Fin.

I never thought that Fin took much notice of me until one day in the park he came over to me and said that he liked my "aura." I must have looked confused, for he began to elaborate. "You have an essence that radiates from you," he asserted with calm authority. "It's a sign that you are a very giving person."

I could feel the heat rising into my cheeks. "I've never been told that before."

"Well, now you have." He looked me in the eye, as if waiting for a response. Not knowing what to say, I looked down. And before I knew it, he turned and walked off in the opposite direction, his bare feet padding lightly on the grass.

My heart was beating wildly. I had no idea what to make of that strange encounter. Was Fin expressing interest in me? Or was he merely being friendly? I knew that I shouldn't get too excited about it, but I couldn't help thinking about him for the rest of the day. His penetrating eyes. His mellow voice that resonated slightly when he spoke. Like a deep purr.

Yet why would he choose me? I was considered to be one of the quieter, more studious girls at my high school. Besides, I didn't have the blond hair–blue-eyes–button-nose combination that made for instant popularity. It's true that people often said that I was pretty. But wavy brown hair, olive skin, and grey-green eyes were not what attracted most of the boys that I knew. I felt as if Fin had plucked me out of a random bunch of fruit and, for some strange reason, placed me on the top of the pile. I must admit that being elevated to the top was kind of nice. In fact, I relished the change. It wasn't every day that the most desirable boy at school decided to single me out for attention. The question remained: would it ever happen again?

4

Artur Mandelkorn
Baranya County, Hungary
November 1944

We marched for an entire day until we came to a forced labour camp where we were shoved into barracks with a hundred other men and given no food to speak of. That night, I could barely sleep because of the hunger gnawing at my empty stomach like an angry beast. I reached for my backpack, hoping to find a scrap of food inside, only to discover that it wasn't my pack at all—it was Manya's. I must have grabbed it by mistake in the chaos after the shooting. I desperately tore it open and dug through its contents in the hope of finding some small morsel to eat. But no such luck. Manya's pack was mostly filled with odds and ends such as a hairbrush and a pair of wool stockings. But among them I found something else—the small hurdy-gurdy that my sister loved so dearly. Somehow the sight of that toy tore me up inside. I cried for the first time since we'd left our parents and I couldn't stop. The only thing that helped calm me down was the idea of hiding the hurdy-gurdy to keep it safe. Spying some loose floorboards beneath my bunk I pried them open and wedged the hurdy-gurdy into the space below. After doing that, I made a silent vow: somehow, I would escape and rescue Manya, even if it meant risking my life to find her.

During those long months at the labour camp, my job was to shovel coal into large storage bins that were then loaded onto trucks. The men who drove the trucks were Hungarian youths recruited by the Germans from the surrounding villages. One day, one of these drivers pulled me aside and told me to load some of the coal into a separate bin while he stood watch down the hill from the truck. I figured he was trying to steal some of the coal for himself. I started to do what he asked but before either of us realized what was happening, the truck started rolling backward and ran right over him. I rushed over to where the truck had stopped and with all my strength, I managed to drag the young man out from underneath. It was immediately clear that he was dead—his head had been crushed so badly by the truck's enormous wheels that his face was unrecognizable.

In that gruesome moment I saw my opportunity. I stripped off his clothes and quickly exchanged them for my own prison garb; I then leapt behind the wheel of his vehicle, and drove toward the camp gate. As I neared it though, I noticed that the front of my newly acquired jacket was smeared with blood. I had no choice but to stop the truck just long enough to tear off the jacket and turn it inside out. In the process, something fell out of its pocket—an identification card. My passport to freedom! I clung to that piece of paper as a dying man clings to his last breath.

Making it past the guard at the gate was the easy part—I simply flashed the card in his direction, and he waved me through the exit line without flinching. However, finding my way back to Manya was the problem, as I had no idea which way to go. I didn't even know if Manya was still at the holding station. Most likely she'd already been taken somewhere else. All I knew was that I had to somehow find my way back to Komló, the city closest to where Manya had been when we were torn apart. Perhaps there I could find out where she and the others had been sent.

I drove for about an hour until I reached a village and asked for directions. My accent was good enough that I could pass as a Hungarian gentile. And it didn't hurt that I was fair-haired and had a straight nose, features that weren't identifiably Jewish.

As it turned out, I had gone in the wrong direction. I was forced to turn around and drive for a full day until I finally reached the vicinity of Komló. I knew that I couldn't approach the holding station during daylight, so I waited until dark and drove to the edge of town, where I remembered the buildings had been. I say *had been* because when I got there, the buildings were gone. Vanished. As if they never existed. My first thought was that I had gotten my directions mixed up once again and was in the wrong place. But no—it *was* the place! I recognized the row of linden trees standing just outside the fence. How could this be? How could the buildings just disappear?

I drove like a crazy man back to the nearest village to find someone to ask. Someone must know about that place. I didn't care if I aroused suspicion. I had to find out. I first asked a young couple on the road, but they said that they weren't from around there. Travelling further, I came upon a skew-eyed woman wearing a faded kerchief and boots tied up to her knees. She was standing in front of a low stone hut, calling her dogs inside. I went over to her and asked, "There were buildings, at the edge of town, near the linden trees. Do you know them?"

"Know them?" she said, moving her teeth from side to side. "The smell lasted for weeks. People from outside must think we live in a dung-pit."

"Smell? I don't understand."

Jabbing her chin close to my ear, she muttered, "It was from the Jews, of course. They burned them all. Locked them inside and set the whole place on fire. We needed that site cleared anyway. Those buildings were supposed to be torn down years ago. The Germans just wanted it done fast." She laughed, then spit to one side.

I froze. "When—when did this happen?" I asked, trying to control the tremour in my voice.

"Oh, not long ago," she said pulling the ends of her kerchief tightly around her neck. "Last week sometime."

A wave of relief swept through me. Manya could not have been there. We had been separated months ago. The guards themselves had said they were shipping off the rest of them, those they considered unfit. She must be far away by now. Poland is where they sent Jews. Yes, I reassured myself, she must be in Poland.

I jumped into the truck and started driving, not knowing where I was heading, or even caring. All I knew was that Manya was still alive. This I was certain of. And she was waiting for me, waiting for me to come back. As I promised. As I vowed to myself I would do.

By early '45, there were rumours flying that Hitler was finished for good. Jews were still being rounded up, but more often than not they were being shot rather than sent to the death camps for mass extermination. Everyday life became more unpredictable. Food was in short supply and so was petrol. I even traded my truck for bread. I managed to stay alive by moving from one village to the next, often sleeping in abandoned buildings or sheds to survive the cold.

Finally news arrived that Germany had surrendered and the war was over. In every town, people rejoiced openly in the streets. Yet it was hard for me to feel much joy. All I could think about was finding Manya. But before I could begin my search, there was one thing I had to do. I knew it made no sense, but I had to retrieve Manya's hurdy-gurdy from the place I'd hidden it at the labour camp. When I'd made my escape from the camp, I had fled without giving any thought to what I'd left behind. Now, for some reason, I was consumed by the need to rescue that toy.

I made my way back to the labour camp and as I approached, I instantly recognized the dirt-stained buildings with their blackened chimneys. But without the screeching guards and barking dogs, it was like a different place. There wasn't a soul around so I was able to saunter in like some kind of morbid tourist. Yet once I entered the building where I had once been confined, I was stricken by the familiar stench of disease and death. Holding my hand over my mouth and nostrils, I stepped over piles of stinking refuse until at last I found the spot I was looking for—my bunk, or what was left of it. All that remained of it were a few sticks of rotting wood held together with iron clamps.

The floorboards close to my bunk were not easy to lift, but I managed to pry a few of them up with my belt buckle. Yet when I finally looked inside, there was nothing there. I was sure I had hidden the hurdy-gurdy in that spot, along with several other small items. Could I be searching the wrong space? Or maybe someone had stolen it. I started yanking up the boards on the lower side of the bunk, jamming my fingers deep into every corner of the hole. At last, I found my cache—an old postcard, a metal spoon— trinkets I had secretly hoarded for God knows what purpose. And there it was, buried sideways beneath the dirt and mire, the little toy organ waiting for my return. A surge of joy ran through me. I felt as though I had unearthed heaven itself.

Now I felt equipped to return home, or at least to what used to be my home. Even if Manya was not there yet, I would get word of her and bring her back. I tried not to think about the rest of my family. Whenever images of them surfaced, I quickly dispelled them. Only Manya was part of my living world, tipping it like a scale in the direction of hope.

I made the long journey home mostly on foot. At one point I got a ride on the back of a wagon belonging to an eccentric jack-of-all-trades who let me squeeze in among his piles of tools and crockery while he regaled me with wild tales of his "heroism" during the war. He even claimed that, while patching a leaky roof in a makeshift army hostel, he had stabbed a Nazi general in his sleep.

When I first reached my hometown of Szegda, it looked oddly similar to the way I remembered it. In the central square, I passed the giant statue of the war hero Count Miklós Zrínyi, still riding tall on his iron horse. And there was my favourite pastry shop, Violeta's, with its front blind pulled down as always in order to keep the sun from melting the cakes.

But when I started down the muddy stretch of road that led to my old house, I barely made it a few steps before I heard a piercing squeal followed by a loud voice calling out my name. Turning, I saw a figure lunging toward me with arms as wide as paddles and a face as broad as a smiling moon. It was Rikka, the washerwoman, who used to do laundry and mending for my mother when times were good. She grabbed my cheeks and held them fast, and once she realized it was really me, she started weeping and babbling with hardly a gulp.

"It really is you, Artur. I can't—I can't believe it's you. We all thought you were dead. Look how thin you are. You look like death itself!"

Dazed to see someone who knew me, I couldn't bring myself to ask the questions that were burning in my brain. Soon, I didn't have to.

"Your Mama and Papa," Rikka sobbed, "they took them away with all the rest of the Jews. I'm just happy they caught that scoundrel Imre Pik who betrayed them to the Germans. Much good it did him—the Nazis shot him anyway because he was a hunchback. But, you know, I cried the most when I heard that they took your baby sister, Kati. Did you know that I nursed her for months after your poor Mama got the influenza and her milk dried up?" She began to weep into the huge apron that hung from her neck like a trough.

An icy chill spread up my neck, entering my skull, my ears, the craters of my eyes. Until now, I still held onto the hope that my family had been spared. Hearing that they'd been betrayed and taken away by the Germans, I felt as if the earth was crumbling beneath me, causing my legs to buckle. As my knees started to sink, Rikka swiftly grabbed me by the shoulders until I was steadied.

She then leaned in so close to me that her eyes were level with my own. "I heard a rumour," she said, "that your brother, Karl, survived. I only heard it once. Later I heard that he was killed in Poland. But maybe, Artur, maybe—"

"And Manya? Have you seen Manya?" I stammered.

Rikka shook her head and looked away, as if she could not bear to see the pain on my face. Turning back, she said, "Listen, Artur. The Germans spared some of the young people. Put them to work in their factories. Manya was strong. She might be alive."

I pulled away from her and said that I had to go home. Maybe there was word of Manya there. Or my parents. Rikka was right— I'd heard stories about Jews who'd somehow managed to survive the Nazi slaughter. But as soon as I mentioned my home, Rikka turned white and began shaking her head, murmuring, "No, no, no." In a surge of fierce whispers, she warned me not to go there, that I would be in danger. Though I didn't understand what she was telling me, I didn't have the strength to question her further. I finally gave in and agreed to go back to her place and take some nourishment.

Once we were back at Rikka's tiny hut, she began to speak more freely. After lowering a blackened pot onto the fire, she said, "You should know, Artur, that there are other people living in your house. They moved straight in after your family left—claimed it was theirs. Ach, such lies. And, after everything your father did for them. The husband worked in your Papa's shop for a while and was given his wages even when he didn't show up for work. Your father felt sorry for him because his wife had a club foot and used to beat the children whenever it ached."

"Who are they?" I asked. "I need to go there."

"No. Stay away," Rikka said, her voice hard. "Jews are being shot when they return to their homes."

"But—"

"Listen to me, Artur. I know what they're like. Those horse thieves will kill you like a skunk and steal your shirt to make a cloth for their table," she said, wrinkling her chin into a fist.

So for three days I stayed with Rikka. She made me a bed of straw and fed me buckwheat groats and sour cream, insisting that it was what I needed to thicken my blood. She refused to let me out of her sight, afraid that I might be tempted to return to my house despite her warnings. Finally, she packed a sack of food for me and sent me to her older sister in a neighbouring town. "There," she told me, "you'll be safe. And I'll send you word if there's any news of your family." Though not a devout Catholic, she crossed herself and said, "May the Lord save them as He saved you."

Rikka's sister Agnes lived in Nagy Sárvár, a larger town than ours, almost the size of a small city. Before the Germans invaded, it had been home to a sizeable Jewish population. I had agreed to go since I knew that my father had a distant cousin who owned a foundry there. Agnes' house was a squat frame building with sagging grey shutters that I soon discovered was packed with lodgers, some of whom were entire families sleeping in one room. There was hardly space for another living soul. Agnes led me to the only remaining space—a small stoop at the back of the house that was used to store potatoes and onions. She pointed to some empty sacks and told me that I could use them as a bed. "Now listen to me," Agnes said, her reddened nostrils flaring. "I'm only taking you in short-term. I should never have agreed to this in the first place. My sister is such a mutton-head—she feels sorry for every beggar she meets."

I understood right away that Agnes had made up her mind against me. Even after I became her chore boy, hauling wood and carting loads from the marketplace, she railed at me and accused me of stealing from her. What made her even more ill-tempered was the fact that she was a terminal asthmatic who frequently coughed and gasped until she was blue in the face, often forcing her to thrust her head out an open window until she could catch her breath.

Normally, I would never have put up with her invectives against me, but I was determined to stay until I could locate my father's cousin—or at least someone who knew him. I hoped that through him I might obtain some help in finding my family.

I discovered that there were several areas where Jews had lived in Nagy Sárvár. One was a neighbourhood that had been home to the religious Jews of the town, and I made my way there one day after completing my early morning chores. The dank peeling shops and public buildings were all boarded up, save for a small synagogue down the side of an alleyway that was so narrow I scraped my knuckles on the walls as I edged down its cobbled path. Noticing some faded Hebrew letters carved into an arch above a doorway, I went down a few steps and entered the synagogue. Inside were several hunched old men wound in phylacteries and prayer shawls chanting verses from the Psalms as a prelude to the Morning Prayer service. One man with watery blue eyes and a sunken jaw approached me as I came in. He gestured to me with his chin and pushed his prayer book into my hands, all the while moving his lips in prayer.

As I looked down at the siddur, the Hebrew words on the pages startled me by their familiarity. There was even something oddly fragrant about the yellowed pages clinging tightly to their frayed threads, as if there were drops of sacramental wine concealed in their binding. When the old men removed the Torah scrolls from the ark, I could hardly believe how mighty these frail old men had become. As they lifted the scrolls high in the air, before my eyes they seemed to transform into warriors carrying their regal banners into battle. Images of my father flooded my mind—I saw him standing erect beside the *bimah* in synagogue every Sabbath morning, handing out tiny place cards to those whose turn it was to chant the blessings. Although he was a modest shopkeeper who never put on airs or graces, my father was lifted out of his ordinary existence whenever he entered the synagogue, becoming a member of a kind of noble assembly.

When the morning service ended, the man with the watery eyes invited me to join them for some food and drink. "We can't promise you a feast," he rasped, "but as long as there's food, we eat." We filed into a small anteroom crammed from floor to ceiling with crumbling books, papers, and stacks of what appeared to be aging manuscripts. I had never seen so much paper in one place; even the table where we sat to eat our brine-soaked eggs and coffee was covered in brown paper that smelled faintly of ink.

A talkative little man with a flat nose sat beside me. He asked, Where was I from? Who were my family? How many had survived? When I mentioned that I was from Szegda, he told a story of a panic-prone dentist who had once lived there and was forced to flee after he mistakenly extracted the wrong tooth of a prominent government official. The little man laughed so hard that he began to hiccough uncontrollably until someone at the table finally told him to put a sugar cube under his tongue and count backward. After the hiccoughs had subsided, I asked the man if he knew my relative, a man named Mandelkorn who had once owned a foundry in town. He whistled through his teeth and said, "Sure—of course—he was a very important man. But," he said, "I don't think they kept themselves as Jews. They were part of the in-tel-i-*gen*-cia."

Before I could respond, a gaunt man across the table interjected. "Who did they think they were fooling? Do you think the Germans treated them any differently because they wore fur mantles and read Schiller? Bah! They hated them all the more for it. I saw firsthand what they did to those 'baptized Jews.' They promised them protection and then stole everything they owned. After that, they sent them to the death camps like the rest of us." He gulped down his drink and ended in a sort of slow growl, "How many dead Jews does it take for us to learn?"

44

Hugging my arms to my chest, I felt tainted in his eyes by being related to Jews who had betrayed their faith. "Tell me," I said, my voice faltering, "Do you know what became of those Mandelkorns? Are any still alive?"

He paused for a moment, then stated flatly, "None—I heard they were all sent to the ovens."

I suddenly felt as if I couldn't get out of there fast enough. When I got up from my chair, however, a bald man with spectacles and pink splotches on his cheeks came over to me. "Perhaps I can help you," he said, shaking my hand. "I'm Oskar Hyman, former magistrate's clerk."

"Pleased to meet you," I replied. "Artur Mandelkorn."

"Tell me," Mr. Hyman continued, "Do you know that there's an organization in town that helps reunite Jews with their families? I cannot guarantee you success, but I am confident they would at least try to assist you." He paused to take off his spectacles and clean them with an immense handkerchief that he pulled out of his breast pocket. He kept glancing at me, as if he were trying to gauge how serious I was about pursuing the matter.

"Yes," I said, with a quick bow of my head. "I am willing to give it a try."

Hearing that, he settled his glasses back on his face. "In that case, I would be honoured to escort you there myself tomorrow."

The next afternoon, after I'd completed my chores, Mr. Hyman took me to a neighbourhood marked by wide streets and tall stately houses, each with its own courtyard. He explained to me that this was where the most prosperous Jewish families had lived before the war. After walking a few blocks, we came to a boulevard lined with tasteful shops and coffeehouses, most of them shaded by scalloped awnings. My guide then stopped in front of a small haberdashery and said, "We've now arrived at our destination." Inside, Mr. Hyman asked the shop girl in German whether Mrs. Kartash was available. The girl took us into the back of the shop, where a staircase led us to an apartment above the store. The flat had been transformed into a huge office and was filled with files stacked on tables in long rows. Several people were sitting at desks, while others milled about or sat on worn sofas, speaking to each other in either German or Hungarian, or a combination of the two. Mr. Hyman brought me over to meet a petite woman with thin eyebrows and pale red hair who was sitting at a broad wooden desk.

"This fine lady," he said, "is Mrs. Hélène Kartash. She will help you as best as she can."

Mrs. Kartash gestured for me to take a chair and offered me some biscuits from a metal box decorated with a faded portrait of Franz Josef. She then proceeded to ask me a variety of questions. She spoke with a slight French accent, gliding over each consonant like a fine silk thread.

I answered all her questions about my home town, providing as much information as I could about each member of my family. I also described the last time I had seen Manya and mentioned the contradictory rumours about Karl's fate. I even told her about Ferko, in the vague hope that perhaps he too had survived. She wrote everything down in a lined ledger, assuring me that she would check her files for any matching information. I was afraid to be too hopeful and asked Mrs. Kartash bluntly whether she had ever found any matches. She looked down at her desk and gently shook her head before answering. "There are—a few," she said quietly. As she looked back up at me and pushed a loose strand of hair from her eyes, I saw the strain and exhaustion written on her face. A web of tiny red veins encircled her pupils, making her eyes look pink and swollen. Deep furrows were etched into her forehead while creases gathered along the sides of her mouth. For some reason, I averted her gaze when she asked if I had any further questions. Not knowing what to say I shrugged and got up to go. She walked me to the door and just as I was about to leave, she placed her arm gently around my shoulders. "It may take weeks, even months until we find out anything," she said. "But we never stop searching. Never."

After meeting with Mrs. Kartash, Mr. Hyman took me to a Viennese-style pastry shop nearby and bought me a cup of cocoa sprinkled with cinnamon. As we sat at a faded checker-top table, he told me a little about Mrs. Kartash and the work that she did.

"She is a remarkable woman," he began. "She has contacts throughout Europe and is said to be trusted even by the Russians. She has ways of getting her hands on documents that no one else can. Not only that, she is a tireless worker, especially where children are concerned. She herself lost her husband and two babies in the war—twins."

He told me that she was from an old French Jewish family, but had married a Hungarian doctor and moved to Budapest before the war. She had also been a gifted flutist and had played with the national symphony orchestra. He paused. "Since the war," he said, shaking his head, "she refuses to touch the flute."

A few weeks later, Mrs. Kartash sent me a note summoning me to her office above the haberdashery shop. As soon as I arrived, she took my hand and silently guided me into a secluded area of the room. My stomach sank: I could feel her hand trembling lightly in mine and noticed the tense lines stretched across her forehead. "Artur," she said gently, "I have received a report that refers to your sister Manya." She looked down before continuing. "According to the document, Manya was among a group of Jews who jumped from a train en route to a concentration camp in Poland. Those who escaped were apparently shot. Only one person survived, a young man by the name of Emil Lenzner. It is he who reported the incident."

"It's not true," I cried, my voice shaking. "He must have made a mistake. Manya would never jump from a train. She was afraid of heights. She wouldn't climb a tree because she was afraid to look down. It was somebody else. I'm sure of it!" My voice must have carried because several people rushed into the room and asked if they could help. A row of faces stared at me with helpless eyes but I couldn't stop myself—I began shouting at them, too. Mrs. Kartash put her arm around me and led me over to a low sofa. She sat with me and listened to the torrent of words that spewed out of me like water from a sinking vessel.

"Please. I beg you," I pleaded. "There must be another witness. Or some other documents. It must be a mistake."

Mrs. Kartash held my hands tightly in hers as if she were trying to transfer to me whatever strength she possessed. She repeated the words, "Yes, yes. I understand," but said no more.

Still, I couldn't stop my own flood of words. I demanded to meet this Emil Lenzner who claimed that Manya was among the victims. I was sure that when I spoke to him I would find that he never actually saw her jump from the train. Even if she did jump, was there any proof that she'd been shot? To calm me down, Mrs. Kartash finally agreed to try to contact the young man, although she confessed that it might be difficult to find him. The last documented address for him was in White Russia, but in recent days fighting had broken out in that vicinity between the Soviets and the Poles. Communication had become virtually impossible.

She also said that so far she had not yet learned anything about the rest of my family, including my brother, Karl. She promised once again that as soon as she heard anything, she would send word to me.

At this point, I'd lost the ability to take in anything Mrs. Kartash was saying—I could see her lips moving, but her words seemed to dissolve before they reached my ears. My head was pounding and my cheeks were burning. All I could think about was finding Emil Lenzner and proving him wrong. I didn't care how hard it would be to find him. I would track him down and disprove his story about my sister's fate. I was determined to do so, no matter how long it would take.

5

Suzy Kohn
Toronto, Ontario
October 1968

Though Bella was not even forty, she'd begun to look as old and frayed as a hand-me-down sweater. She spent most of her time sitting in her velvet bergère chair staring at the television set that stood in a corner. It was hard to have any real conversations with her. Whenever I tried asking her how she was feeling, the best I could hope for was a one-word answer. Finally, I tried a different approach. "Do you remember how we used to take trips downtown?" I asked her. "To the Colonnade? To Gerrard Village?"

Bella stared at me as if she barely understood what I was saying.

"How about that rainy day when we visited the Museum?" I persisted. "Do you remember how I helped that old woman down the steps? And she wanted to give me a five-dollar reward?"

At first, Bella's vacant eyes showed no sign of recognition. But gradually a thin smile began to spread across her lips. "Yes, yes, I do recall that."

"Of course, I didn't accept the money."

"Charles always said you were a good-natured girl," Bella sighed.

"Really? When did he say that?"

Bella looked away without answering.

I swallowed. "Did he say anything else about me?"

"No, no." Bella pulled her crossed arms close to her body. "Just—"

"Just what?"

"Once or twice—he said—that you reminded him of someone he once knew."

"Did he mention a name?"

"No. Never." She closed her eyes and leaned forward a little, as if she was trying to remember. "I think—it was a childhood friend."

I instantly recalled the name that Uncle Charles had once called me—Manya. Could Manya have been his girlfriend? Someone he'd been in love with before he came to Canada? Why, I wondered, did I remind him of her?

Bella slid back into her seat, and turned her head toward the television screen.

I didn't have the nerve to ask her anything more. Nor the heart.

Unlike that day, most of my visits with Bella were spent in complete silence. Despite my efforts, I just couldn't get much response from her. Eventually, I became so bored that I decided to make myself useful and tidy up the place. It certainly needed it. There were plates of half-eaten food and cold cups of coffee under the sofa, on top of the bookshelves, and wedged inside the wicker plant stand. The garbage cans were so stuffed with crumpled tissues and wrappers that they were spilling onto the floor. The only clear surface was the dining room table, which had formerly been covered with beads and fabrics, but now was entirely bare. Yet it was odd—no matter how much I straightened up, when I returned the next day, Bella's place looked much the way it had before I cleaned it. It was as if I had never been there. Perhaps that's why I grew tired of my visits and started coming less often. Why should I bother if my help wasn't appreciated? Besides, Bella hardly acknowledged my presence. I felt no different from the Staffordshire figurines gazing down at us from her mantelpiece: a grinning poodle or a wide-eyed shepherd strumming on a lute.

Not that I didn't feel guilty about it. I remembered Fin saying that I was a "giving person." How wrong he was. But I suppose I was wrong about him, too. For weeks after our encounter in the park, I held on to the idea that he was attracted to me. Granted, it was strange that he didn't talk to me after that first conversation. In fact, he barely made eye contact with me, passing me in the halls at school as if he didn't know me. When I went to the park with the rest of the gang at lunchtime, he paid no attention to me at all. Nevertheless, I continued to replay the memory of his piercing blue eyes gazing into mine. At first, I told myself that he was ignoring me because he'd interpreted my quietness as a rejection. But after a while, I had to admit it. Our encounter had meant nothing to him. Just like it meant nothing to Bella that I went to her house and worked like a slave. Or sat with her for hours like a stone.

My home life was not much better. My father seemed to be in a constant state of irritation over one thing or another. He demanded absolute quiet whenever he was home so that he could immerse himself in the files he brought home from the accounting firm where he worked. My thirteen year-old sister Julia particularly got under his skin—for speaking too loudly, for being rude, for arriving late for dinner. This prompted ten-year year-old Jan to join in and defend Julia by hollering louder than anyone. The result was a shouting match that always ended in slammed doors and tears. That was followed by muttered recriminations from my parents, generally directed at the children. And, more recently, at each other.

One night, the situation at home reached an all-time low. It started with Julia playing a Rolling Stones album in her bedroom. Mother sped upstairs and banged on her door. "Turn down the volume!"

"What are you screaming about? It's not even loud." Julia shrieked through the door.

"It's that thumping," Mother shouted. "Your father can't take it. It's right over his head in the den."

"So, tell him to change rooms."

"How dare you speak to your parents like that! Get out here. Now."

Julia burst out of her room, her face twisted with fury. "I can say what I want. I don't give a damn!"

Mother's eyes bulged and her cheeks were on fire. She slapped Julia across the face so hard that she fell backward against the wall. There was a moment of shocked silence, then Mother slumped onto the floor and began crying. "I'm so sorry," she sobbed. "I never meant to hit you." Julia was clearly not hurt, but she knew how to play the part of the victim. Rubbing her head and moaning, she acted as if she'd had been beaten with a club.

Meanwhile, Father raced up the stairs and tried to console my mother, intermittently yelling at the rest of us to go to our rooms. We all disappeared quickly. But I was too restless to stay in my room for long, so I decided to go out for a smoke. As I passed the den on my way to the porch, I saw Father pouring himself a drink out of a heavily carved glass bottle full of something that looked like whisky. What? My father drinking? He usually only drank liquour when he invited his co-workers over, and even then he barely took more than a sip. Mother used to joke that the liquour in our cabinet was so old, it must have come over on the Mayflower. What was going on? More than ever, I really needed that cigarette. But instead of going out, I decided to go back upstairs and smoke in my room. The way my family was behaving these days, who would even notice? Or care?

6

Artur Mandelkorn
Nagy Sárvár, Hungary
November 1945

After I had gone back to the office above the haberdashery several more times, Mrs. Kartash finally had some news for me—news that would make my search all the more daunting. She'd received a report that Emil Lenzner had left Europe on a ship bound for Palestine. No other information was available, she said, probably because, with Jewish immigration so restricted by the British, the groups that were responsible for smuggling Jews into the Holy Land had to operate in secret. There was no sailing date or ship manifest, only a private disclosure that she managed to obtain through her ongoing ties to Jewish underground organizations. Mrs. Kartash made it clear, however, that it was impossible to know if Emil Lenzner had even landed in Palestine, since many of the ships were being turned back if the British discovered that they were carrying Jews.

I didn't know what to do next. Day after day, I tossed ideas back and forth in my brain about how I could make any progress in searching for my family. Should I stay where I was and wait for news? Should I pack my few dismal belongings and continue the search elsewhere?

Nothing in fact was keeping me in Nagy Sárvár except for my relationship with Mrs. Kartash. Certainly my reluctance to leave was partly based on the fact that I'd put all my trust in her to find my family. But that was only half of it. The truth is that I'd also begun to enjoy my increasingly frequent visits with her. We didn't only talk about my family; we talked about everything under the sun—the theatre, card games, the cinema. Sometimes, she even spoke about her girlhood in Lyon. She had grown up in a home filled with culture—her father was a well-known art collector and her mother was a pianist who also gave lessons. Artists and musicians gathered in their home most evenings; her fondest memory, she said, was falling asleep at night lulled by the soothing sounds of music, eating, and laughter.

Mrs. Kartash also talked a great deal about the books she had read as a girl—mostly adventure tales and biographies. She encouraged me to read, saying that it helped to dispel the notion that you are alone in your suffering. Knowing that I had no access to books, she brought me some of her own to borrow: Hungarian translations of Robinson Crusoe, Don Quixote, Ivanhoe, and others. I devoured them all, particularly the stories by Cervantes. I hadn't had any chance to read for over a year and I missed the thrill of living someone else's life for a while. Mrs. Kartash was not familiar with the authors I had read as a child—books by writers such as Ferenc Móra and Elek Benedek—and I encouraged her to read them, too.

One day Mrs. Kartash surprised me with an illustrated copy of Benedek's Hungarian folktales that she had found at a used bookshop. Looking at the colour-tinted drawings of magical creatures reminded me of the hours I had spent sketching pictures of insects in jars. But even more than that, the mythical creatures took me back to a childlike reality I had all but forgotten—when the possibility of an enchanted world was accepted implicitly. Much as I appreciated seeing those illustrations, they made me realize how much I had changed. Those same creatures that had once filled me with wonder now looked completely foreign and even a little grotesque.

We also talked about our plans for the future, though a future without my family was difficult for me to imagine. I figured I would learn a practical trade such as carpentry, so that I could help provide for my family members after I found them. Mrs. Kartash, on the other hand, was quietly devising a way to join the *halutzim* who were building a Jewish homeland in Palestine. She had been in contact with a girlhood friend who had survived the war in hiding and was now in a displaced persons camp in Austria. They hoped to reunite in Palestine and join a collective farm that had been co-founded before the war by residents of their city. In truth, I had difficulty imagining Mrs. Kartash working on a farm—with her thin eyebrows and delicate hands she hardly fit the image of a rugged farm labourer. When she told me her plans, I couldn't help but laugh. But she merely teased me playfully in return, "And will you look any less absurd hammering nails into wood while quoting Cervantes to your fellow carpenters?"

Over the next several months, I continued working for Agnes, or to be precise, working around her—carrying out her orders while trying to ward off her rages. As often as possible, I spent time with Mrs. Kartash, who always tried to make time for me despite the long and wearying hours she spent sifting through files for the tiniest specks of life.

One day in early February when I arrived at her office, Mrs. Kartash told me that she had some exciting news. My heart leaped in my chest. She must have gotten word of my family! Her face was glowing as she held up a document in her slender fingers like a trophy. "Artur," she said breathlessly. "I have managed to get you travel papers to sail to Palestine! You can leave next week for Italy, via France. This is a rare opportunity. You must grab hold of it."

I could hardly speak. "Me?" I sputtered. "I don't understand. I have no plans to go to Palestine. That was where *you* wanted to go."

"Hear me out," she insisted. "The British are only allowing a tiny number of Jews to enter Palestine legally. But with tens of thousands of Jewish refugees vying for a spot, the chances of obtaining a ticket are virtually impossible." She paused, pressing her hands together. "I can't disclose the details, but one of my contacts in the underground—with great difficulty—managed to secure legal passage for the sole surviving son of a comrade who was murdered in the death camps. Tragically, this boy succumbed to typhus three days ago." She tapped her fingernails restlessly on her desk. "I can't tell you how precious this ticket is—it would bring thousands on the black market. But, Artur, I decided to make a case for sending you in his place."

"I—I just don't know."

"You would, of course, have to assume the dead boy's identity," Mrs. Kartash said. "But only as long as you are on the ship. Once you are safely in Palestine, you can go back to using your real name."

Palestine? Going there never entered my mind. There had been Zionist clubs such as Hashomer Hatzair or the Maccabee Society in my town, but my parents had always regarded them with trepidation. They thought that openly endorsing such groups would give credence to the growing slander that Jews were disloyal to Hungary. For that reason, I'd never joined any Zionist youth groups, and knew little about Jewish life in Palestine. However, I once discovered something curious about my father. While he'd kept his beliefs to himself as an adult, when he was young he'd been an admirer of Theodor Herzl. In fact, he possessed a whole file of newspaper clippings about him, most of them dating back to his own boyhood. On one occasion, I came across him leafing through his file of clippings and asked him about it. Though at first he was reluctant, he slowly drew the clippings out one by one. His eyes gleamed as he described Herzl's accomplishments—he even had a yellowed photo of Herzl meeting with the Turkish Sultan—but said that after Herzl died, he lost hope that the Zionists would be able to accomplish their goals.

But me? Leave here now? It was true that there was little to hold me in Hungary—there were even days when I would have been happy to be anywhere but here. But there was a buzzing inside me, like a needle in my ear, which kept telling me to wait. Wait here, it said. Wait, and your family will come back.

"I'm sorry," I said. "I cannot leave. It's very kind of you. But I won't go. I won't go to Palestine."

"Artur, please re-consider—"

"No. I can't leave Hungary. Not now. Not until I find my family." Though my tone was rigid, my thoughts glided softly toward Manya. I still hoped that she was waiting for me to come for her. She couldn't be far away.

Mrs. Kartash leaned forward. "Listen to me, Artur. This opportunity is not just for you. It's for your family as well. Just think. If you are lucky enough to find anyone alive, you will be in a position to provide for them. To sponsor their exit from Europe. Do you know what most people would give for that?"

I shifted uncomfortably in my seat and said nothing.

Shaking her head, Mrs. Kartash sighed. "There is little you can do here. You know that I will continue doing all I can to find your family. You can rely on that. But in Palestine," she said, "you can track down Emil Lenzner and find out what he knows about your sister."

I continued to give her reasons why I couldn't go along with her plan—I would never be able to impersonate the dead boy, I said, and if I were found out, I might be sent to prison, or worse. Nevertheless, when I went back to my room that night, the idea of going to Palestine began to burrow its way into my brain. I knew from my geography books that all of Palestine was no bigger than most Hungarian provinces. Surely I could find Emil Lenzner in such a small place. With his help, perhaps I would be able to find Manya at last. I envisioned bringing her to the country of the Jews, where she could learn the songs of her people and become a famous singer, a young Alma Gluck or Lilly Pons of the Hebrew stage.

The notion of sailing to Palestine also reawakened a desire for the kind of boyish adventures that I thought I had long abandoned. Just imagining the sea voyage produced a flurry of romantic associations. As a young boy, I had spent hours reading books about sailing vessels, imagining myself a sea captain or navigator charting a course through undiscovered waters. Now these dreams returned to me like old friends.

I hadn't made a firm decision when I went to bed that night, but the moment I woke up the next morning I knew that I would go. And once I'd made up my mind, there was no turning back. Yes, I would sail to Palestine and start my life again. It was all so clear to me now. How could I not have seen it before?

7

Suzy Kohn
Toronto, Ontario
November 1968

My parents hardly mentioned Uncle Charles anymore, even in passing. Yet he was there. Like a phantom whose presence aroused fears that no one wanted to confront. I could sense their fright. If Charles could die so young from a heart attack, who knows when tragedy could strike next? It could target anyone. Including us.

I tried broaching the subject of Uncle Charles' past several times. I wanted to learn about his life in Europe and how he survived the war. But whenever I started asking questions, I was stopped short—as if I was about to enter territory that was out of bounds. True, my mother had always been prickly when it came to talking about the past. And who could blame her? She was the only one of her nine siblings to escape the Holocaust, because an aunt in Toronto happened to bring her over at age fourteen to work in her drapery factory before the war. If it hadn't been for that, she would have been murdered in the camps along with all the other members of her family.

But now even the simplest questions set Mother on edge.

"What did Uncle Charles do before he came to Canada?" I asked. "Did he have a profession in Europe?"

"I don't know anything about it," she said stiffly. "Why does it matter?"

"Just curious."

"You shouldn't be wasting your time thinking about such things." Her voice sounded strained, almost brittle.

"But you must know *something* about him. He once mentioned a girl named Manya. From his childhood. Do you know anything about her?"

"Nothing. He never mentioned her to me."

"Maybe she was a girlfriend. Or a relative."

"I wouldn't know."

"But aren't you curious? Maybe she's still alive."

"Well, if she is, there's no way we'll find out. Uncle Charles is gone. Just leave it at that."

By her sharp tone, I knew not to ask anything further. And after a few further attempts, I realized the subject was closed.

My father was only slightly more willing to talk about Uncle Charles. Recently, while he was giving me a lift to school, I nonchalantly asked why Bella blamed herself for Charles' death.

Father snorted, "You're listening to Bella? I wouldn't put much stock in anything she says."

"But she must have had something in mind," I insisted.

"Listen, Suzy. Bella has not been well lately. Look at the way she lives. It's a pigsty in there. Your mother helps out every day and still nothing changes. It's taking a toll on her, too. I'm not blaming Bella, mind you. It was a big shock, losing Charles so suddenly like that."

"Was it really so sudden? I thought Mother said that Uncle Charles had been sick for a while."

Father hesitated for a moment before answering. "That's true—but—"

"So it wasn't sudden."

"No. I guess it wasn't. But I'm sure Bella never expected him to, you know, die." Then, unexpectedly, his voice turned cold. "Suzy, I really don't want to discuss this anymore."

"But—"

"That's enough," he snapped. His grip tightened on the steering wheel, turning his knuckles white.

All I could think was that the entire family had become unhinged. Why was everyone so agitated? I was beginning to feel like the only sane one in the bunch. Or maybe it was the reverse. Perhaps they were the normal ones and I was the one who was crazy. Was I deluding myself that there was more to the story of Charles and Bella than everyone was letting on?

After not visiting Bella for several weeks, my guilt got the better of me and I decided that I'd better look in on her. When I got there, I sat down on the couch and tried to look casual, as if everything was the same as it used to be. I made some attempts at small talk. Was she pleased that Trudeau had swept the recent election? Did she think that *Funny Girl* would win an Academy Award? But Bella had no opinion to offer on either subject. Next I tried asking whether she was still following her favourite television drama, *Ironside*. To which she answered: "I can't watch it anymore. Raymond Burr has gotten fat."

After several moments of silence, I began leafing through one of the leather-bound photo albums that were stacked in their usual place on the walnut coffee table. Most of the pictures were ones I had seen before—childhood shots of my father and Bella at various woodland sites on the outskirts of Budapest; brown-speckled photos of my late grandparents in formal attire looking stern and unyielding. There were also some pictures of Renata, my father and Bella's older sister who had been an actress of some repute in Hungary. She had refused to leave Europe with the rest of the family and eventually starved to death in the Budapest ghetto.

Flipping through the pages, I was hoping to find some pictures I'd never noticed before. Perhaps from Uncle Charles' youth. Maybe even a photo of someone who looks like me, the girl he called Manya. But as I turned the pages without finding anything, I realized that it was unlikely. Charles had come to America with nothing. Where would he get photos from his childhood or youth? So instead, I focused my attention on one of my favourite shots of Bella, taken when she was sixteen and had just discovered lipstick. Mugging for the camera, her deep red lips were puckered and saucy. Apparently Bella had been quite the rebel. She once told me that around that age, she had started seeing a young man who sold live chickens in Kensington Market, close to where the family had lived when they first arrived in Canada. When my grandparents found out about the romance, they locked her in the house for a week and immediately started looking for a new place to live in another part of town. I remember laughing out loud when I heard this story. Though my grandparents had died when I was too young to remember them, I could well imagine how these cultured Hungarians must have felt when faced with the idea of a chicken seller as a son-in-law.

Stuck between the pages of the album, I found a small wedding portrait of Charles and Bella, signed in a lavish scrawl by a wedding photographer in Toronto. Since the picture was loose, I lifted it out of the album to take a closer look at it. Turning it over, I noticed some writing on the back: "Karl and Bella Mandelkorn, August 14, 1953."

"Aunt Bella," I asked, "why does it say Karl on the back of this photograph?"

Bella was silent for a minute, then answered in a slow monotone. "Your uncle changed his name. From Karl to Charles. Not long after he arrived in Canada. He thought Karl sounded too European."

I had never heard that before. Yet I had no trouble understanding why Uncle Charles had done it. In a way, I'd done the same thing myself. I rarely told anyone my full name—Zsuzsana Rochel Kohn. I even toyed with the idea of changing it completely. I dreamt of calling myself something simple, like Sue Cole or Susan Connor. Those names were so much easier to pronounce. And not foreign in the least.

Thumbing through the pages of some of the other albums, I asked Bella if she had any pictures of Uncle Charles' family. I knew that he had lost everyone in the war, but I thought that maybe some photos had survived.

"I don't know," Bella said, looking down at her hands.

"What do you mean?"

"I simply don't know. He told me nothing."

"You mean he had no photos?"

"No. I mean he had no memories."

"I don't get it. Everyone has memories."

"Not him. He never spoke about his family. Ever. I don't even know if he had brothers or sisters."

"But—what about his parents? Didn't he ever say anything about them?"

"No. He just said that everyone was killed. That he doesn't remember anything else."

"You mean he had amnesia?"

"Who knows..." Bella's voice trailed off as she sighed and shook her head.

"But you were married to him for fifteen years."

All of a sudden, Bella buried her face in her hands and began to sob, "Yes. Fifteen years—he hid it from me—and look what it led to. I didn't know him. I didn't know him at all."

As her crying grew louder I tried to put my arm around her. But she pushed me away. "Nobody understands," she whimpered.

I wasn't sure what to do. Should I call my mother? She might blame me for asking too many questions and upsetting Bella. Or should I quietly retreat and pretend it never happened? Choosing the latter, I got up to leave, first asking Bella if I could get her anything. Without looking up, she waved me away with her handkerchief, as if she was swiping at a fly.

I went straight home and up to my room without saying anything to my parents about what happened. But I kept hearing Bella's words echoing in my ears: "He hid it from me—and look what it led to." What did she mean? Was Bella's mental condition making her imagine things that never happened? This was the likeliest explanation. Yet I couldn't leave it alone. I kept wondering, what could Uncle Charles have possibly been hiding from Bella? And why did it cause Bella such guilt and anguish?

I found it hard to concentrate at school the next day. So when my closest friend Lynne asked if I wanted to skip classes that afternoon, I took her up on it. Lynne and I had become friends at the end of last year when we gravitated toward each other at school—both of us shy and awkward, but with an underlying streak of quiet impudence. In the past few months, we shed some of our shyness and allowed our impudence to break free. It didn't take long before Lynne bleached her hair white-blond and started to smoke. And it was Lynne who gave me my first cigarette.

We headed over to Steve's Restaurant, a dimly lit greasy spoon not far from the school. As we flopped down at one of the tables, a voice called out from behind us, "Skipping classes, girls? I didn't think you had it in you." I spun around to see Fin sitting at a table with a few of his friends, clearly amused by the look of panic on my face.

I recovered quickly, "Why not? School's such a bore."

"In that case, maybe you want to come with us to a sit-in at Queen's Park. It's an anti-war protest. Now *that* is where you'll see some real action. I hear the cops are going to be out in full force."

I glanced back at Lynne who was nodding her head in approval.

"Sure, we'll come along," I countered.

Fin gazed at me with a look of satisfaction—as if he'd succeeded in capturing his prey.

Turning back to Lynne, I could see her silently mouthing the words, "I think he likes you."

I blushed wildly. At that moment, I felt it too.

8

Artur Mandelkorn
The SS Sentinel
April 1946

In some ways, I had already experienced so much in my young life, but in other ways I was as innocent as a pup. Once I was on board the ship sailing for Palestine, it occurred to me how little I knew about the world and the ways of most people. This applied especially to girls. Before the Germans reached our town, I had just reached the age when boys were beginning to express interest in the opposite sex. But before I had the chance to learn much about girls, I was swept up into the war and the daily battle to survive. Now that the war was over, I was beginning to notice girls all the time. And I longed to gather the courage to speak to one of them— *any* one. It did not much matter.

At age sixteen, I was sprouting a moustache and was as restless as a fish on the shore. There were girls on the ship who occasionally glanced in my direction and one or two who giggled when I tried to tip my hat to them. But despite such opportunities to make the acquaintance of a young lady, it was always the same problem: a feeling of unbearable shyness would come over me and I would quiver like an aspen leaf. Before I could even utter a word, I would turn on my heels and make a quick departure. What complicated matters even more was how shocked I was by this sudden change in my character. Only a few months earlier I had been a self-confident—though not quite brash—young fellow who never thought twice about engaging in conversation with anyone. Now all of that seemed to have changed. I had become consumed with doubts about myself, especially about my ability to be pleasing to others. I blamed some of it on the conditions of life on board the ship—and the hours I spent alone with nothing to do but listen to the thrashing of the waves. If I had previously thought that sea-travel would be an exciting adventure, I was now sure it was quite the opposite: a time of loneliness, tedium, and desperate longing for the shore.

One night when I was having trouble sleeping, I went for a stroll on one of the lower decks, hoping that the fresh air would relieve my insomnia. It was windy outside and the spray had coated the deck with a slick film. No one was around except a tiny grey-haired woman tramping down the steps carrying an oversized laundry pail. When she reached the bottom and put her foot on the deck, she slipped and fell. Hearing her cries of pain, I rushed over and found her lying on her back, her arms and legs waving helplessly. I offered to help her to her feet, but she was in so much pain that I had to lift her up in my arms and carry her back to her cabin.

We must have made an unlikely pair—me with my long legs and awkward gait and she a grey-haired bundle cradled in my arms as if she were a stray rabbit I'd caught in the woods. When I pushed open the door to her compartment, I saw a young lady sitting up in one of the beds reading by the light of a small kerosene lamp. I had never seen anyone so beautiful. Her porcelain skin glowed in the lamplight while her copper-coloured hair spilled over the bed-cushions like a shimmering flame. Startled at the sight of the injured woman in my arms, she immediately jumped to her feet. "Elsabet! What happened?" she cried in German.

"I—I'm fine," the old woman said haltingly, drawing short, quick breaths in an effort to conceal her pain. "Do not—fret—my dear." Ignoring Elsabet's pleas for her to stay in bed, the young lady hastily wrapped herself in a large woollen shawl. She rushed to Elsabet's side and helped me lower the old woman onto the adjoining cot. When she was assured that her elderly companion was resting as comfortably as possible, the young lady assailed me with questions. "Do you think she fractured her spine?" she asked. "Is there a doctor or nurse on board?" "Should we inform the captain?"

I offered to find a member of the crew and see what could be done. Since it was almost midnight, I couldn't find anyone right away. I ran around the ship until I remembered a middle-aged gentleman on board whom other passengers referred to as "Herr Doktor." I had no idea whether he would turn out to be a medical doctor or a doctor of philosophy, but I decided that he was my only option. Like me, he was travelling in steerage, packed into the lower level of the ship with a horde of other refugees. I remembered where he slept and made my way to his bunk. Although he appeared to be in a deep sleep when I found him, the moment I leaned over him, his eyelids popped open and he seemed fully awake. I apologized repeatedly for disturbing him, but explained that there was a medical emergency. Was he a physician? He jumped out of bed, pulled on his trousers, and spoke hastily as we strode rapidly toward the women's compartment. "I'm actually a psychoanalyst," he said panting heavily, "but I received excellent medical training in Marburg—better than any *quacksalber*," which I knew was German for "quack."

When the doctor and I entered the tiny quarters, the young lady was sitting on the side of Elsabet's bed, stroking the old woman's pale forehead. Although Elsabet insisted that she was fine, it was clear that she was in pain, for whenever she tried to move her face contorted and she emitted tiny cat-like cries. The doctor asked us to leave the room while he examined the patient, so we went out into the dim corridor. The young lady introduced herself as Fanny, adding that Elsabet was her maid and travelling companion. Wringing her hands as she paced back and forth, Fanny revealed to me that she had been seasick for part of the voyage and could not have survived without Elsabet.

As I listened to Fanny, my mind scrambled for something to say that would not sound forced or awkward. But Fanny did not seem to notice. Her soft brown eyes were half-covered in shadow as she spoke about Elsabet's unselfish devotion to her. Soon her voice began to crack, "If it had not been for me," she said, "Elsabet would never have gone out on the deck at night." Burying her face in her hands, she began to weep. I fumbled for some words of comfort, but all I could manage was something banal. "I'm sure it will be all right in the end," I said lamely. For the most part, I just stood beside her, nodding my head sympathetically. Perhaps that was all she needed. For when the doctor motioned us back into the room and announced that Elsabet was fine—"nothing that bed rest cannot cure"—Fanny turned to me with such a grateful look that it seemed as if I was the one who deserved full credit for the doctor's prognosis. I must admit that I was feeling somewhat heroic, although it was not because of Elsabet. It had more to do with Fanny and how I felt transformed by her appreciative gaze. Indeed, I was now a young man who had earned a woman's gratitude. Dared I also hope to win her affection?

In the days that followed, Fanny and I gradually became inseparable friends. Fanny's seasickness had started to pass and, with my help, she was soon able to walk on the deck without faltering. Being of service to Fanny also helped dispel my shyness, for the more I was able to assist her, the less I was concerned about what to say and how to say it. In fact, it was not long before I was so much at ease with her that I felt as if I could tell her almost anything. On most days, I also helped her care for Elsabet who was recovering from her fall, and as we shared our duties, we also shared secrets from our pasts with each other. The only secret that, of course, I could not tell her was my real name; I had promised Mrs. Kartash that under no circumstances would I disclose it to anyone until I landed safely in Palestine. That meant that I also couldn't tell her about Manya and my real reason for being on this voyage. As far as everyone on board was concerned, I was Beno Vislassy, son of Zoltan and Rela Vislassy from the town of Sarga, just outside of Budapest.

Other than the difficulty of keeping the truth from Fanny, it wasn't hard to maintain the fiction. Perhaps it was because Beno and I had so much in common. Our fathers had both been shopkeepers who had owned stores in their respective towns, and, like me, Beno had been a student at a local *Gimnázium*. Beno also had several siblings who had been similar in age to mine. The main difference between us, of course, was that unlike Beno, I had managed to escape the Angel of Death, while Beno was felled at the last moment, like the proverbial tree that topples after the storm has passed.

Fanny revealed her own survival story in bits and pieces as we strolled from one end of the ship to the other, exploring the narrow walkways like children in a garden maze. She told me that she was an only child, born in the German city of Frankfurt am Main, where her family had lived for generations. Her mother died when she was three and she was raised by her father with the help of their housekeeper, Elsabet. She had studied music from the time she was able to hold a violin and her dream was to join a chamber orchestra. Her father had been an attorney, but after the infamous anti-Jewish Nuremberg laws went into effect, barring Jews from the professions, he could no longer practice. Fearing that the situation for Jews would only get worse, her father tried desperately to arrange passage for Fanny to England, with the idea that he would follow. But it was too late. He was arrested on false charges, sent to a concentration camp with other "political agitators," and was eventually murdered.

When the mass deportations of Jews from Frankfurt began in 1941, Elsabet had taken Fanny into her home and hidden her there, first in the basement, and later, when that became too risky, in a closet concealed behind a large painted chifforobe. Fanny hid in that closet for more than three years. Several times, the Gestapo came to Elsabet's house looking for Jews since people knew that she had worked for a Jewish family. But Elsabet cleverly made it look as though the chifforobe was built into the wall by creating a false rim that looked like one of the wall panels. As a result, the Gestapo men never once tried to move it.

Fanny tried to describe the lengths to which Elsabet had gone to keep her safe. But whenever she attempted to talk about it, her voice began to tremble. She would take a deep breath and hold her palms together in an effort to calm herself enough to speak. "I still don't understand how Elsabet found the strength to do it. Every evening she'd move the heavy chifforobe by herself so that I could come out for a short time, just long enough to eat, wash, and stretch. She shared everything she had with me—whatever scraps of food she possessed. After I returned to the closet each night, she would sing bedtime songs to me as I crouched inside. They were the same tunes that comforted me after my mother died."

At one point I asked Fanny how she'd been able to endure the long hours of confinement. She was silent for several moments, then whispered, "The worst thing was the darkness." She seemed unwilling to say anything more, so I dropped the subject and vowed to myself never to raise it with her again. One thing I did notice after that was that she never seemed able to get enough light—she was always turning up the lamps in her room even when the sun was pouring in and the room seemed perfectly bright. I even teased her about it once, saying, "You better be careful. Your skin may become freckled from all the lamplight."

As for me, I trained myself to get used to being called Beno, and I actually started to like the name, probably because it became associated in my mind with the charming way that Fanny pronounced it. I regarded it as a kind of nickname, nothing more. I knew, however, that I would eventually have to tell Fanny my real name once we landed in Palestine. I dreaded the thought of it, fearing that somehow her feelings toward me would change along with the change in name. I even toyed with the idea of switching my name permanently to Beno. But I knew inside that I could never do that. I had been named Avrum-Mordechai after my mother's father, a Polish Jew who had died the year before I was born. I remembered the way my mother used to rock me in her arms when I was little, telling me that I had her father's eyes, and that someday I would grow up to be a learned man like him. I had always felt an obligation to Avrum-Mordechai to become at least a little like him. Now I felt an even stronger obligation to be merely me.

Fanny and I spent many hours during the voyage talking about what we anticipated our lives would be like in Palestine. Since I had no family there, Mrs. Kartash had arranged for me to go to a kibbutz that had opened its doors to orphans from Europe. I was to learn Hebrew there and be introduced to life in Palestine. Fanny, however, was going to live with her great-uncle Chaim in Tel Aviv. Though he had gone to Palestine as a pioneer before World War I, he had stayed in touch with her family over the years. Since he had been unsuccessful as a farmer, he left his agricultural community and found a position in the city with the Histadrut, the Labour Council. He had risen in the ranks and was now a man of considerable influence, which allowed him to "pull strings" in order to sponsor Fanny's immigration to Palestine. Fanny was quick to explain, though, that she had paid for her own ticket and Elsabet's as well, for she'd inherited several pieces of precious jewellery that belonged to her late mother and had managed to take them into hiding with her. When the war was over, she sold most of it, with little regret. Her thought was that if selling the jewellery would help get her to the Jewish homeland, then that would do more honour to her mother's memory than wearing the jewels ever could.

I was curious however about why Elsabet would want to start a new life in Palestine. Fanny put it in the simplest possible terms: "When people learned after the war that Elsabet had hidden a Jew," she said, "her entire family shunned her. Now Elsabet has no family other than me."

When the ship finally docked in the port of Haifa, there were hundreds of people waiting for the passengers to disembark. Several people held up signs with names scrawled in large letters—most in Hebrew but also some in Yiddish, German, and Polish. Some were waving and shouting, trying to get the attention of individual passengers. Fanny and I helped Elsabet navigate the long staircase leading down to the dock and I was so consumed by this task that I had little time to notice my new surroundings. I was further distracted by the fact that as soon as our feet touched the ground, we were immediately conducted into long line-ups to wait for the immigration authorities to approve our entry. Worried that the dour-faced British officer who processed my papers would suspect that I wasn't Beno Vislassy, I avoided looking him straight in the eye. He examined my documents, then paused and glanced up at me for a moment, as if something about me was doubtful. My stomach grew queasy as he squinted at the photo on my doctored passport and, with a tight-lipped scowl, looked up and glared at me, this time longer and harder. Then without uttering a single word, he stamped my entry papers with a loud bang and waved his arm impatiently for me to move along.

When Fanny's Uncle Chaim appeared and took charge of his great-niece and her companion, I realized with a shock that I'd have to leave Fanny and go my own way.

"I'll write to you," I said.

"Please," she whispered, her eyes downcast before turning to her uncle Chaim who was calling her away. Before I could say anything more, Fanny and Elsabet were ushered into the back seat of a tiny European car. As her uncle revved the engine, Fanny looked out the window and waved to me, mouthing something that I couldn't make out. Watching the car leave, all I could hope was that the words she uttered were more than just goodbye.

9

Suzy Kohn
Toronto, Ontario
January 1969

Fin was now the centre of my life, though I couldn't say for sure that we were "dating." He certainly never used that term. Ever since I'd gone to the sit-in with him and his friends—though, as it turned out, the police barred us from entering—our relationship seemed to take off. Even on the way there, I could tell something was happening. As soon as we took our seats on the subway, Fin casually slung his arm around my shoulders and started massaging the back of my neck. When I looked up at him, he said that he was teaching me how to relax.

"Mmm—that feels good," I murmured.

"Of course it does. Your neck is really tight."

"I never noticed. I suppose it's true."

"You sure are tense," he said. "I've never met anyone so uptight."

I thought about it a minute before asking, "Is that why you've been avoiding me these past few months?"

Fin pulled back slightly. "No, I just thought you were too straight for me. I generally go out with girls who are a little more—hip."

"So what changed your mind?"

"I don't know. Maybe I suspected that you're not as straight as you appear."

"And were you right about that?"

He smiled mysteriously, "I'll just have to wait and find out."

When I told my parents in passing that I was seeing someone—a boy from my year at school—they jumped on me as if I'd told them I was dating the Wild Man of Borneo. Father was sitting in the kitchen reading the newspaper while my mother and I cleared the dinner dishes.

"Who is this person?" Father asked, throwing down the paper. "Does he have a name?"

"Ned. But he goes by Fin."

"Fin?" said Father. "What kind of name is that? Is he Scandinavian?"

"No, he's Canadian."

Mother wrinkled her brow. "He's Jewish, I hope."

I could feel my shoulders tightening. "Yes, as a matter of fact he is," I stated coolly. "His family name is Finberg."

"Well, that's a relief." She rubbed her hands on her apron and went back to the dishes.

"A relief? Why do you care if he's Jewish? I certainly don't."

Mother swung around. "Well, you should care," she said sharply. "No matter how much the gentiles pretend to like us, we'll never be accepted. I'm glad you're sticking with your own."

"Oh, come on. This isn't Europe in the forties. People aren't like that anymore."

Father snorted. "Oh no? You should hear what people say about Jews. Even at work I hear it. If I had a nickel for every time I heard someone say that he was 'Jew'ed.' Some things never change."

"Well, maybe that's true for your generation, but not for mine."

"You just wait and see."

After my father's last remark, I walked out of the room, my head steaming. My parents' views made no sense. Why did they suddenly care so much about being Jewish? They weren't at all religious. Sure, they'd sent me to Hebrew school when I was younger, but we never went to synagogue and only celebrated the Jewish holidays in the most perfunctory way—a box of matzo on the table during Passover; a Chanukah menorah hauled up from the basement, generally left unlit. Yet, strangely enough, all of my parents' friends were Jewish, most of them having fled Europe just after the Nazis came to power. Who knows—after that trauma, maybe they would never get over their fear of persecution. But certainly I didn't have to live my life that way. Besides, all of that happened years ago. The world had changed. If my parents wanted to stay in their ghetto, that was their choice. They shouldn't expect me to follow their lead.

Whenever Fin and I went out, he always brought along his guitar, a steel-string Gibson that he slung over his shoulder like a rifle. No matter where we were, he had no qualms about pulling out his guitar and singing, even while waiting on a subway platform or riding the train. Since he often remarked that I had a nice—though undeveloped—singing voice, I tried to keep up with him and occasionally made an attempt at harmonizing.

Fin was a regular in the alternative music scene in Toronto and soon initiated me into its nocturnal venues—underground blues clubs, coffee houses, jam sessions in vacant warehouses. On Saturday nights, we usually stayed out late and by the time we wanted something to eat, most of the restaurants were closed. We often ended up at an all-night coffee shop or diner. Most of these places looked the same—orange vinyl booths filled with shift workers, loners, and the occasional college kid smoking Gitanes and reading Kafka. Fin loved these places. Arching his back against the cracked orange vinyl, he would survey his surroundings with an air of quiet satisfaction. "This is the place to find *real* people," he'd say. I'd nod in agreement, trying to see the world through his eyes.

Fin never came to my house to pick me up; we always arranged to meet somewhere near a subway station or a park. It wasn't because I had any reservations about introducing him to my parents. Though Fin had long hair and sometimes wore a tie-dyed scarf wrapped around his forehead, he was Jewish and that seemed to be all that mattered to them.

I once told Fin about their "Jewish obsession." He guffawed. "Ha—I don't even consider myself Jewish. Wouldn't that give them a shock."

"What do you mean?"

"Sure, I was born Jewish. But organized religion's not my thing. I'm a human being. That's all that matters to me."

"What about your parents? Didn't they make you have a bar mitzvah?"

"No, my parents are cool. I said I wasn't interested and they never asked again. Besides, these days my parents are more into eastern religions."

Despite his bold assertions, I could tell that Fin was hesitant about coming to my house. I understood why—meeting my parents would raise expectations, tie him down. And if there was one thing Fin was afraid of losing, it was his freedom. Being with Fin meant agreeing to a kind of unspoken pact. Of course, it was never stated explicitly. But I knew the terms. His offhand comments made it clear from the outset. We would be together as long as we were both happy. No possessiveness was allowed. If one of us became jealous or suspicious, it would be a sign that the relationship had run its course.

And what, I thought, could be wrong with that? I was overjoyed to finally have a boyfriend, even if I was not supposed to call him that. It changed everything at school. Boys started noticing me and craned their necks in my direction when I passed by. And girls who had hardly spoken to me before now wanted to be my friend. They told me that they admired my naturally wavy hair and the unique way I dressed—embroidered peasant blouses had become my trademark. I guess I was what people call a late bloomer. Before Fin, I had only been out on occasional dates, generally with boys who liked me more than I liked them. Or vice versa. This was the first time that the attraction was mutual. I felt as if I'd struck gold.

10

Artur Mandelkorn
Haifa, Israel
June 1946

As I stood on the dock in Haifa, I felt a sense of inner calm that I had not experienced in years. It was certainly not a reflection of my surroundings, which were anything but serene. Looking around at the crowds of people shouting, laughing, embracing, and arguing, I revelled at being in a place where Jews were free to be exactly how they are, without apology. Even as a young child I remember my mother telling me not to talk too loudly or with too much expression because people would say that I was acting like a Jew. Behaving like a Jew was something to be trained out of you, like a bad habit or a vice that you learned to control. If you were proficient at it, you could even learn to rid yourself completely of any outward signs of Jewishness, and take secret pride in being told that you didn't "seem Jewish." Here, in Palestine, I felt as though a mask had dropped from my face. Though I didn't know a soul among the throngs of people around me, I was more at home than I had ever been.

I was supposed to be picked up by someone from the kibbutz, but no one claimed me for the longest time. Not that I cared. I was content to just sit on top of my trunk and savour the unruly din around me. Eventually, a short stocky man wearing shorts and sandals approached me and asked in Yiddish if I was Beno Vislassy. He introduced himself as Shmulik Goldvasser, and told me that he'd been assigned to drive me to the kibbutz. He led me to a truck that was loaded with machinery parts; after making room for my belongings, we clambered into our seats and were on our way. Shmulik, I soon learned, was an assistant to one of the *madrichim,* the group leaders, of the educational program on the kibbutz. After telling me this, he was silent for the rest of the journey, driving with one hand on the steering wheel while the other hand held a cigarette, flicking the ashes out the window at regular intervals. I didn't mind that he was the silent type; I was happy to just look out the window and quietly absorb the unfamiliar surroundings.

Despite Shmulik's lack of conversation, it was anything but a leisurely drive. Even though the narrow, winding streets of Haifa were crowded with people, Shmulik manoeuvred through the city at full speed, swerving sharply around corners and honking at every person or animal that had the audacity to stray into his path. Occasionally someone cursed at him, but for the most part everyone just moved out of the way and continued to go about their business. As if they had already seen a hundred such drivers whiz by them that day.

From the truck window, the images that flashed by me changed so quickly that I felt as though I was travelling across the centuries, moving more through time than space. But if this was time-travel, it was not chronological. As we left Haifa and drove through a series of tiny parched towns and villages, we seemed to shift from modern times to the biblical past and then back again, all within a matter of minutes—signs in Hebrew for soda pop, Arabs pulling donkeys, a Hassidic Jew in gabardine thumbing a ride.

We soon came to a stretch of emerald fields that covered the grey earth like a dense green blanket. This was the Palestine I had read about in books, a place where the desert had been transformed into vineyards and orchards. It reminded me of a Yiddish expression that my mother often used in order to describe someone who was satisfied with his lot in life. "Vi baym tatn in vayngortn," she would say with a hint of wistful irony, "Like being in his father's vineyard." It is doubtful that my mother had ever seen a real vineyard in her life. But as we turned down a stony road that cut through the waving emerald fields and arrived at the entrance to Kibbutz Tivon, I knew at that moment exactly what she meant.

Living in close quarters with the fifty or so other young refugees was not an easy adjustment. Most of us spoke little or no Hebrew when we arrived, so we were required to learn it as quickly as possible, which also meant that we were strongly discouraged from using our various native languages. In my kibbutz house alone, there must have been boys from seven or eight different countries. Like me, many of them spoke a number of languages, such as Yiddish, German and Hungarian, but there were some who only spoke French or Polish or Russian.

It was not the language barriers though that proved to be the major stumbling block. More than a few of the young refugees were emotionally scarred from the effects of the war, often in unpredictable ways. One boy who seemed easygoing on the surface flew into a rage if anyone touched his possessions. Another tried to frighten us by saying that the food was poisoned or that the air was contaminated. I was never sure if he actually believed these things himself, or if he was merely trying to strike fear in those weaker than him. The thing that unsettled me most was that you couldn't always detect that there was anything abnormal about them at first, but after living with them for a while, it became obvious, and, at times, unbearable.

And then there were the nicknames. Everyone seemed to be given one, almost as if it were an initiation rite devised by the group leaders. Although I'd formally returned to using my real name when I arrived in Palestine, I don't think that anyone on the kibbutz ever called me Artur. Nor was I called Avi, which was short for my Hebrew name, Avrum-Mordechai. From the beginning, I was called Muki and that was that. I'm not sure where I got that nickname, although it might have been short for my middle name, Mordechai. In any event, I became Muki to everyone and it stuck like glue. I suppose I should have been thankful that I didn't get branded with something worse, like some poor devils who were given nicknames that highlighted their flaws, like "pig-nose" or "featherbrain."

Over time, I came to the conclusion that the group leaders teased and badgered us on purpose in order to make us less sensitive to such things. And it worked to a large degree. They also kept us so busy that we had little time to worry much about our individual feelings. Half the day we spent learning Hebrew, and the other half doing physical labour—mostly agricultural—but there were other kinds of work, too, such as kitchen and laundry duty. Once we learned enough Hebrew, most of us were also enrolled in high school courses in order to catch up on the education we were denied in Europe. The evenings were often dedicated to cultural programs: we sang Hebrew pioneer songs, danced horas by torch light, and attended outdoor lectures, swatting at mosquitoes as we tried to focus our attention on such topics such as "Ber Borochov and the origins of Labour Zionism." It was only late at night when I returned to my bunk that I was able to find a few minutes to write letters to Fanny, hoping that she would answer them before too long.

I soon made friends with one of the other young refugees on the kibbutz, a fellow everyone called Dudu, though his real name was Dovid Meir Kligerman. Short, muscular, and agile as a tiger, Dudu could perform most chores in half the time it took anyone else. But it was Dudu's crooked smile and dry sense of humour that drew me to him most. While we were taking a break from picking olives one day, I asked him where he was from.

He shot me a sardonic glance. "I hail from the illustrious city of Lodz. I'm sure you've heard of it—they call it the Manchester of Poland. I suppose it was no worse than anywhere else in that God-forsaken country. When the Nazis invaded, we were forced into a ghetto with the rest of the Jews. Just think—we were a family of eight, squeezed into a single apartment with six other families. There were more lice in that apartment than food."

I winced.

"Don't look so shocked. You get used to it—people everywhere starving to death. Seeing shrivelled bodies on the streets of the ghetto every day will do that. Actually, we were lucky compared to some. My father was a printer by trade, so once a week the Jewish underground gave us bits of food—an onion, some blackened potatoes—in exchange for his services. They recruited him to print material that was secretly distributed throughout the ghetto—newspapers, poems, jokes. Can you believe it? Even the dying crave some form of entertainment. As we used to say: they could beat us and torture us, but they couldn't stop us from telling jokes."

"They actually managed to distribute that material?" I asked.

"Sure, for a while. In fact, they recruited me as well. I helped them transport materials by concealing them inside of barrels and garbage bins. Once I even hid a load of pamphlets in an empty coffin and helped move it from one end of the ghetto to the other without detection."

I was struck by how easily Dudu spoke about his past. He described his experiences in the war in the way that others would talk about eating a meal or riding a bicycle—bluntly and with no expectation of sympathy. One humid summer evening when the two of us were sprawled on the ground under the twisted branches of an olive tree, Dudu told me about how he had occasionally made clandestine deliveries outside of the Lodz ghetto late at night. Be-

cause he was slight for his age—and was helped by guards suscep-
tible to bribery—he managed to slip through a small gap in the
fence and meet his contacts on the other side. They were mostly
Jews working for the underground who were able to "pass" as gentiles. "Sure, I was risking my life every time I left the ghetto," he
said matter-of-factly. "But the irony is, instead of getting me killed,
it ended up saving my life."

When I raised an eyebrow at that, Dudu reached over and patted me on the shoulder as if I were an innocent when it came to
matters of life and death. Staring up at the sky, his tone grew un-
characteristically sombre. "In late June of 1944, I was sent out of
the ghetto after midnight to deliver some vital documents to my
contact on the outside. He never showed up, so I had to decide
whether to wait or go back to the ghetto. I decided to stay where I
was—a dangerous choice, given that it was close to daybreak. Finally a woman came and told me that the Gestapo had picked up
my contact. She urged me to stay with her, since I couldn't possibly go back to the ghetto in daylight. I followed her—Irina was her
code name—to her place of work at a large textile mill where she
was a manager. Introducing me as a new apprentice, she put me to
work in the mill. But by the end of the day, the news broke that the
Nazis had begun liquidating the ghetto, systematically forcing all
the Jews onto trains. Everyone knew what that meant—the dreaded concentration camp in Chelmno."

Dudu hugged his arms to his body and rocked slightly as he
resumed his account. "I ended up spending the rest of the war in
Nazi-occupied Lodz. I continued to work at the mill and, with the
help of false documents, I blended into my surroundings."

"And after?" I asked, my voice a mere whisper.

I could hear him swallow before he spoke, "It was not until after the war that my worst fears were confirmed: my entire family—mother, father, and all five sisters—had been sent to the show-
ers and gassed."

Unlike Dudu, I had no desire to speak about my own experiences during the war. In fact, I didn't want to share any details about my life. I told him nothing about Manya and the reason I had come to Palestine. I didn't want anyone prying into my affairs, asking questions, passing judgment.

Yet my attempt to hide my private affairs was thwarted when Dudu found a postcard from Mrs. Kartash that accidentally dropped out of my jacket pocket one evening as we lined up for food in the dining hall. "Is this yours?" he asked, scanning the writing on the back of the postcard.

"Yes, thanks," I mumbled, grabbing the card from his hand. "It's nothing important."

"Don't worry, I didn't read it," Dudu smirked. "At least, not the whole thing."

I quickly scanned the postcard, and saw that Mrs. Kartash had written to find out whether I'd had any luck in locating Emil Lenzner in Israel.

When Dudu and I sat down in a quiet corner of the dining hall, I saw by the quizzical look on my friend's face that it was time to finally open up about myself (at least as much as I could). I started off by explaining that I was searching for this young man named Emil Lenzner because he claimed to have met my sister during the war. This, of course, led to me telling him all about Manya. By the time I finished my story, we were the last ones left in the room.

Dudu sighed. "So the mystery man finally speaks!"

I could feel my face reddening. "I didn't know that people perceived me that way," I said.

Dudu smiled and slapped me on the back. "Well, you have to admit that you are a bit aloof. But I admire your discretion. People like me talk too much and say things we regret."

Although Dudu was intrigued by my plan to search for Emil Lenzner, he warned me not to raise my hopes too high. He had a blunt kind of realism that was likely born of his own crushing experience. In short, he did not believe in expecting anything from anybody. "If you expect others to do unto you as you would do unto them," he said, "you'll get a sock in the nose."

I began my search for Emil Lenzner by seeking the help of a *madricha*, a female group leader on my kibbutz named Ruti. Of all the *madrichim*, Ruti was the most approachable. She was a robust girl of twenty-two with black eyes, hazelnut skin, and a husky voice that vibrated slightly when she talked. But it was her wide smile and devil-may-care attitude that attracted everyone to her. Sensing that I could trust her, I decided to ask for her help.

My opportunity came when I spied Ruti sitting alone on the wooden steps outside of the dining hall. It was one of those cool evenings in early spring when the sun emerged briefly from behind the clouds, dispersing brief pools of warmth before setting onto the fields. Taking a deep breath, I walked up to her and made my request in the best textbook Hebrew I could muster.

"Ruti, would you be so kind as to help me with a matter of great importance?"

She threw back her head and laughed so loudly that I thought the whole kibbutz would come running to hear the joke. My mortification must have shown on my face because when she realized how her laughter upset me, she grabbed my hand and started patting it rapidly saying how sorry she was for laughing.

"It was the way you spoke, Muki—so formal and solemn—like a lawyer making a plea to the court."

When she saw that I was not so easily consoled, she tried to make it up to me by making me laugh as well. She solemnly declared that she would be my slave for a week and would even scrub my muddy shoes every morning by hand if I would only forgive her. She even fell to the ground, grabbing my feet and pleading with me for mercy in a mock show of grovelling. Her antics worked—I finally broke down, laughing so hard that my ribs ached.

86

When I regained my composure, I sat down beside Ruti on the steps and briefly told her about my sister and my need to find Emil Lenzner. "The problem is," I explained, "I have no idea how to find him. We're kind of isolated up here on the kibbutz. I wouldn't know where to begin."

"Don't worry, Muki. I'll be glad to help. I was born and raised in this country and know all about its crazy bureaucracy. You can hardly buy a cup of coffee without filling out a form. But there are ways of cutting through the red tape, if you know how to do it. Leave it to me. I'll find out which office to contact—Jerusalem or Tel Aviv—and try to arrange an appointment for you."

"I don't know how to thank you."

"No need for thanks, Muki—I have an ulterior motive. Once I arrange an appointment, I figure you'll need the help of an interpreter at the meeting. I can use a break from the kibbutz. A taste of big-city bureaucracy may be just the excitement I need."

Several weeks passed before Ruti at last arranged for the two of us to travel to Jerusalem for an appointment at a branch office of the Jewish Agency. The bus ride took us through rugged hillsides leading up to the legendary city that sat perched like a queen on her rocky throne. It was still early morning in Jerusalem and the air was cool and fragrant as we climbed out of the bus onto the streets of the city. Women in kerchiefs were carrying fresh loaves from the market, while men in shirtsleeves gathered on street corners to buy newspapers and cigarettes.

We found our destination easily—a ramshackle building that was half covered in sheets of perforated tin—and entered an office that was hardly bigger than a vestibule. Space was at a premium in Jerusalem, since the British were doing all they could to discourage Jews from acquiring property. We could hear the sound of typing from behind a desk piled high with boxes, but it was impossible to see who was behind the tower of cartons that seemed to quiver with each tap of the keys. Finally a woman's voice called out in a nasal drone, "Sha-lom. I'll be with you in a moment," though the tapping of the typewriter continued unabated.

Ruti swiftly retorted, "And when will that be? When the messiah comes?"

At last, a stout woman with a sharp nose and eyes like two black beetles appeared from behind the barricade and introduced herself as Tziona Afek, the assistant manager. Ruti started by reminding her that she had written to her about my search a few weeks ago. Miss Afek immediately told us to sit down while she began flipping through some papers on her desk. When she found what she was looking for, she donned a pair of enormous spectacles that covered half her face and began reading the contents aloud line by line. "Yes, here we go. Emil Lenchner, born in Prague, 1924. Parents George and Sabina, deceased. Siblings, unknown. Interned at Theresienstadt. Arrived Palestine, 19—"

"No, no, no," I cried out, trying to make her stop. "Not Lenchner. *Lenzner.* You have the wrong name!"

She scowled, raising her beetle eyes suspiciously from beneath her glasses, and said, "You know, young man, it is entirely possible that it is you who are mistaken."

"No, I have repeated that name to myself a thousand times. It's *Lenzner*—Emil *Lenzner.*"

Miss Afek shuffled through more papers, muttering to herself about people giving her the wrong information, that it wasn't her fault if people were not precise. Finally, after scurrying back and forth between towers of boxes, she returned and announced definitively, "No, I have nothing on anyone named Lenzner. Not a thing. No one named Lenzner has entered Palestine within the past year. Nobody."

Before I could express my indignation, Ruti turned to me and said, "Listen, Muki. Perhaps it is the same person. It could be that his name got written down incorrectly. Why don't we go and meet him?"

At first I felt there was little use in doing that. But then in order to please Ruti who seemed so set on the idea, I finally agreed. Miss Afek copied Emil Lenchner's last recorded address onto a slip of paper and handed it to me. In lieu of a farewell, she shrugged her shoulders and remarked dryly, "Nu, so now you decided you do know this boy Lenchner? Good luck to you." Out on the street, I unfolded the slip of paper and found that it contained only four words: EMIL LENCHNER, BE'ER YAAKOV. I was puzzled, but Ruti explained that Be'er Yaakov was such a small town that no one needed a formal address. Everyone knew everyone; you couldn't hide in Be'er Yaakov, she told me, even if you tried.

We trudged several blocks in the blazing sun through the centre of Jerusalem's shopping district—rows of shabby stores packed tightly together like herring in a jar—until Ruti suggested that we stop for a cold drink. We entered a narrow bakery that was even hotter than it was outside, but we managed to find a table squeezed into the back of the shop where the rear door was open to the breeze. As we took our seats, the proprietor called out to us from behind the counter and requested our order. Humming a tune as he brought us our fruit drinks, he asked us if we were brother and sister. Ruti laughed and said, "Almost." To which she added, "I'm thinking of adopting him as my brother. Right, Muki?" It may have been the heat in the bakery, but her comment felt like a warm embrace. I'd forgotten how good it felt to be wanted, even though I rarely thought about missing it.

Before tasting our drinks, Ruti drummed on the table rapidly and declared, "I am so excited about going to Be'er Yaakov to find Emil Lenchner."

I smiled weakly. "I'm willing to go, but I think it's a waste of time. For one thing, I doubt whether *my* Emil came from Prague as this Lenchner did. My guess is that he was from Hungary since he was sent to Poland so late in the war."

Ruti grimaced. "I wouldn't jump to that conclusion. You never know."

"It's unlikely."

As Ruti sipped her drink, I thought about another possibility. What if my Emil had entered Palestine under a false name just like I had? Or changed his name, once he arrived. If that were the case, how would I ever find him? When I shared this idea with Ruti, her eyes lit up, "You're right! He might have changed his name deliberately in order to assume a more Hebrew-sounding name. Loads of Jews did that. To rid themselves of Europe for good."

The prospect of a changed name created a new challenge for us. What kind of name would be the equivalent of Emil Lenzner in Hebrew? Some of our speculations were serious, others humourous. We came up with a whole range of possibilities. He could have translated the literal meaning of Lenzner into Hebrew. I knew that in German the word "Linz" (or Lenz, as some Yiddish speakers pronounced it) had two meanings: lentil and lens. Therefore, a *lenzner* could be a lentil-grower, or a lens-grinder. We also tried to think of Hebrew names that sounded similar to Lenzner. As a joke, Ruti suggested that he might have changed his name to Leytzan, which, she explained, meant clown or buffoon.

In any event, Ruti reminded me that we were expected back at the kibbutz for the afternoon chores, so it was time to put an end to our fanciful conjectures. For my part, however, I held them in reserve, thinking that they might yet be useful—that is, after the trip to Be'er Yaakov to investigate the unlikely possibility that Emil Lenchner and Emil Lenzner were one and the same.

Knowing that a journey to Be'er Yaakov would require a full day's leave from the kibbutz, I was prepared to wait a few weeks for permission to carry out the next phase of my quest. I didn't mind. I was still sure that the journey would prove to be a wild goose chase, so putting it off meant that I could delay having to endure yet another certain disappointment.

I tried to keep my mind off the coming foray to Be'er Yaakov by concentrating on someone else who was always in my thoughts—

my beloved Fanny. I hadn't seen her since our hasty parting at the dock in Haifa. It was now February and eight months had passed since that day in June. Although we'd exchanged several letters, we hadn't yet broached the subject of seeing each other again. It was getting to the point that the more I tried to picture her face, the harder it got. It was only when I wasn't trying that, out of the blue, I would see her lifelike image flash in front of me and then just as quickly disappear like a phantom.

And then one day at the end of the month, she suddenly appeared in the doorway of our kibbutz dining hall, looking more real than any of the phantoms I could ever conjure. I surely must have looked as though I had seen a ghost, for she broke into laughter at the sight of me. But she didn't appear ghost-like in the least. Her porcelain skin was tanned and she looked healthy and radiant. I must have been shaking my head in disbelief, for as she approached me the first thing she said was, "Yes, it is I. I hope it's a good surprise."

I felt all eyes on me as I fumbled around trying to find an extra chair. In an effort to appear calm, I introduced Fanny individually to everyone at the table. Dudu, who was sitting across from me, shook her hand and shot me a teasing glance as if to say, "You sly devil. How did you snare this beauty?" The other boys and girls at the table—Benny, Moshe, Dov, Esti—all greeted her warmly before going back to their usual lunchtime joking and bickering. Fanny explained that her uncle happened to be travelling in this direction and had offered to bring her to the kibbutz while he attended to his business in nearby Afula.

"In that case," I responded, "I am very much in his debt." Hearing this, she looked down and I noticed that the edges of her ears had turned pink. Glancing back up at me, she quietly requested that I give her a tour of the kibbutz. Seizing this opportunity to be alone with her, I escorted her out of the dining hall, hoping that she couldn't hear the thumping of my heart in my chest.

I began by showing her the layout of the kibbutz—the barn

and chicken coop, the dairy, the woodworking shop, the small cultural centre and library. As we strolled along the paths, I asked her what life was like in Tel Aviv. At first, she spoke in general terms—about the high school she was attending, her supplemental Hebrew studies, her classmates. But I detected a note of hesitation in her voice when I asked about her uncle and aunt. "My uncle Chaim is so kind," she began. "He has done everything possible to make me feel welcome. He even made a small party and invited some of the neighbours to meet me." When I asked about her aunt, she started twisting her fingers and then changed the subject. I knew from Fanny's letters that her uncle, who had been a widower for many years, had recently married a woman named Varda. Seeing that Fanny was uncomfortable with the topic, I dropped it for the time being. Instead I spoke about myself and my own adjustments to life in Palestine.

Talking about this gave me the opening I needed to broach the subject of my name. I had already disclosed the entire story of my false identity as Beno Vislassy in my first letter to her and begged forgiveness for having to deceive her when we first met. In that first letter I also told her my real name and said that I hoped that she could begin thinking of me as Artur Mandelkorn. Although I feared that she would feel angry and betrayed, nothing could be less true, judging by her complete lack of reproach. In fact, she tried to comfort me. She wrote back immediately and said that she cared little about names, adding that a person should be judged by what he has experienced in life and by who he is *inside*. She ended the letter by quoting some lines from Goethe:

> *Who never ate his bread in sorrow,*
> *Who never spent the darksome hours*
> *Weeping and watching for the morrow—*
> *He knows you not, ye heavenly powers.*

Though I'd repeated those lines to myself many times since receiving that letter, once I was face to face with Fanny, it was a different story. In person, I was filled with uncertainty about how she would feel about me now that I was no longer Beno. Would I, Artur Mandelkorn, be disappointing to her in some way? Instead of raising the subject directly, I tried to bring it up in a roundabout sort of way.

"Do you know, Fanny, that here on the kibbutz, everyone calls me Muki."

"Muki?" she giggled, her nose crinkling. "Where did they find that name?"

"I'm not sure how it happened. My Hebrew name is Avrum-Mordechai, but somehow it evolved into Muki. Now the real question is," I said turning to face her directly, "what would *you* like to call me?"

Without a moment's hesitation, she replied, "Artur, of course. It's a lovely name."

I was so buoyed by her words that I threw my arms up in the air and shouted something about the glorious beauty of the land of Israel. And before I knew what came over me, I grabbed her hand and we began to run up the side of a nearby hill. When we reached the top, she bit her lower lip and started to retract her hand from mine. But before she could do so, I cupped her hand in both of mine and wouldn't let it go. It was then that I stopped and for the first time looked deeply into her eyes. She returned my gaze and smiled with a sense of deep recognition, as if to say, "Yes, it *is* wonderful to be alive, despite everything." No actual words were spoken between us. Not one. Yet I knew that something powerful had occurred between us that could not be taken away.

Fanny's uncle Chaim soon appeared in the distance, ready to fetch Fanny for the long drive back to Tel Aviv. Fanny and I quickly dropped each other's hands and descended the hill toward him as if we were making our way there anyhow. Uncle Chaim didn't seem perturbed. Shaking my hand, this tall white-haired man in khaki shorts, had a grip as strong as a youth. But lodged between the creases of his rugged face, were brown eyes that were warm and knowing.

"You'll come to us soon I hope. There is much to see in Tel Aviv these days," he said with a grin. He then winked at me to let me know that he meant more than just the buildings.

11

Suzy Kohn
Toronto, Ontario
February 1969

There was never any question in Fin's mind that we were going to sleep together. If not sooner then later. But, not *too* much later, as Fin constantly reminded me. Yet as much as I was head over heels about him, I simply wasn't ready. Call it old-fashioned, but I couldn't have sex with someone who cared more about himself than he cared about me. In that sense, Fin's persistent prodding worked against him. The more he pressed me, the less willing I became. No matter how many authorities he cited—Sigmund Freud, Alfred Kinsey, John Lennon, the Kama Sutra—I still wasn't completely swayed.

One evening Fin persuaded me to come to his house. His parents were out of town, he told me, and we'd have the entire place to ourselves. They were publishers of a travel journal and were often away on business. And being an only child, Fin was used to fending for himself.

The moment I arrived, Fin turned down the lights and lit some patchouli incense he picked up at a shop in Yorkville. Pulling out an open bottle of Sangria from his parents' liquor cabinet, he poured us two tall glasses. He then took out his guitar and announced that he had a surprise for me—a new song that he'd just written. While tuning his guitar, he gazed up at me and began to speak, his voice low and resonant, smooth as honey. "Suzy, I know you don't realize it, but you are so beautiful. I tried to express my feelings in this song—I wrote it just for you."

As he began to sing in his soft hypnotic voice, a swell of warmth flooded through me, like a current pulling me out to sea. His words were sheer poetry. And, even more amazing, they were all about me.

When Fin ended the song, he took my hand and led me to the couch. Unbuttoning my blouse, he planted rows of tiny kisses up and down my neck, causing shivers to run from my spine to my toes. Using his one hand to unhook my bra, he slid the other hand up my skirt and began stroking my thigh in a slow circular motion. My head was swimming from the Sangria and my body was growing limp. Colours were bursting in my brain, opening and swirling like a kaleidoscope, spinning to Fin's song still dancing in my ears.

Just as Fin pulled down his jeans and climbed on top of me, a thought filtered through the haze. My limbs stiffened. That song— I knew it from somewhere. I'd heard it recently. At Lynne's place. Wasn't it a song by that folksinger—Tim Hardin? Yes. It was Tim Hardin's song. But wait—how could Fin say that he wrote it for me? I sat up, yanked Fin's hands off my body, and frantically started searching for my clothes.

"Hey," Fin asked, half-dazed. "What's the matter?"

"How could you?" I cried, buttoning up my blouse. "How could you lie to me like that?"

"What? I don't get it."

"That song. You didn't write it for me. You didn't write it at all."

"What are you talking about?"

"I know that song. It's by Tim Hardin. Did you really think I was that dumb? I guess you thought, Suzy's so straight, she'd never know Tim Hardin's songs. Only cool people know him. Well, I have news for you. I do know his music and that song is not yours!"

Fin's eyes blinked rapidly. Slowly, he began to speak. And once he got going, his pace quickened and his face turned red as a fire-cracker. "So what if I didn't write it?" he said. "What's the big deal? I borrowed the song. Anyway, who's to say what's original and what's not? All artists borrow from each other. That's how they learn. How do you think the Old Masters learned their craft? They were apprentices—all painting the same pictures. Who knows if Da Vinci even painted the Mona Lisa? Or if Shakespeare wrote his plays? It doesn't matter. Those dudes weren't obsessed with their egos, like the bourgeoisie today. Go read Marcuse. You'll see how screwed up our system has become."

I couldn't think of anything to say. Fin had a way of twisting an argument that made my brain fizzle. I got up and grabbed my coat.

"Where are you going?" Fin asked, now sounding more deject-ed than angry. "I thought we were having a good time."

"I have to go. It's late."

"Well, suit yourself." Fin hung his head and shielded his eyes with his hand as if he was blinking back tears. Suddenly I felt as if I were the one to blame. For a split-second, I considered rushing over to console him, to apologize for my reaction. But somehow, that thought passed quickly. I kept thinking: Oh my God. Oh my God. I almost slept with him. How could I have been so gullible? How could I have let myself believe that he loved me? I felt as though I'd almost fallen into a deep pit and was saved at the last minute.

I ran all the way back to my house, tears streaming down my face, seeping into my mouth. What was I going to do now? How could I go on? Despite everything, I didn't want to lose Fin. And then it hit me: what if I misjudged him? Maybe he didn't have the confidence to write a song of his own. Why had I been so hard on him? No wonder he looked so sad when I left. As if I'd stomped on him. And crushed his spirit.

I prayed that he would call me the next day. I had to tell him how much I cared about him. That I believed in his talent. That I didn't mean it when I accused him of lying. I had to get him back. But was it too late? Would he possibly be willing to forgive me?

As soon as I got home, I called Lynne and told her everything.

"You're unbelievable," she said. "You refused to sleep with him because of a dumb song?" She'd lost her virginity the summer before and couldn't understand why I was making such a big deal of it.

"I was angry," I tried to explain. "I thought he was trying to trick me."

"Who cares? Most girls would love to get that kind of attention from Ned Finberg. Everyone at school envies you."

A wave of regret swept over me. "Lynne, I'm worried that I've lost him."

"Are you kidding? He's wild about you. He just needs to know that you feel the same way. Maybe you should write a song for *him*."

That idea made me laugh momentarily—until I realized how unlikely it was that Fin would ever forgive me. I feared our relationship was over. Gone forever. And as I tried to envision my life without Fin, all I could think about was how much I missed him already.

12

Artur Mandelkorn
Be'er Yaakov, Israel
March 1947

I finally received permission to leave the kibbutz and travel to Be'er Yaakov. It took a while to find it on the sprawling map pinned on the wall of the kibbutz cultural centre. Yet there it was: a tiny red dot south of Tel Aviv near the town of Ramla. Although Ruti was supposed to come with me, she had to bow out at the last minute because she had promised to help her sister sew a dress for her upcoming wedding. As Ruti put it, it was useless trying to argue with a hysterical bride-to-be. Luckily, though, Dudu stepped in to take her place, happy for an excuse to get away from the kibbutz for a little while. He recently began reading Martin Buber's *I and Thou* and was complaining that the *kibbutzniks* lacked "a spiritual consciousness." This, he imagined, could be found elsewhere—especially in the big city cafés and tearooms where artists and intellectuals gathered. The fact that we would be passing through Tel Aviv on the way to Be'er Yaakov was enough to fire up Dudu's enthusiasm for the trip.

Early on a humid morning, while the dew was still heavy in the fields, Dudu and I set out. Once we were settled on the bus, I felt positively giddy to be embarking on this journey. One might think that after wandering through Europe, I would have completely lost my wanderlust. But this was different. Then, I was being hunted. Now I was free to roam as I pleased.

Our first stop was Hadera, where we had to get off the first bus and wait for another to take us as far as Tel Aviv. With an hour to spare, we decided to explore the town sights, even though the grimy storefronts were hardly appealing. Several blocks away from the centre of town, however, we came upon a sight that made me catch my breath—there, out of nowhere, were row upon row of shimmering eucalyptus trees. What stunned me was not so much the sight of the glistening trees—though their beauty was breathtaking—but the incongruity of finding them so close to this desolate town. Dudu and I grew quiet as we approached them, stopping to stare at the vast assembly of trees wrapped in their silver-green robes.

Dudu sighed, and in a voice quite unlike his own, he murmured, "Baruch ... she-kacha lo be-olamo," the prayer that religious Jews recite when they encounter a wondrous sight. I was startled—not only by hearing Dudu say a prayer, but by the reverent tone of his voice. There was no trace of the familiar irony that Dudu wore like an identity tag. But his pious mood didn't last long—before I had a chance to say anything, he turned to me and quipped, "Let's get out of this place. If I see one more tree, I'll be tempted to swing from it like a monkey."

We made our way back to the small bus station in Hadera where we joined a teeming crowd of people waiting for the Tel Aviv bus. When the bus finally arrived, the entire crowd lunged forward in one seismic thrust, people using their bodies like assault weapons to get through the door. Since missing this bus meant a long wait for the next one, we too pressed and squeezed along with the others and somehow managed to get inside. Once on board, we wedged ourselves into a corner behind the driver where there was barely enough room to place both feet on the ground at the same time.

The driver hollered at the people to move to the back so that others could get on, though it did little good. What further complicated matters was an elderly gentleman carrying a large birdcage who planted himself in the centre of the bus and refused to move an inch. The people on the bus began shouting at him to move back, but he insisted that he needed space for his bird who, he asserted, had a delicate constitution. This started a series of jokes that seemed to erupt spontaneously from one end of the bus to the other. "Maybe your bird needs a hotel room!" someone shouted, making the crowd heave with laughter. Someone else began doing birdcalls, prompting another round of jokes and hoots of laughter.

The taunting and jeering continued unabated until an angry voice cut through the din, bellowing, "Stop it—enough—leave the poor man alone! Can't you see he has a number on his arm?" The entire busload of people immediately fell silent. A cloud of shame settled on the bus with no one daring to look his neighbour in the eye. But that didn't last long. A man with a heavy lisp broke the silence, "So what if he does have a number on his arm? We've all suffered. What gives him the right to clog up the bus?"

Some people turned on the man with the lisp saying, "What kind of Jew are you?" while others chanted, *Rachmanut! Rachmanut!* Show some compassion!" until the man with the lisp stormed out of his seat and angrily pushed his way to the door of the bus and dismounted.

"Good riddance to him," someone pronounced. And with that, the door snapped shut, the driver started his engine, and the bus sped off toward Tel Aviv, seemingly unperturbed by its troublesome cargo.

The first thing that struck me when we arrived in Tel Aviv was the smell. As soon as I stepped onto the street, my nostrils were filled with the acrid odour of exhaust fumes from the horde of buses converging on the city. But only a block or two further, the stench dissipated, overtaken by the peppery-sweet aroma of cumin and fried chickpeas coming from the ramshackle food stalls that were clustered around the station.

Drawn by the tantalizing smells, Dudu and I stopped at one of the stands and bought falafel from a coarsely-shaven seller, his thick fingers stained black with grease. As tahini slid down our chins from the overfilled pita, the vendor pulled us aside and whispered that he had other items for sale as well. He opened his jacket a few inches to reveal an array of gaudy trinkets pinned to the inner lining of his faded jacket—watch chains, key rings, sunglasses, and some miniature decks of cards. When we showed little interest, he stepped up his sales pitch, promising that we would never find prices like his anywhere else. The more we hesitated, the lower his prices fell until he swore that he was offering them to us below cost. "At these prices, it's like I'm giving them away!" he cried. Leaning forward and lowering his voice, he wagged a blackened finger, saying, "I'm only offering you these prices because I can see that you are special people. For no one else do I give these prices. No one else!"

In the end, we declined his offer, not because we didn't want his wares—I actually coveted a small bone-covered pocket knife pinned to the inside of his lapel—but because it was time to catch our connecting bus to Be'er Yaakov. The vendor, however, did not give up so easily. He continued to shout after us, vowing that we would regret passing up his offer. As we hurried toward the bus station, I looked back momentarily and could still dimly see him standing with his arms outstretched, pleading for us to return.

Be'er Yaakov looked much like any other small village in Palestine—a bleak crossroads with a few dusty shops bearing handwritten signs advertising cigarettes and gasoline. Yet one thing was different—the inhabitants. Clad in embroidered cloaks and round turban-like hats, they looked as though they had come from another world, or even from another century. They reminded me of the Hungarian peasants of my childhood who donned their traditional garb for the harvest festival, the men in square-edged hats and flowing robes, and the women in apron-covered dirndl skirts.

We weren't sure where to go to find Emil Lenchner, so Dudu and I went into one of the shops and asked the proprietor if he knew a young man by that name. The shopkeeper, a portly fellow with a thin black moustache and a nose like a quill, immediately revealed himself to be a man who would talk your ear off given half a chance. Before answering our query, he proceeded to give us a detailed account of the origin of every group that had settled in the village since its founding. It turned out that the people in the strange garb were, to my astonishment, Jews. Known as "mountain Jews," they had, according to the shopkeeper, come from Dagastan in deepest Russia and were the first Jews to settle Be'er Yaakov at the turn of the century. Nonetheless, he made a point of adding, if it had not been for Turkish Jews like himself, who arrived in the 1920s, the place would still be a swamp. "The Dagastanis know nothing about farming," he sneered. "All they know are goats and knives, knives and goats."

I had no idea what he meant by this, but fearing another long discourse, I tried to return the conversation to Emil Lenchner. When I repeated my question about whether Lenchner was a resident of the town, the proprietor stretched his moustache into a perfect horizontal line and slowly calculated his response. Instead of answering directly, he grinned slyly and challenged us with a riddle: "What," he asked, "rhymes with Emil but has his face buried in a book?"

I was confused by his riddle, but Dudu, who had a talent for word games, chimed in from the other side of the shop, "Maskil." It was the Hebrew word for a modern scholar or intellectual. Pleased with Dudu's answer, the merchant opened the door of his shop and pointed to a small frame structure across the road. "Do you see that building with the flag on the roof?" he said. "That's where our children go to school. You'll find your *maskil* there." We instantly realized that Emil Lenchner was not only a resident of Be'er Yaakov, but he was also the village schoolteacher.

We thanked the shopkeeper and hurried out. As soon as we crossed the road in the direction of the small schoolhouse, we heard children's voices singing a familiar tune. I recognized it as the melody of an old German carol that we had sung in school at Christmastime when I was a child, except now the words in Hebrew were about tilling the soil in the land of Israel. Dudu and I waited outside until the singing stopped and minutes later, the door burst open and children of all sizes came running out to play in the scraggly yard. Some of the children were wearing the peasant attire of the mountain Jews, while the rest looked like most other children in Palestine, only poorer. Some did not even have shoes on their feet. Following closely behind the children was a pale curly-haired young man with protruding ears and a silver whistle dangling from a string around his neck. Could this be Emil Lenchner?

When the children had dispersed like a band of wild pigeons, we introduced ourselves to the young man. With Germanic formality, he shook our hands and identified himself by saying, "Emil Lenchner, Head Schoolmaster, Be'er Yaakov Primary School." Before I could stop myself, I launched into my story. I was searching for my sister, I blurted out, and had reason to believe that she was last seen by someone who had the same name as him. The words poured out of me like water from a broken cistern. Yet Emil Lenchner stood there in silence, not moving a muscle. I was trying to read his eyes but they were flat and lifeless, like the button eyes sewn on the faces of marionettes. Finally, he raised his hand and stopped me from speaking further. "Let us go inside," he said, "and discuss this matter further. I'll prepare some tea." The abrupt way he cut me off made me wonder if he thought that I needed a salve to calm my nerves.

We entered the schoolhouse, which was comprised of one long room lined with tidy rows of wooden desks and chairs. Dudu and I each took a seat at one of the undersized desks while Emil went to the back of the room and boiled water on a small kerosene stove. Then, instead of taking his place at the front of the room at the teacher's desk, Emil sat down backward on one of the children's chairs so he could speak to us at eye-level. I noticed that he had deep creases on either side of his mouth, which, along with his large protruding ears, gave him an almost dog-like appearance. Turning to me he said, "I am not the man you are looking for. I'm sorry if that is a disappointment to you. I have never met your sister, but please—perhaps I can help you anyway."

My jaw tightened and I swallowed hard. I knew it was a mistake to come here. How could this stranger possibly help me?

Emil Lenchner took a long sip of tea and chose his next words carefully, as if he were rehearsing each sentence in his mind before saying it out loud. "I was born and raised in Prague. As were my parents. And their parents before them. We were a large family—like a world unto ourselves. That is not to say that we didn't mix in gentile society. My father had a government post and we lived a privileged life. We spoke German like the upper classes, attended good schools, hosted dignitaries in our home. We knew, of course, that we were Jews, but it meant little to us. I did attend a local *cheder* for a few years, but only as a concession to my maternal grandparents. Our one source of Jewish pride was that on my mother's side, we could trace our lineage back to the great rabbi of Prague, the MaHaral.

"When the Nazis invaded Czechoslovakia, however, my family and I were sent to the camps like all the other Jews. My whole family perished there—my parents, my three sisters, my older brother with his wife and baby daughter, all my aunts and uncles and cousins. I was the only one to survive. How that happened is another story—perhaps for another time." Leaning forward, his words emerged more quickly. "The point I am leading to is this: my father had a brother who went to live in Hungary and he also had a son named Emil. We were named after the same great-grandfather. I had not seen this cousin Emil since we were small children and assumed that my uncle and his eleven children had all been killed. Not long ago, however, I received a letter postmarked Cyprus. It was from my cousin Emil, who had somehow also managed to survive the war. What a strange coincidence that of all our extended family, the two Emils were the only ones to come out of the inferno alive.

"My cousin Emil's letter was written in rudimentary Hebrew, but I was able to make it out. He had been in several labour camps in Hungary and Poland before he escaped and joined a group of Jewish partisans in the forest. At the end of the war, he boarded an illegal ship to Palestine—but his was one of the vessels diverted to Cyprus by the British. His letter was full of bitterness toward them for not allowing the refugees to reach their homeland after all the suffering they had endured.

"The way that he found me was highly coincidental. You see, I write occasional articles of an educational nature for some of the local newspapers. Apparently, one of my pieces about teaching Hebrew to immigrant children was reproduced in a leaflet that was distributed to the internees on Cyprus. He had seen my name and school affiliation on the bottom of the article, so he sent his letter to this address.

"I am sorry to bore you with these details," he concluded. "Of what interest could they be to you? But, you see, I am wondering whether it is not my cousin Emil whom you are seeking. After all, he and I share the same name, although I think that in Hungary, it is pronounced Lenzner, rather than Lenchner."

On hearing this, I must have yelped or shouted in glee, for I could hear my voice bouncing down the length of the cavernous schoolroom. How strange—only moments earlier I had been in despair. Now, what had been upside-down unexpectedly became right side up. *This* Emil may not have been the right man, but his cousin surely was. I was convinced of it! It was all so clear now—the Emil Lenzner I was seeking could not be found in Palestine because he had never actually arrived. He was in Cyprus along with thousands of other hapless Jewish refugees who were trying to get into Palestine. The question of how I would contact him did not concern me then. It was just a matter of time before I could finally confront him and learn the truth about Manya.

I jumped out of my chair and grabbed Emil's hand, shaking it up and down. "Thank you for sharing your story. I am truly indebted to you. I am certain that this information will bear fruit."

Without warning, however, Emil's face suddenly turned dark, as if a shade had been pulled down over it. Lowering his eyes, he buried his chin in his chest. "Never be certain of anything," he said, his tone hollow. "Even if I am able to contact my cousin, I cannot vouch for his soundness of mind. In my experience, not everyone is capable of retrieving the past. For some, it is an utter impossibility. Even if he is the person you are looking for, he may not help you. He may not be capable of it."

I noticed that his hands were clenched and thick blue veins bulged from his neck. Just as I was about to apologize for burdening him with my story, he cut me off before I could begin. "Look," he said, his mouth hardening. "I am just trying to tell you what I've experienced. Do not count on finding anyone alive. Assume all is lost. Finished. *Kaput.* If you find anyone alive, it's a fluke. A mistake in your favour."

I bristled when I heard those words that were swift and final like a judge's gavel. At that moment, I had only one desire—to leave. But Dudu, who was silent up until now, cut in. "You're right," he said evenly. "We cannot expect miracles. But every once and a while they do happen. I could not have survived the war if I hadn't believed that." Emil countered by firing a second volley, this time aimed at Dudu point-blank. "So how do you account for all the miracles that didn't happen? Can you tell me why the millions of murdered Jewish children did not merit a miracle? What gives you a right to expect one? Your virtue? Your faith?"

I was dumbfounded by how calmly Dudu received this attack—until I noticed the fingers of his right hand drumming furiously on the underside of his chair. I tried to intercede before tempers grew hotter. "I beg you—if I have caused either of you grief by asking you to help me in my search, then please—treat it as if it never occurred. Forgive me—I am entirely to blame."

A nervous silence hung in the air. All of a sudden, Emil Lenchner sprang out of his seat, his lips suppressing an embarrassed grin. Striding over to Dudu, he extended his hand. "You are a good man—much better than I. I lost my faith completely during the war and I doubt I'll ever find it again. But I'm not totally lost—not yet. The children here give me some comfort. Not because they're pure and innocent and all that nonsense. They're little scoundrels most of the time. You see—how can I put it? They are a different sort of Jew. Just imagine, growing up and never caring about what the *goyim* think. Never having to worry about being called a pushy Jew, a cheap Jew, a rich Jew, or a Jew who controls the world. What freedom! These children are their own masters."

Stunned by his rapid turnaround, I glanced briefly at Dudu and saw by his pensive nodding that he understood Emil perfectly.

There was another brief silence before Dudu and I gestured to each other that it was getting late. Soon we got up to go, and as we walked toward the door, Emil followed closely behind. "Wait," he said. "Permit me to show you something before you leave." Once outside, he led us to the edge of the playing field and pointed to the sparse landscape around us.

"You see those saplings beside the road? Jews planted them one by one. Clearing the stones was only half the battle. This place was so barren before we came here that the soil was like dust. That's why we teach the children agriculture, just like we teach them reading and writing. Can you believe it? Jewish farm labourers! I remember studying the agricultural laws in *cheder* as a child and thinking— what does this have to do with me? In Prague, I was as estranged from farm life as, excuse the comparison, a priest is from a brothel."

Kicking the stones beneath his feet he continued, "I used to wonder why we Jews refer to God as our 'Rock.' Now it is clear, although I cannot say that I believe it in any metaphysical sense. I see these stones and I know that without us, they are nothing but dead objects in need of transformation. They are a permanent re-minder that the land is in constant need of work. Every morning I say to myself: Who has time to give in to despair when there is so much work to be done?"

On that note, Emil Lenchner ended his speech and turned to bid us farewell. Carefully inscribing my address on a scrap of paper, he assured me that he would write to his cousin in Cyprus and would let me know when he heard back from him. Instead of warning me not to hope for miracles, this time he shook my hand vigorously and wished me the best of luck with my search.

I did not know what to make of Emil Lenchner. Despite his moodiness, he was a peculiarly inspirational character. Though he'd certainly deny it if he heard it said, he possessed a kind of religious zeal—certainly not for God—but for rebuilding the land and its people from the bottom up. He was the first person I'd met who seemed to live solely for that ideal. I had the feeling that his words would stay with me for a long time, that his dedication would be a kind of yardstick by which to measure my own short-comings. Though I doubted that I would ever see him again, I was certain that if I wanted to, I could always find him—still toiling in Be'er Yaakov, instructing another generation of immigrant chil-dren how to be, as he put it, "their own masters."

I left Be'er Yaakov on that day with the growing sense that having made this breakthrough in my search for Manya, I too would have to become my own master. I had been given an "opening" and it was up to me to act on it. I didn't have to wait for Emil Lenchner to write to his cousin on my behalf—I could write to him myself. After all, I was the one who should be posing the crucial questions that only he, Emil Lenzner, could answer: How had he known Manya's full name to report it in his testimony? How late in the war had he met her? Who else might have seen her last? Has he been in contact with any other survivors of that deportation?

All of these questions turned round and round in my brain as Dudu and I headed back to the kibbutz, both of us keyed up but weary from the day's emotional events. Our going was much like our coming, except for one thing. This time when we stopped in Tel Aviv to change buses, we found our way to the same vendor's stall and, much to Dudu's astonishment, I bought the bone-covered pocket knife that I'd coveted earlier in the day. The vendor showed no surprise that we had come back. "I knew you would return," he said. "I could see it written on your face. You will need a knife now that you are a grown man, yes?"

I nodded in agreement. Before I'd gone to Be'er Yaakov, I might not have seen it that way. But now I knew that even if I could not quite call myself a man, I would have to become one in very short order.

13

Suzy Kohn
Toronto, Ontario
March 1969

Fin now refused to speak to me at all. I tried everything—letters
of apology, phone calls, notes slipped into his locker. I even asked
Lynne to intercede for me. But he wouldn't speak to her either.
The hardest part was getting through the day at school. I imagined
that everyone was talking about us, gloating over what happened.
Mocking me behind my back, saying, Suzy Kohn is such a fool.
Letting Fin get away. Who does she think she is? She'll never get
anyone half as cool as him.

Fin was always surrounded by girls at school. Whenever I saw
them fawning over him, I wanted to shake them by their skinny
shoulders and slap their lip-glossed faces until they begged me to
stop. Of course, that was fantasy. In reality, I just rushed past them,
averting my gaze. I tried to carry on as best I could, but I wasn't
myself anymore. It was as if I were living in a sort of fuzzy haze,
on the other side of a thick glass wall that separated me from everyone around me. I began to feel awkward and unattractive again;
all the old self-doubts that had been bubbling beneath the surface
started to re-emerge.

One memory in particular kept coming back to me. At the end of junior high, I was befriended by a girl in my grade named Frances Mason, France for short. Like most of her crowd, France had all the trappings of popularity: straight blond bangs, lustrous teeth, and a winter tan. A ski-lift tag dangled from her jacket zipper long after all the snow had melted. I didn't think to wonder why she suddenly included me in her circle of friends until one day I overheard her telling one of her gang how she planned to "re-make Suzy Kohn." I had no idea what she meant, so I ignored the comment. But I slowly began to notice that whenever France invited me to her home, she would insist on doing my nails, plucking my eyebrows, or ironing my hair. At first I was flattered by the attention, but after a while I started to feel like some kind of ugly duckling. I found myself staring in the mirror all the time with a growing sense of despair. It was no use—I would never be able to look like France and her friends, no matter how hard I tried.

I remembered broaching the subject of my appearance with Bella. Though my aunt was inclined to be a little erratic—the result of her "artistic nature," my parents often commented—I could usually depend on her to offer me advice. When I told her about France and her friends, she threw me a knowing sidelong glance indicating that she grasped the entire situation. "Don't worry, honey," she said, "you have the kind of looks that women will always be jealous of. I should know. You remind me a lot of myself at your age. Girls like us have a different sort of beauty. Not the kind that takes people's breath away. It's softer. But it's the kind that lasts." Bella's comments had been soothing at the time, like a cool compress on an injured limb. But that was so long ago. The situation now was completely different. When I stared at myself in the mirror, why did I still feel like that same ugly duckling? How I wished I had Bella to talk to now. She still barely responded to any attempts at conversation.

My parents had also become more remote than ever. Mother

stumbled from room to room like a wounded bird, pecking at anyone who got in her way. And we rarely saw Father. He came home from work later and later every night, then spent most of the evening in the den with the door closed. When he finally emerged to go to bed, he'd mumble something vague as he passed me on the stairs leaving a cloud of whisky-breath behind him.

Even Lynne was getting tired of hearing about my troubles. After we'd spent many evenings sprawled out on the shag rug in her basement discussing my breakup with Fin, she finally threw up her hands and told me to snap out of it. I jumped up to leave, tears welling in my eyes. Lynne grabbed me by the elbow. "Suzy, wait. I didn't mean to hurt you. It's all this talking and analyzing. You're bringing me down. I can't take all the negativity."

"Well, sorry if I'm a burden," I sneered, my voice quivering.

"Don't take it like that. It's just that—Fin's not worth it. No boy is."

"How can you say that? You're always hung up on some guy or other."

"Sure. But then I go on to another one. They're all the same. All they want is one thing. Why fool yourself?"

Maybe she was right. And yet—I couldn't be like her. I didn't want to look at boys as if they were predators, always plotting to snare their bait, discarding it when they had their fill. As I turned toward the door, Lynne rushed over and gave me a hug, whispering in my ear, "Lighten up, okay?" I bit my lip and nodded, but knew I couldn't change how I felt. Lynne meant well, but she simply didn't understand. How do you lighten up when your thoughts are so heavy that you're about to crumble from the weight?

In desperation, I turned to writing, hoping that getting my feelings down on paper might help. Yet, seeing my loneliness in black and white just made me feel even more pathetic. In the end, I tore up everything I wrote. And burned the scraps with the end of my cigarette. Sitting on the floor of my bedroom, staring at the ashes of those burnt-up pages, I realized how deflated I'd become. Like a bottle of soda gone flat. Losing Fin was bad enough. But worse still was losing my spirit. I seemed to have lost all my enthusiasm for life. And I was so afraid that I'd never get it back.

14

Artur Mandelkorn
Kibbutz Tivon, Israel
March 1947

It started to rain heavily on our return from Be'er Yaakov and by the time we got off the bus near the kibbutz, Dudu and I had to run to our lodgings through a heavy downpour. Soaking wet, we arrived at our rooms only to find them empty. A note attached to the door informed us that the whole kibbutz population had been summoned to an emergency meeting in the dining hall. After changing into dry clothes, we hurried down to find out what had prompted this unexpected gathering.

When I walked into the dining hall, I saw a speaker with a British accent addressing the crowd from a makeshift podium. He was broad-shouldered but lean, with an angular face and sharp cheekbones that framed a pair of darting black eyes. Impeccably groomed, he had the taut look of a well-trained British officer. My first thought was that he was there to warn us against harbouring members of the Haganah, the Jewish defense force. Rumour had it that the British, in their attempt to appease the oil-rich Arab countries, had become increasingly hostile to the Haganah. They were well aware that many kibbutzim had close ties to the defense organization and that some served as safe havens for the Haganah's caches of illegal weapons.

But it didn't take long for me to realize that the speaker was not a British soldier—quite the opposite. He was an English Jew who was on a special assignment to recruit for the Haganah. He told us that he belonged to the group of Jews who had fought for the Allies as part of the Jewish Brigade during the war. In an urgent tone, he explained that the situation for the Jews in Palestine was becoming dire. "Without new recruits to relieve the ranks of volunteers who are already stretched thin," he said, "the results could be catastrophic." He scanned the faces in the room. "As you may know, Arab attacks against Jewish targets have increased twenty-fold in recent months. And," he added, "there are signs that the British government wants out of Palestine. They are drawing up a plan to partition the land into separate Jewish and Arab states. We all know what that means. Once Britain gives up the administration of Palestine and withdraws its forces, the Arab countries that surround us will attack."

I soon learned that the speaker's name was Harold Davidson, although he preferred to be called by his Hebrew name Tzvi. To my eyes, he seemed to embody the fighting spirit of the young Jewish nation while also being in full control of his emotions. This combination appealed to me, since my experiences in Europe during the war had made me wary of people who look at army life as a chance to give free rein to their animal natures.

It was evident that I was not the only one who was inspired by the figure of Tzvi Davidson—for many of the young people in the room began to crowd around him after he finished speaking. Some of them wanted to join up immediately, although he made it clear that there was a formal procedure that had to be followed. I knew that several of these enthusiastic youths would likely be rejected, as many of them were too emotionally damaged from the war. But there were others who I thought would make excellent soldiers since they had what I would call an aggressive resilience. They confronted adversity as if it were a personal test of strength and, like prizefighters, became tougher with each fight. I wasn't sure where I fit in or, indeed, whether I fit in at all. My habit of thinking too long and hard about things didn't, to my mind, make me well-suited to being a soldier.

Once the crowd began to clear, Ruti spotted me standing at the edge of the room and called me over so she could introduce me to Tzvi Davidson personally. She seemed to be on close terms with him and referred to him as Tzvika. He asked if I was interested in becoming a recruit. I cleared my throat, not sure how to answer. "Yes—of course. I would like to do my part. I'm just not sure how someone like me could be of use." He didn't seem bothered by my hesitation. "You appear to be a bright sort of chap," he said. "Perhaps we could use you in intelligence."

At first I thought he was merely being facetious. But when he went on to describe the type of work he had in mind, I realized that he was speaking in earnest. "It wouldn't be anything glamorous, of course," he said. "No spying on Arab sheikhs or anything of that sort. Mostly information gathering. Keeping records."

"Hmmm," I said. "I would need some time to think about it."

His reply was swift. "Perfectly understandable. But don't dwell on it too long or I might not be around to offer it again. The Brits are arresting us by the dozens." It sounded peculiar to hear him use the term "Brits" when he was obviously from Britain himself. But I suppose he'd become so much a part of the *Yishuv* since coming to Palestine that he no longer thought of himself as an Englishman—no more than David Ben-Gurion considered himself a Russian.

Lying in bed that night, I had trouble falling asleep. The combination of heat and rain made me feel chilled one moment and sweat-soaked the next. On top of that, my head was in a complete stew. When I arrived back from Be'er Yaakov, I had thought that my plans were firmly laid out—I would write to Emil Lenzner in Cyprus and, depending on what I heard from him, embark on the next stage of my search for Manya. Now, a new possibility presented itself: working for the Haganah. Ever since I'd arrived in Palestine, I hadn't given much thought to what I would like to do with my life. In childhood, I vaguely remembered that I'd wanted to become an airplane pilot or an inventor of mechanical devices. More recently I'd toyed with the idea of becoming a carpenter. But after arriving in Palestine, those distant dreams seemed to belong to someone else. These days, a part of me just wanted to stay on the kibbutz and live out my life as a farmer.

Thoughts of joining the Haganah dogged me throughout the night, until I finally gave up and went for a walk before the sun came up. The heat had lifted and the rain had stopped. I looked up and saw a hazy moon reclining on the treetops. Such perfect tranquility. It was hard to believe that a war might break out at any time. But experience told me otherwise—I knew only too well that the most frightful things often happen at the very moment you least expect them.

15

Suzy Kohn
Toronto, Ontario
April 1969

After losing Fin, music was the only thing that helped ease my loneliness, offering me refuge in a world where I felt I belonged. Every evening, I spent hours in my room with the door closed, listening to songs on my record player, studying the album covers and inserts, meditating on the words. To me, it wasn't just music. It was truth and beauty and wisdom all rolled into one. Joni Mitchell, Judy Collins, Simon and Garfunkel, Leonard Cohen—they were prophets of sorrow and heartbreak. Of the yearning for simplicity. Of the child in all of us asking to be loved. More than any other, I was drawn to the song "Michael from Mountains" by Joni Mitchell. It embodied all my bottled-up feelings about Fin that I couldn't express myself. I pictured him in my mind every time I listened to her sing that song. And when she came to the refrain, "someday I may know you very well," my stomach turned hollow and my eyes welled with tears. How could Joni Mitchell know *me* so very well?

After listening to that song countless times, something that Lynne had said suddenly came back to me. It was what she'd flippantly suggested I do after Fin and I broke up—that I should write a song for him. At the time, I'd simply dismissed the idea as a joke. But now it started to make sense to me. Of course, I had long given up on ever getting back together with Fin. That was over and done with. I just wanted to let him know that I finally understood him. And what could convey that better than a song? "Michael from Mountains" was the ideal choice—all I had to do was adapt the words. Fin once told me that he was born in Fort William in northwestern Ontario and hadn't moved to Toronto until he was six. How simple: I would re-name the song "Fin from Fort William." It fit so perfectly. I wrote out all the words and practiced the song over and over until I was sure I could sing it flawlessly. I then made a tape recording of it and mailed the cassette to Fin, along with a note:

Dear Fin, I finally understand what you meant when you said that all artists learn from each another. You were right. So I borrowed this song by Joni Mitchell and made it a song for you. I send it with no expectations. I just want you to have it. Please know that I wish you much peace and contentment. Suzy

A week passed and I didn't hear back from Fin. Not that I really expected to. Who knows? Maybe he threw out the tape, once he saw it was from me. Or listened to it and had a good laugh.

The following week, Lynne and I made plans to meet downtown on Saturday to check out an art exhibit in Nathan Phillips Square. When I arrived, there was a fierce wind tearing at the flags surrounding the reflecting pool. I finally found Lynne huddled behind Henry Moore's sculpture "The Archer," sheltering herself from the wind. "Let's go somewhere warm," I said. "We can grab some coffee and come back to see the exhibit later."

"No. We have to wait for Margot. I asked her to join us. I hope you don't mind." My stomach sank—I was in no mood to deal with Margot Brandt. Even at the best of times, she had a smug manner that made me feel small, even though she was barely five-foot tall herself. As we stood there shivering, waiting for Margot to appear, Lynne pinched my arm. "Look. Over there," she said. "Is that who I think it is?"

Squinting my eyes, I saw a young man with a lanky torso walking toward us, buffeted by the wind. The rambling black curls, the long-footed stride, the jean jacket emblazoned with a Swedish flag. I knew it was Fin. I looked down at the ground, my heart pounding, pretending not to see him. But he obviously saw me. Before I knew it, I was staring at Fin's tawny Birkenstocks that were planted directly in front of me. I heard him chuckle as he waited for me to look up. "Suzy, aren't you going to say hello?"

"Um—yes. Hello."

"How've you been?" Fin cupped his hand over his eyes, shielding them from the wind. Two sapphire slivers shone through the lashes.

"I'm fine. Great. Yes—everything's great."

"Hey," he said. "Could we talk—just for a minute? If you're cold, we can walk around a bit."

I turned to Lynne with a questioning glance, wondering if she minded. She waved her hand to indicate it was fine with her. Fin and I crossed the square, braced against the forceful gusts, neither of us saying a word. Dodging through the traffic to cross Bay Street, my feet seemed to be hardly touching the ground. It wasn't until we reached the gothic walls of Trinity Church that I felt the cobblestones under my feet. Fin stopped and broke the silence, "Listen, Suzy, I got your cassette—I was very touched by it. I mean, it really blew my mind."

"I don't know what to say," I mumbled, not daring to look him in the eye.

"I guess I just wanted to tell you that I—I really miss you."

My head began to swim. Had I heard him correctly? Perhaps I'd imagined it —like seeing a mirage, or hearing the ocean inside of a shell. But when I turned to look at him, I saw it was real. There he stood, smiling widely, his luminous blue eyes seeking mine. "I miss you too," I heard myself whisper. Fin reached out and touched my arm, tracing his finger up my neck toward my face. My cheeks, my head, my toes, were singing. And in that split second, I knew. Our relationship was going to begin again.

16

Artur Mandelkorn
Kibbutz Tivon, Israel
March 1947

Despite my dread of an imminent war and the sleeplessness that followed, when morning came and my chores began, all my anxieties dissolved like dew. After finishing my usual breakfast of boiled egg, yogurt, and diced cucumber, I received an unexpected surprise—a letter arrived in the mail from Fanny, inviting me to join her in Tel Aviv next month for her uncle's Passover seder.

Passover was still several weeks away, but I immediately looked for Ruti to see about getting permission to go. Although Ruti wasn't in charge of such decisions, she possessed what was commonly known as *protektzia*—that is, she could pull strings to make things happen. When I found Ruti and told her that I had been invited to Tel Aviv to spend Passover with Fanny, she shook her head from side to side in mock disapproval.

"So, you've already got a sweetheart. I hope you'll invite me to the *chupah!*"

I could feel the heat creeping into my cheeks as I hastened to explain that Fanny was merely a friend I'd met on the ship. Ruti chortled, then offered me a bit of sisterly advice. "Muki, listen to one who knows about such things. Don't marry the first girl you fall in love with."

When I started to protest that I wasn't even thinking about getting married, she stopped me and insisted on speaking her mind. "I know your sort, Muki, and I know that you're easy bait for a certain type of girl. You're reliable, serious, a little shy sometimes— just the type some motherly girl would like to lead by the nose. But don't let yourself get caught. I've seen it happen too many times and then, *chik-chuk,* you're stuck for good!"

Although I was indignant that Fanny had no designs on me in that way, I figured it was useless to argue with Ruti. She always managed to twist a dispute in such a way that my very arguing with her was proof to her that she was right. At the same time, I knew that Ruti was only looking out for my welfare, believing it to be her responsibility to warn me against those who might do me harm. Yet I knew in my heart that Fanny was nothing like the kind of girl that Ruti was describing. I was certain that once she met Fanny in person, she would see that she was completely mistaken.

I turned the discussion back to the question of permission for me to travel to Tel Aviv for Passover. Though Ruti claimed that it was not her decision to make, everyone knew that if Ruti wanted something, she could always get her way. People liked to please her, perhaps because her effusive personality made everyone feel good when she was happy. I promised I would make up the time by doing twice the amount of work I was scheduled to do for the entire month before the holiday. But what clinched the deal was this: I also offered to take on Gidon's chores for the upcoming weekend. Gidon, another one of the group leaders, was sweet on Ruti and I was quite sure she was sweet on him. During group meetings, he would often stop in the middle of a sentence, tilt his head to the side, and smile at Ruti in a way that made his teeth glimmer. She would scold him for his sudden silence but then laugh as if she were the happiest person in the world. It was clear to me that they were in love, although I wasn't sure whether they even knew it yet. That night, I wrote Fanny a note telling her that everything looked promising for my visit to Tel Aviv. I didn't mention anything about my search for Emil Lenzner or my recent encounter with his cousin in Be'er Yaakov, as I wanted to share that information with her in person.

Over the next few days, I devoted hours to composing a letter to Lenzner in Cyprus. I began countless times, only to rip up each draft after one or two paragraphs. The first few, I thought, had an angry tone to them and I feared that if I sent a letter like that he might take offense and not answer. The next few were more conciliatory but, to my ear, they sounded insincere. The more I tried to find exactly the right tone, the harder it was to write, and I finally had to stop. But the urgency of writing this letter kept gnawing at me and wouldn't let go.

Most of the kibbutz members were occupied with preparations for the Passover festival. Our kibbutz was not religious, so we marked most of the Jewish holidays by transforming them into national celebrations. Since Passover commemorated the liberation of the Jews from Egyptian slavery, it took on a different significance for those of us who had recently survived the most brutal slavery imaginable. Yet some of the refugees refused to celebrate the holiday at all, having turned their backs on anything that smacked of even the tiniest whiff of religion. As for me, I sometimes felt that coming to Palestine after the war was a more miraculous event than the entire biblical story of slavery and redemption.

One of the Passover traditions that the kibbutz retained was the practice of cleaning one's home from top to bottom in the weeks preceding the holiday. As a result, kibbutz members participated in a thorough scrubbing of all the buildings, including our personal residences. It was similar to the ritual Passover cleaning that I recalled from my childhood, except the aim was different. When my mother scoured our home before Passover, what drove her to near exhaustion was the religious requirement to remove all traces of *chametz*, leaven, from the house. Here, on the kibbutz, we did the same meticulous cleaning but it was done without the sacred purpose in mind.

During the cleaning of our dormitory rooms, one of our final tasks was to empty the storage area beneath our beds. After dragging out a bulging carton that was stuffed beneath my cot, I opened the flaps to peek inside. What I saw made me jump: at the top of the pile was Manya's hurdy-gurdy. It wasn't just the sight of it that stunned me. Holding the toy in my hands, I looked down at it and realized that it was the only remnant I had of my life before the war. The war had robbed me of everything—my parents, my brother, my two sisters, my home. All that remained was this ragged little plaything. Seeing it again made my stomach turn. I didn't even want to look at it. I thought of destroying it, but one thing stopped me: Manya loved it. I had to save it, if only for her sake. Once I found her, it would be the one thing she could point to and say, I once had a regular life. I even had toys like other children. I remember that life. I'm still that person.

So instead of destroying the wretched little toy, I examined it to make sure it was still intact. The fabric on the bellows was so threadbare that I didn't think it could make any sound. But when I cranked the handle, it actually began to play a tune, though off-key and wheezy as if it were gasping for breath. I scrambled around the room looking for something soft to wrap it in. Finding a towel, I laid the hurdy-gurdy on it and rolled it up as gently as I would bundle a baby in swaddling clothes. Then I put it carefully back into the carton and went back to finishing my cleaning.

Strangely enough, that evening I was finally able to write the letter to Emil Lenzner. The words now poured out of me, like milk gushing from a bottle. I knew exactly what to say and how to say it. I told him everything about Manya, describing her as painstakingly as possible so there could be no mistake about her identity. I began with her appearance—her light brown hair that shone gold in the sun; her straight nose that turned neither up nor down; her eyes, brown and velvety, with long black lashes that half-covered them, giving her a wistful, dreamy look; her small mouth and her habit of sucking in her bottom lip when she was tense or afraid. But the most striking thing about Manya was her character. She had an air of gentle refinement that you didn't often see in young people. Our elderly neighbour used to call her *an eydl kind,* Yiddish for "a precious child," though it implied much more—a quality of inner nobility or sweetness of soul that fit my sister to a T. I also described her aptitude for music and her lovely singing voice. I even listed some of her favourite songs and the tunes she liked to hum. Music was so much part of her that I knew it was impossible for anyone to meet her and not be aware of it.

But the most important thing I wanted to tell him in my letter was about Manya's terror of heights, to convince him that my sister could never have jumped from a moving train. Hers was not an abstract fear; it went back to something that happened when she was only three years old. She was leaning on a window in our house when the frame came loose and crashed to the ground, taking Manya with it. She fell several stories and would likely have been killed if it had not been for the fact that a thick mound of boxwood cushioned her fall. As it was, she suffered a mild concussion and a broken leg that left her bedridden for months. She eventually recovered but was left with a morbid fear of heights. For a long time, we could barely persuade her to come near an open window and, even in daytime, she kept the curtains drawn in her room so the windows weren't exposed. Her distrust of windows eventually subsided, but her fear of heights remained constant and she went to great lengths to avoid them. That was why, I wrote passionately, I was so convinced that it could not have been Manya who jumped from the train. Since Emil Lenzner had given Manya's name to the authorities after the war, I acknowledged that he must have met her, that they might have even been on that same train. But I was certain that his depiction of what had happened to her was mistaken.

I ended the letter by begging Emil to search his memory for any recollections of my sister. I implored him to think back to the time on the train and to try to remember who else was on it. Was there someone who might have known my sister and who might have information about her whereabouts? Was there anyone else from that transport who had survived the war? Has he seen or spoken to anyone from that time? What was the eventual fate of that train-load of Jews? Had they all been sent to death camps or were some sent into forced labour?

When I got to the end, I quickly sealed the letter and posted it without an exact address. Perhaps naively, I assumed that a letter sent to a particular person in Cyprus would reach its proper destination. How many people could there be on such a tiny scrap of land? Though I knew that there were thousands of refugees being held in internment camps on the island, I didn't want to even consider the possibility that my letter might not reach him. I sent the letter to Emil Lenzner full of blind faith that he would receive it. I was also certain that once he read my letter and heard my story, he would feel compelled to respond.

The next several weeks brought no response from Emil Lenzner. Nor did I hear anything from his cousin in Be'er Yaakov. The more days that passed without a letter, the more my thoughts grew darker. Like the olive tree whose bark turns blacker over time.

At last Passover arrived, with the promise of a brief respite. With Ruti's help, I'd been granted permission to spend the holiday with Fanny and Uncle Chaim. As I was packing my belongings, Dudu appeared with the day's mail and handed me a fat grey envelope. When I first saw the row of multi-coloured stamps embellished by a series of black wavy lines, I was sure that it was the letter I'd been waiting for. But instead of Cyprus stamped on the envelope, I saw the word Hungary. I then immediately recognized the European hand of Mrs. Kartash, whose writing curled at the end like a row of fishing hooks. But why was she sending me such a thick letter? Mrs. Kartash wrote to me often, but always on post-cards. A heavy packet like this would surely have cost her a week's wages in postage. My fingers were shaking as I grasped the letter, fearful about what the contents might be. My first thought was, No. Not now. I'm not ready to read this. Stuffing the letter into my haversack, I decided that I would open it later, perhaps on the bus.

I left the kibbutz in a daze, as if my mind and my body were divided from each other. It was as if I were watching myself on a cinema screen although I was the only one in the audience. Once I was on the bus, I slumped down into my seat and just stared out the window for at least an hour, maybe more. My body was limp, but my mind was racing like a dog around a track.

An elderly gentleman across the aisle broke my stupour by tapping me on the shoulder, asking me if I had a cigarette. For some reason, I answered, "I'll check and see," even though I didn't smoke, and never carried cigarettes. I pulled out my pockets, which were empty, and apologized to the fellow. I now saw that he was younger than I originally thought. Despite a tangle of wiry grey hair, his skin was surprisingly smooth and sun-burnished, giving it the appearance of deep red leather.

He pulled a toothpick out of his shirt pocket, placed it between his teeth and struck up a conversation with me, first about farming and irrigation—he was a member of a nearby kibbutz—and then a little about himself. After telling me the tale of his *aliyah* from Poland in the 1920s, he proceeded to ask me about myself. Before I knew it, I was talking about my childhood in Hungary, a little about the war, and about my search for Manya. I even told him about the letter in my haversack and how I wasn't sure if I was ready to open it. I don't know why I confided in him of all people— a complete stranger. But he listened quietly, nodding in an understanding sort of way, which caused the toothpick in his mouth to bob up and down. After a short pause, he turned to me and said, "When or where you open the letter is not going to change what's inside of the envelope. You are the one who has to be prepared for what's in it—good or bad. Good news is easy to prepare for. But who is ever prepared for bad news? Nobody."

His words stayed with me even after we said goodbye, although I realized later that I never caught his name. Just before getting off the bus in Tel Aviv, he shook my hand and wished me good luck, adding the common Hebrew expression, "All will be for the good." Though he said it with confidence, I couldn't help wondering: do people really believe that, or are they just hoping it is true?

Arriving an hour earlier than expected in Tel Aviv, I settled myself onto a bench inside the central bus station. The building was dank and gritty with the smell of sweat hanging in the air. Throngs of people looking weary and impatient waited in clusters. When the buses finally appeared, they announced their arrival by roaring into the station one after another with the fanfare of an imperial procession, honking their horns and spewing smoke. The passengers all sprang to life—jostling and fumbling, grabbing packages, suitcases, and children. Everyone was suddenly happy, full of smiles and chatter. The world seemed a better place. And then, as if it were my cue, I sprang into action as well. I reached into my haversack, pulled out the letter, and using my bone-covered pocket knife, I tore it open right there in the hurry-scurry of the Tel Aviv bus station.

From the envelope I extracted a sheaf of official-looking documents that were folded inside a single sheet of notepaper. Mrs. Kartash's ornate penmanship covered less than half the page:

My dear Artur,

It is with great sorrow that I must convey to you the following news: I have received confirmation that your beloved parents, Maxim and Eva Mandelkorn, along with your baby sister, Kati, died in the Nazi concentration camp of Auschwitz-Birkenau on July 3, 1944. The enclosed documents provide verification of their deaths. Two of the documents are sworn testimonies—by Mr. Roman Krall and Mrs. Blanca Lutz—who were acquainted with your parents and sister at the camp and were witnesses to their murder. As you can see from the documents, the cause of their death was gas poisoning.

We have also received an unconfirmed report that your brother, Karl, died of typhus in Auschwitz in January 1945. However, since we have no eyewitness report to verify this information, we await further documentation.

I am sorry to have to be the bearer of this tragic news. But it is better to know the truth than to live with false hope.

Please accept my deepest sympathy.

Yours,

Hélène Kartash

I sat there immobilized, as lifeless as a limb torn from a body. There was no pain, only numbness, the world around me now a dull shade of grey. Time became meaningless, as if I were drifting through a long foggy tunnel. I vaguely remember Uncle Chaim arriving, driving me to his house, and escorting me down the half-lit hallway to his apartment. I also remember Fanny greeting us at the door, her cheeks glowing as she chattered excitedly. Attempting to smile, I heard myself mutter that I was tired from the journey. Varda, Uncle Chaim's wife, shuffled in from another room and introduced herself. With her thick orange lips and painted brows, she reminded me of a clown at a carnival show. Varda asked if I would like a cold drink, but before I could answer, she began rearranging the flowers on a nearby table.

I unpacked my haversack in the spare room and reluctantly joined the others in the salon, where Fanny tried to initiate conversation. I could only manage a few terse words and a shrug of my shoulders. It didn't take long for her to start biting her lip and blinking; eventually she excused herself, muttering something about being needed in the kitchen. I knew my aloofness was hurting her, but I was powerless to explain myself or change my behaviour.

All I could think about was the letter. But I couldn't bear to talk about it to anyone, not even Fanny. I was afraid that if I said anything about it, I would break down completely. As it was, my head was burning and my throat was parched. Yet I could not allow myself to give in. Nothing was worse than releasing into the world what was crushing me inside.

The seder started in a sluggish manner. We sat around the cramped dining table, as Fanny's uncle chanted slowly from the Haggadah, the telling of the story of the Jews' liberation from Egyptian slavery. After every few stanzas, he stopped and looked up from under his heavy reading glasses to ask us what we thought was meant by the previous section. The final time he did this, Varda cut in, saying, "It's enough, Chaim. No one is interested." Fanny tried to come to her uncle's aid by asking him what he thought the passages meant. Drawing on the extensive knowledge he acquired as a youth in a Polish *yeshiva* (he called it his first "battle training"), he explained the words of the Haggadah with ease. Having given up the religious life in order to join the Zionist pioneers in Palestine, however, he ended his comments with a nationalistic message: "Certainly the Israelites in Egypt and the Jews in modern Europe had much in common. Except the Jews in Egypt did something about it: they left en masse."

I could feel my blood rising and my heart began to hammer in my ears. "How can you say that?" I burst out. "Surely Theodor Herzl was a modern-day Moses."

Uncle Chaim drew back. "Yes," he responded calmly. "He could have been like Moses. If more of the Jews followed him."

How can you blame the Jews of Europe for not leaving? I wanted to shout. How could they have known that the people they had lived with for hundreds of years would turn into murderers? Did *you* see it coming? Did *anyone*? But I didn't say it. I just sat and boiled like a pot on the fire. And as I seethed and raged inside, I decided that I wouldn't say another word to anyone that night. That would show them, I thought. That would let them know not to insult me. If they want to cast aspersions on Jews like me and my family, let them speak their ugly words, but I will not give them the satisfaction of witnessing my contempt. I could tell by the scraping of chairs and the clearing of throats that my behaviour was creating an increasingly strained atmosphere, but I didn't care. Even Fanny's doleful eyes did nothing to calm me down—she too had become one of *them*. I could hardly look at her.

Once the supposedly festive meal was served, everyone turned their attention away from me and concentrated on eating. But the food was like lead in my mouth and I left most of it on my plate, pushing it away as if it were contaminated. The matzah was the only thing that tasted good to me. While the others slurped their soup and devoured the brisket, I satisfied myself by breaking off tiny pieces of the unleavened bread, dipping them in salt water, and sucking on them until they dissolved on my tongue.

Uncle Chaim attempted to draw me into conversation, but I refused to engage with him. I figured that a few nods and hand motions were good enough to answer his frivolous questions. At the same time, Fanny kept trying to find out what was wrong, whispering to me and making imploring gestures with her hands. After receiving nothing but a series of sullen shrugs from me, she at last cried out, "How can you act like this, and on Passover of all times? Don't you have any respect? What did we ever do to you?" She jumped up and ran out of the room sobbing.

Her cry cut through me like a knife. I leapt out of my seat and raced into her room, where she lay weeping on the bed. Trying hard to hold back my own tears, I stood beside the bed pleading

with her to forgive me. I said that I didn't know why I was acting that way. I cursed myself for being a scoundrel and said that I
wouldn't blame her if she never spoke to me again. Fanny sobbed
into her pillow for several minutes. Short, gasping sounds soon
came out of her throat as she attempted to speak. With her face still
buried in the pillow, she began to speak, "Artur, I thought I knew
you. We had been like one soul. Now you are like a stranger. Who
are you? Where is the Artur I knew?" She burst into tears once
again, this time crying even louder and with more intensity.

Not knowing what more I could say, I asked if she wanted me
to go. I said I would leave that very evening if that is what she preferred. She pulled the sides of her pillow up around her head as if
she wanted to block out the sound of my voice. I stood there motionless for several seconds before coming to the conclusion that
this was her way of telling me that she wanted nothing more to do
with me. I turned and left the room, determined to grab my belongings and get away from there as fast as I could.

But Uncle Chaim was in the next room waiting for me to
emerge and took hold of my arm as I rushed through the hall to
collect my bag. He urged me to sit down and talk to him before I
did anything rash. I started to apologize for ruining his seder, but
he waved away my words, "What would a seder be without a bit
of excitement? Come, we'll sit on the balcony. There's a breeze tonight. It's good. We'll talk."

As soon as we sat down, Uncle Chaim started talking about
Fanny.

"You know, it has been very hard on the girl, very hard . . ." Hearing this, I felt sick with shame all over again and expected him to
chastise me for my despicable behaviour. But I quickly learned that
the subject of his speech had nothing to do with me at all. Leaning
forward, Uncle Chaim spoke in a subdued tone. "Fanny has had
many burdens in her young life," he began solemnly. "And I admit,
the situation here is hardly ideal." He coughed several times, and

his voice grew even quieter. "Varda is not an easy woman to live with. And, perhaps, I have not been the best uncle to the girl. What do I know about young girls? But the trouble really began a few months ago when Varda told Fanny that her *goyeh*, you know—her maid-servant, Elsabet—is no longer welcome to live with us. It seems that Varda took a fierce dislike to the woman. Said that she didn't want her poking her fingers into every pot. I'm sure you remember Elsabet. Fanny was very devoted to her—and you know that she saved Fanny's life."

I nodded to indicate that I was well informed of Fanny's past. Uncle Chaim continued, "You are likely not aware of the fact that Fanny recently underwent a kind of—how shall I put it?—nervous collapse. Nothing too severe, mind you, but worrisome, very worrisome. It happened in January, not long after Elsabet moved out and found a job with another family. It came on slowly. I blame myself for not seeing the signs: her difficulty sleeping, her refusal to eat. I thought it was just stubbornness. Or an act of spite. But I was mistaken. She was truly lost without Elsabet. The *goyeh* was all she had left. Thank God, she eventually got over it. After a few weeks, she came back from the rest home, returned to her studies, and everything went back to normal. Yet I can't help worrying about her. Take tonight for instance. Clearly, the two of you had a little disagreement, a lovers' quarrel. What's wrong with that? It happens all the time. But look at the reaction. Such tears! Like the world was being blown apart. Look, I want you to know that you must be patient with her. She's experienced enough pain for a hundred lifetimes. But I don't have to remind you about what life was like over there. You lost family members too, I recall. Did any of them make it through?"

"I—I am still searching," I muttered. But I knew I was lying the moment I spoke those words. Who was I kidding? The apprehensive way that Uncle Chaim peered at me from under his thick spectacles convinced me that he could see right through me. I felt ambushed. My only escape route was to turn the conversation back to Fanny. "I would help Fanny if I could," I stammered, "but I'm not sure what I can do. I don't think she wants to speak to me. Not only that, I have to leave early tomorrow morning. I'm needed back on the kibbutz by noon."

Uncle Chaim stood up slowly to end the conversation, but then reached over and squeezed my shoulder as if to comfort me. I was stunned that he was willing to accept my story without questioning me further. After that, he tried to break the tension by joking that young people are always in such a hurry to get to the next place, even if that place is worse than the one they're in. I didn't pause to think about what he said—I was just happy to be released from the conversation.

I went back to my room and attempted to get some sleep, but without much success. Before the sun rose, my bag was packed and I left the apartment before anyone stirred. The streets of Tel Aviv were silent and empty. And once again, I was alone in the world.

17

Suzy Kohn
Toronto, Ontario
May 1969

My relationship with Fin resumed with all its old intensity. The only thing that changed was that Fin stopped pressuring me to have sex with him—he respected my decision, saying he was willing to wait until I was sure I was ready. Of course, whenever we were alone together, we indulged in some lengthy make-out sessions and it was getting harder and harder for me to resist him. But he never tried to do anything without my consent. That fact alone made me love him all the more, and I knew that I was just about ready to give myself to him completely.

Fin and I now spent all our free time together. Occasionally, he even came with me to visit Bella. He wasn't at all bothered by her long silences and saw her as a woman of unique sensitivity. "Bella's really got her head together," he remarked. "More than most people I know." I wasn't sure how he had come to that conclusion, glad as I was to hear it. Bella hardly spoke more than two words when we were with her.

One afternoon Fin and I found her slumped in her velvet chair staring at the television. She was watching a news report on America's plan to send a man to the moon. Fin sat down on the couch and joined her while I cleared away some of the clutter on the coffee table. I collected the bills and bank statements buried under a pile of newspapers and went upstairs to put them in the bureau drawer where Bella kept all her important documents. Sliding open the drawer, I spotted a note written in Uncle Charles' characteristic script: *I'm sorry, Bella, but I have to leave you. You know that I always loved this spot by the water. Please forgive me. Love, Charles.* I had no idea what to make of it. What did he mean by "I have to leave you"? Had Uncle Charles walked out on Bella? Had they been on the verge of divorce? And what did "the spot by the water" refer to?

I knew I couldn't ask Bella about the note. I probably wouldn't get an answer anyway, so what was the use? Besides, I was afraid she would think I was snooping. Nor could I talk to Fin about it, as I didn't want to betray Bella's trust—or her privacy. And asking my parents was out of the question. Lately, they were as closed as a cast-iron safe. I had to figure this out on my own. But no matter how much I thought about it, I couldn't find any answers. Finally I gave up and decided to put my questions aside. I would try to forget about events from the past. Live for the present—that was how Fin saw the world. Why not follow his lead?

Fin constantly encouraged me to open myself up and to embrace new perspectives. He introduced me to books and movies that were mind-expanding and profound. On his advice, I read R.D. Laing's *The Divided Self,* Richard Brautigan's *In Watermelon Sugar,* and Hermann Hesse's *Magister Ludi.* I watched films by Truffaut, Bergman, Fellini, and Kurosawa and tried to decipher their symbolism. Though I was never confident that I understood them completely, Fin assured me that by exposing myself to great works of art I was raising my consciousness.

Fin's favourite film by far was *King of Hearts,* a satire about inmates in an insane asylum. We went to see it three times at a beat-up old movie theatre near High Park where the frayed seats and sticky floors only added to the atmosphere. The part of the movie I liked best came at the end when the patients in the asylum were revealed to be saner than everyone else in society. It left me with the heady feeling that my eyes had been opened to a truer perspective on life.

My mother wasn't pleased that I was spending so much time with Fin. One night I came home and found her waiting up for me in the living room. Her brows were pinched and her eyes were blazing. "Do you know what time it is? This is a school night. Where were you?"

"It doesn't matter," I retorted. "I can take care of myself. I'm not a child."

"Well, you're certainly acting like one."

"What's that supposed to mean?"

"You know very well what it means. You're behaving irresponsibly. Staying up late. Running around until all hours. Don't you realize that you're jeopardizing your grades at school?"

"My grades? Is that all anyone cares about? Anyway, I'm doing fine at school," I said, though I knew it wasn't exactly true. Some of my grades had begun to slip lately, but I wasn't about to admit that to her.

"And what about university? Doesn't that concern you?"

"I got early acceptance to York. Isn't that good enough?"

"I thought you had your heart set on U of T."

"It doesn't matter to me anymore."

"What?"

"You heard me. I really don't care. Besides, I wouldn't fit into one of those elitist schools anyway."

Mother's eyes narrowed, "Does this have something to do with that boyfriend of yours?"

I rolled my eyes, though I could feel the pressure rising in my throat.

She continued undeterred. "As far as I'm concerned, you've been spending too much time with him. You shouldn't be so wrapped up in one boy at this stage of your life."

"So I should live like a nun?"

"Who said anything about nuns?" Mother threw up her arms, then paused for a moment, tapping her nails on the coffee table. "But since you mention it, I hope you and Fin are not doing anything that you would regret."

"I don't believe we're having this conversation!" I gasped. "Is that why you were waiting up for me? You want to know if I'm having sex? Well, you can rest easy. Your chaste daughter is not doing anything 'sordid.' In fact, Fin respects me and wouldn't do anything to hurt me. We trust each other. Not like some people in this family." With that parting shot, I turned and walked out of the room. Briskly. Before I could see the injured look carved into Mother's face.

18

Artur Mandelkorn
Kibbutz Tivon, Israel
April 1947

After my disastrous visit to Tel Aviv for Passover, I returned to the kibbutz with the sense that it was the only place I belonged. I was aching to get back to the uncomplicated routine of my chores and attacked them with a single-minded intensity. I was beginning to find joy in the hard physical labour of ploughing fields, sawing posts, and hauling loads of grain. In fact, the very idea of labour held a kind of enchantment for me. In the kibbutz library, I found books by A. D. Gordon and read about the purification of the Jew by means of physical labour. I thought that I had discovered an unknown genius in Gordon—that is, until I learned that his works were well known among the *kibbutzniks* and that they considered his ideas out-dated. But I didn't care. All I knew was that it felt good to be dead tired at the end of each day and then read a few pages by my friend Mr. Gordon before falling into a deep tranquilizing sleep.

I felt much older than my eighteen years and no longer considered myself a boy. And I was now so tall that other people often mistook me for being older, too. When I looked at myself in the mirror I could see myself changing before my eyes. Overnight, it seemed, my nose took on a bony shape and my skin was so ruddy that my eyes were like thin strips of cloud between hills of burnt sand. I was also getting much stronger and could lift twenty kilos of ice on my back without flinching. Girls started to tease me about being a "catch," although I didn't feel particularly worthy of being caught. After my sorry experience with Fanny, I was in no hurry to involve myself with any other young women, at least for a while. I tried to put Fanny out of my mind completely, concentrating instead on performing feats that tested my physical strength and stamina.

It was not surprising, I suppose, that I also began to involve myself in the Haganah's clandestine military activities. The official line was that the organization only provided Jewish self-defence against Arab assaults. But in reality, it was developing into an underground army, especially since the British were now making it clear that they had no intention of remaining in Palestine. We knew that once they cut and run, the Jews had better be prepared to defend themselves against the surrounding Arab armies. I didn't just drift into the Haganah, as some of the boys did. I made a conscious decision to join and become one of them. I admit that I may have been drawn to the romance of being part of an underground organization. But I also truly believed that this was the "moment of truth" for the Jews: we either fought back now or we would be cast out of our homeland forever. Or at least for another two thousand years.

While I was training with the Haganah, I devoted my entire being to its harsh regimen. If I showed myself to be an exemplary trainee, I thought, I might qualify for the Palmach—the elite combat unit that we all dreamed of joining. Several of the kibbutz boys had already become *Palmachniks* and were looked up to like gods.

I never did get the chance to become a *Palmachnik.* When Israel affirmed its independence on May 14, 1948, five Arab countries declared war the very next day, putting all our soldiers on emergency assignment. We all knew that we were vastly outnumbered in soldiers and weaponry. But we couldn't allow the word "defeat" to enter our vocabulary. It was a fight for our very existence. I was sent to join a patrol manning a lookout post near the Syrian border. We had to do everything—from tracking enemy manoeuvres to burying our dead. Although the battles went on for weeks, I never got used to the sight of dying soldiers writhing in pain from their wounds. Most of them were just boys, the same age as me, yet for the most part they endured their injuries like men. The one thing I noticed was that most of them reverted to the language of their childhood—Yiddish, Arabic, German, French—just before they died. Who knows—perhaps the child in us is never outgrown. It just waits for us in some small corner of our being in order to reclaim us just before death.

After months of battle in the searing heat of summer—losing some territories, reclaiming others—we were able to gain control of the Negev in the south and the Galilee in the north. The invading armies were pushed back and in a matter of months, armistice agreements were signed. Near the end of the war, I was transferred to the coastal plain to help secure towns that were still vulnerable to attack. It was in one of these deserted towns that something extraordinary happened—I saw Fanny again. It happened in the middle of the day on an ordinary street corner. There she was, standing there in a melon-coloured dress, waiting for a bus. Seconds before the bus arrived, I saw her from across the road and called out her name. But before I could run over and try to stop it, the bus pulled away. I had missed my chance. Empty and despairing, I was just about to turn in the opposite direction, when I saw a solitary figure far down the road, walking toward me, waving her arms, and calling out my name. Could it be? Yes, it was unmistakeable. It was Fanny. She must have seen me from the window and asked the driver to stop. She was laughing as she came closer and saw me shaking my head in disbelief and grinning widely.

The first words she spoke were golden. "Artur! How fine you look as a soldier." To my mind, I looked anything but fine. I was as gaunt as a scarecrow, my beard was overgrown, and my uniform was covered in oil stains. But Fanny! She was as fresh and fair as a morning glory. When she pulled a strand of red-gold hair away from her soft brown eyes and studied my face, I felt as handsome as a prince. And I knew that I was just as smitten with her as I had been when I first met her on the ship to Palestine.

We found a bench and sat talking for hours until the sun began to sink behind the rooftops. Our conversation wasn't strange or awkward in the least. Quite the opposite. We were as easy together as if we had seen each other yesterday. I learned that she was now studying music at the Tel Aviv conservatory and played viola in a youth chamber orchestra. When the War of Independence broke out, she had taken a leave from her studies in order to work as a volunteer teacher, travelling to nearby schools to fill in for teachers who had been called up for military duty. That's what had brought her to this town. She added that she was no longer living with Uncle Chaim and Varda, but was boarding at a student residence close to the conservatory. Her roommate, Etti, was also a refugee from Germany who was studying to be a psychoanalyst. "Sharing an apartment with Etti is like living with a chameleon," Fanny chuckled. "One day she's a passionate believer in the theories of Freud and the next day she's switched to becoming a devoted follower of Jung."

"And you're able to remain friends through it all?" I asked.

"Of course. Sometimes she even tests out her theories of analysis on me, depending on what she's studying that week."

"You don't mind being her guinea pig?"

"Not at all," Fanny replied. "It may sound strange, but I find it enlightening." Pausing for a moment, she looked down at her hands. "For the first time," she said quietly, "I feel as though I am able to confront my fears without worrying that they will destroy me."

When Fanny uttered those words, I sensed that it was her way of letting me know that she was ready to talk to me about everything, even the most painful subject of all—what had driven us apart on that terrible Passover evening. She had given me my cue and it was up to me to take it. I started by speaking in the abstract—about fear and how it can be made worse when it dwells too long in one's imagination. Then, with some hesitation, I admitted that I knew this all too well from personal experience. "Tell me," she whispered. And so I began to speak, slowly at first, grasping for the right words but knowing that this conversation was necessary and—how shall I put it?—fateful. She listened so intently to every word I said that I felt as though I were placing my soul in her lap. And, to my surprise, it felt good. Very good.

It was the first time that I had spoken about my family in over a year. I thought it would be impossible to even mention them without breaking down, but I managed to maintain my equilibrium. I guess being a soldier had taught me some measure of self-control. It was Fanny however who became distraught. When I told her about the murder of my parents and my baby sister in the concentration camp, and how I had learned of it on the very day of my arrival at her uncle's seder, she was so stricken that she grabbed hold of my arm and held on as if she were about to faint. I put my arm around her waist and steadied her. When she'd regained her composure, she urged me to continue.

I tried to explain the effect that my parents' deaths had on me, and how alone and isolated it had made me feel. I could only describe it as a kind of temporary madness. Acknowledging my ghastly behaviour at the seder, I started to apologize. But Fanny stopped me. "I understand everything now," she said. "There's no need to punish yourself further."

I soon found myself telling her about my childhood, especially my close relationship with my parents. I rarely thought about it anymore, yet here I was telling her detailed stories about my boyhood in Hungary. Some of the things I mentioned were trivial—the way my father swept under my bed with a broom to scare away the ghosts that I imagined living there. How my mother fed me a raw egg every night before bed to strengthen my voice before my bar mitzvah. Somehow I was able to talk about these things without feeling that it was morbid. Fanny had such a guileless curiosity about my past that I found myself telling her one story after another.

At one point during our conversation, Fanny asked me about my brother, Karl, and whether I had received any news of him. I told her about the unconfirmed report that he'd died of typhus. With no reason to suspect that he might have survived, I knew it was futile to hold on to any hope. Cautiously, Fanny then broached the subject of Manya. Knowing how close we'd been, she uttered her name with hesitation, as if it would open an unhealed wound.

"Not a day passes when I don't think of Manya." I said. "And I'll tell you something—I know that she's thinking of me as well." Fanny's eyes widened, as if she were expecting me to reveal some happy news. "No, no," I said quickly. "I haven't found her. At least, not yet. But, I just know she's alive. I can feel it. Just as I can feel the sun on my back and the ground beneath my feet."

"Then you must trust your instincts and never give up hope."

"At one point," I continued, "I almost did despair of ever finding her. I had written to a fellow in Cyprus who may have known her during the war. But he never answered. I still sometimes think that I might track him down. But once I joined the Haganah and the fighting started, I had no opportunity to continue my search."

Fanny wanted to know all about my hunt for Emil Lenzner and

I told her everything, right down to the last detail. Realizing how long I'd been speaking, I teased her that her roommate must be having a powerful influence on her. Maybe, I told her, she herself should think about becoming a psychoanalyst. "What!" she exclaimed. "And do this for money? That would take all the pleasure out of it!" Her voice softened. "Seriously, Artur, I just want to know everything about you. Is there anything wrong with that?" I assured her that I was flattered, but worried that I was becoming a bore. I never thought that my experiences were that interesting. But Fanny refused to listen to my protests and urged me to go on.

When the sun began to set and the few remaining vendors locked up their stalls, I started worrying about making it back to the army camp on time. I was also concerned about Fanny travelling to Tel Aviv on her own in the dark. Still, I had to face the fact that it was time for us to part. I walked her to the bus stop and then asked if she was willing to see me again. When she hesitated, I thought for sure that I was doomed. That is, until she looked at me with an impish gleam in her eye and said, "I was wondering what took you so long to ask."

19

Suzy Kohn
Toronto, Ontario
June 1969

University acceptance letters were already being delivered, so I thought it was strange that Fin didn't say a word about which school he hoped to attend. In fact, whenever I raised the topic, he grimaced and treated it as a worthless topic of conversation. He wasn't interested in formal education, he said, and planned to hitch-hike through Europe instead. More and more, he tried to convince me to do the same. "How can you learn anything about the real world by sitting in a lecture hall? You've gotta live it, not study it."

I agreed with him in theory. Yet knowledge gained from books and professors appealed to me and I tried to defend the benefits of higher education as best I could. Besides, Fin hadn't exactly asked me to come with him on his European adventure. He just thought I should value the idea of it as much as he did.

Our final school prom was about to take place and though Fin and I mocked it as shallow and pretentious, we decided at the last minute to attend—but not in the usual prom style. We put togeth-er outfits from things we'd picked up at a thrift store on Queen Street, along with the remains from past Halloween costumes. Fin donned an old tuxedo jacket with tails, which he wore along with his blue jeans. Coupled with a top hat and pince-nez glasses, he looked like the Count of Monte Cristo in denims. I sewed some picture-frame wire into the hem of an old bridal dress and transformed it into a hoop-skirted ball gown à la Scarlett O'Hara. I'd also dug up a cream-coloured umbrella, which I trimmed with lace to create a makeshift parasol. When we arrived at the school, Fin suggested that we go around to the back of the building before going in. In a secluded corner behind the darkened windows of the auditorium, he pulled a small plastic bag from the back pocket of his jeans, took some weed from the bag, and skilfully rolled a few joints. He was just about to light up when he removed his top hat with a flourish and bowed to me. "Mademoiselle, will you join me in some finely cultivated marijuana? Methinks it will add to the surrealism of the experience."

"Much obliged," I replied giddily. "Your wish is my command."

Fin and I made quite the pair. Making our entrance, we swooshed our way through the school gym and onto the dance floor. Gasps and squeals spread throughout the room as everyone pushed closer to the dance floor to get a good look at us. Boisterous laughter and excitement surrounded us. We revelled in it. Mr. McCurdy, the school vice-principal—a bald, vinegar-faced man in his fifties who looked as if he'd been born with a ruler up his back— came over and made a dry remark about our "interesting attire." He then asked Fin to step outside with him; I insisted on going too and followed them into the foyer. Standing to one side, I watched Mr. McCurdy's scalp turn red as he launched into a tirade. "What do you think you're doing coming to the prom dressed like that? You think you're being clever, I suppose?"

"Not really," Fin answered flippantly.

McCurdy's response was like a pistol shot. "Wipe that smirk off your face, young man."

Fin glanced up at the ceiling as if he was bored. McCurdy paced back and forth, his hands on his hips, clearly trying to come up with some punishment that would fit our supposed crime. All of a sudden, my chest tightened, remembering the marijuana hidden in Fin's pocket. McCurdy continued to pace, then abruptly pivoted and faced Fin head-on. His voice was now cold as steel. "Have you familiarized yourself with our rules on prom attire? If you had taken the time to read them, you would know that we take these rules very seriously. In fact, we adhere to them scrupulously. You would also realize, young man, that you are guilty of breaking one of our primary ordinances: no blue jeans allowed. Of course, that is only one of your many indiscretions. By arriving at the prom dressed like a buffoon, you have succeeded in causing a disturbance. Not to mention making a mockery of the event."

Fin glanced furtively in my direction. I could see beads of sweat gathering under his pince-nez.

"Your parents," Mr. McCurdy continued, "will be duly informed of your transgressions." Turning in my direction, he added, "As will yours, young lady."

Fin shifted his weight from one foot to the other. "So, can we go now?" he asked.

"You will leave when I tell you to," McCurdy snapped. "And if I ever catch you—" Stopping himself, he swallowed and clenched his bony fists into two tight knots. "All right. Get out of here. Both of you. And, I'll be happy if you never show your faces here again."

As we crossed the playing field, I whispered to Fin how lucky it was that McCurdy hadn't searched his pockets. "It wouldn't have mattered if he did," said Fin smoothly. Seeing the perplexed look on my face, he explained, "You know how I value silence? Keeping things under my hat? Well, voila!" Like a magician pulling a rabbit out of a hat, he pulled a thin plastic bag filled with marijuana out from under the inner lining of his top hat. I couldn't help laughing out loud. But just for a moment. I knew only too well how close we'd come to getting into serious trouble. Even more than we were already in.

20

Artur Mandelkorn
Kibbutz Tivon, Israel
May 1949

When I was finally released from the army, I returned to the kibbutz. Though several members of our community had been killed or wounded in the war, there was now a greater sense of common purpose that bound us together even in our mourning. At the same time, an enormous change had taken place in my own life. Fanny and I entered our second round of courtship, this time leading to a much happier conclusion—after seeing each other constantly for several months, we became engaged and decided to marry the following year.

Our wedding took place in the spring of 1949, right after the first anniversary of the founding of the state. We had a simple kibbutz wedding without fancy trimmings. Fanny wore a plain white shift with a garland of flowers around her forehead, looking more like a Greek goddess than a traditional Jewish bride. Our only wedding decorations were the blue-and-white Independence Day banners that were still hanging limply on the walls of the dining hall, where a simple reception would take place after the marriage ceremony.

As Fanny and I stood beneath the *chupah* set up outside in the shade of the lemon grove, I looked out at the group assembled around us. I picked out Ruti and Dudu from among the *kibbutzniks*, as well as Elsabet, who had accompanied Uncle Chaim to the event. Everyone sang and clapped as I slipped the ring on Fanny's finger and readied myself to say the ancient Hebrew prayer. I searched for Fanny's eyes as I began with the words, "At mekudeshet li," but for some reason, her eyes were squeezed shut, though a tranquil smile was spread across her lips. At the end of the prayer, I leaned over and whispered, "You can open your eyes. We are now man and wife."

"I know," she answered. "I memorized each word as you said them. I want to hold them forever inside my ears."

We began our married life on the kibbutz and lived there content-edly for a full year until Fanny gave birth to our son, Menachem. Though he was named after my late father, Maxim, the baby was a tiny replica of me: long-limbed, with a look of puzzled contempla-tion on his face. But as much as Fanny embraced communal living before the baby arrived, it became impossible for her to endure its rules once Menachem was born. She simply couldn't accept the kibbutz practice of raising children in separate children's houses rather than in their parents' homes. Because of that, we finally agreed that it was time to leave.

It was difficult for me to say goodbye to the kibbutz; it was the only home I had known since coming to Israel. The friends I'd made there were like my family—which meant that I had grown as used to their individual oddities as they had to mine. The hardest person to leave was my "big sister" Ruti, who had recently married her sweetheart, Gidon, and settled into a house on the kibbutz just down the road from ours. Every evening Ruti and Gidon stopped by our tiny cottage and joined us on the front stoop where we sat and drank seltzer mixed with mashed fruit. The two of them inevi-tably started to bicker over some issue or other until Gidon muttered that Ruti was no better than a fishwife and she accused him of being a stubborn ox. In the end, they always patched things up and sometimes even walked home together in a tight embrace. Fanny and I often remarked after they left that we had never seen a couple who seemed to thrive more on arguing than on making up.

The day before we left the kibbutz, Ruti and Gidon organized a farewell picnic. The kibbutz executive usually frowned on such events but, as usual, Ruti found a way to bend the rules. Even Dudu, who was now studying philosophy at a college in Jerusalem, made a surprise appearance in honour of the occasion. Compared to Dudu who was merely regarded by the *kibbutzniks* as an egghead, Fanny and I were looked upon as misguided souls who failed to appreciate the virtues of pure socialism in action. In the middle of the picnic, one member even began to recite the anthem of the proletariat, both in Russian and in Hebrew translation—albeit after drinking a quantity of plum cider spiked with alcohol.

The transition from the kibbutz to life in the city wasn't easy. With a baby to care for and rent to pay for our tiny apartment in Haifa, there was little time for the friends and conversation we'd enjoyed on the kibbutz. Since I didn't have any formal training in a trade or profession, I had to take a series of menial jobs, sometimes doing double shifts. I worked as a presser in a laundry, a dishwasher in an old folks' home, and a packer for a shipping company that exported dried fruit to Africa and Europe.

Though life in the city was more stressful than kibbutz living, it did offer me one vital opportunity—I was able to make use of the city's resources to continue my search for Manya. I first tried the Jewish Agency, which had amassed copious information about Jews around the world. But with thousands of other survivors hounding them for news about their own relatives, I had to wait my turn. I was told it might take up to a year before they got to my query. Next I turned to the newspapers, since I'd discovered that the daily papers carried dozens of ads submitted by survivors who were hunting for lost family members. There was even talk that the Jewish Agency would soon start broadcasting such ads on the radio.

I began to read the newspapers regularly, scouring the survivors' ads for a family member or someone from my hometown. After weeks of not finding anyone even remotely familiar, I decided to submit an ad of my own. I composed it carefully, citing all the relevant details—Manya's full name and place of birth, the names of our family members, and a description of my sister. I realized that she would now look different from the way I remembered her—she would be eighteen and almost a grown woman. But I couldn't help thinking that there were some characteristics that would never change, such as her gentleness and air of refinement. And just in case it helped, I added a sentence about Emil Lenzner, requesting information about his whereabouts as well.

Again, months passed with no response. The longer I waited, the more I started doubting whether my efforts would bear any fruit. Gradually, I began to think about other tactics. I thought back to my trip with Dudu to Be'er Yaakov and our meeting with Emil Lenchner. And then it dawned on me: hadn't Lenchner promised to write his cousin in Cyprus on my behalf? It was strange that I'd never heard from him. Maybe it was time to pay him another visit. I was hesitant about approaching him on my own, so I decided to ask Dudu if he would accompany me. Dudu was still pursuing a university degree in Jerusalem while working part-time as a photographer for various newspapers and magazines. Since Fanny and I didn't have a phone of our own, I went to a phone booth on the main street and rang his rooming house. I was surprised to hear him answer, as he was often at school or out on an assignment.

When I asked him about coming with me to see Emil Lenchner, he hesitated for several seconds before answering, "I guess you don't know," he said.

"Know what?"

"Lenchner is dead. He was killed in the war, back in '48. Didn't I ever mention it?"

"Killed? I had no idea."

"Sorry, I thought I told you back then," said Dudu. "I read about it in one of the papers. If I remember correctly, he joined up as soon as the Arabs declared war. Became a jeep driver, I think. Apparently he saved a group of men during a raid. Poor fellow—got blown to bits in the process. I saw his picture in the paper. Same guy. Who'd ever think he'd become a hero?"

My voice shook as I echoed, "Yes, who'd ever think—"

I hung up and headed back toward the apartment, meandering through the streets until I reached our building. My legs were leaden as I walked up the stairs and my thoughts were glum. One by one, every path that led to Manya seemed to reach a dead end. Every scent of her kept drifting away, evaporating like vapour. I didn't know what to do next. Doubts gnawed at me, filling me with gloom. Was there any possibility that I would ever find her? Or was I just tormenting myself with the futile hope that she was still alive waiting for me to find her?

Toward the end of that year, I finally landed a more permanent position as a clerk in a government office that issued building permits. The work was routine, but I enjoyed the job, particularly looking at the architectural drawings submitted for approval. Although I was only responsible for putting these drawings into the correct files, I often took a few minutes to examine them for myself. It was a secret pleasure that I thought had gone unnoticed. That is, until I was found out by the office manager, Yossi, who caught me poring over some proposed drawings for a small commercial building to be erected in downtown Haifa. Noting my interest in the drawing, he asked me what I thought of its feasibility. Without realizing that he was being facetious, I launched into a detailed analysis of what I considered to be the flaws of the design, right down to the location of the sewage pipes. He was shocked by my apparent expertise and casually suggested that maybe I should consider becoming an architect myself. Surely, he added, you would design better buildings than most of what was passing for architecture these days.

Although Yossi's suggestion was clearly an offhand remark, it stuck in my mind. I began to dwell on the idea until one day I decided to broach the subject with Fanny. "What would you say if I told you that I was thinking of studying to become an architect?"

"Hmm. I would say that it is exactly what you need."

"Truly? I thought you would think I'm joking."

"Do you think I haven't noticed how skilled you are at drawing? Architecture would be a perfect career for you—artistic, yet practical."

As a child, drawing had been one of my favourite activities. But since the war, I hardly gave it much thought. It was true that I often found myself doing random sketches on scraps of paper around the house—on the borders of shopping lists, newspapers, and grocery bags. But I never thought of it as "art." I didn't consider it anything more than a nervous habit, like biting one's nails or stuttering.

With Fanny's encouragement, I decided to enrol in a night course on the rudiments of architectural design. It was gruelling work because I was far behind the other students in advanced mathematics, which was a prerequisite for the course. In the end, however, I achieved the highest grade in the class. My professor even recommended me for a fellowship that would allow me to study architecture abroad. Since there were limited spaces available in Israeli schools of design, I was tempted by the possibility. Sure enough, I soon received a letter informing me that I had been awarded funds to attend the Bartlett School of Architecture in London, England. Although I was hesitant about leaving Israel, Fanny convinced me that it was important to seize the opportunity. So within a matter of weeks, we packed up all our worldly possessions and, with two-year old Menachem in tow, sailed for England and yet another new beginning.

21

Suzy Kohn
Toronto, Ontario
June 1969

I could tell from the shrillness of Mother's voice that she'd already received a call from the school about what had happened at the prom. "Suzy," she shouted up from the hall. "Your father and I want to see you in the den."

Father was leaning heavily against the fireplace in the wood-panelled room; he held a tumbler in his hand and stared into its depths as he swirled its contents in circles. My mother sat on the checkered couch, her head bent down, brushing lint off her skirt. When they heard me come in, they both looked up, lips pursed, eyes glowering. Father banged his tumbler down on the mantle. "We are very disappointed in you, Suzy," he said. "What were you thinking, going to the prom dressed like that? We don't know what's come over you."

"It's that boy," Mother muttered from the sidelines.

"That boy?" I cried. "How dare you blame everything on Fin!"

Mother's eyes flared. "Yes, we do blame him. And you too. What were you thinking, getting involved with a boy like that?"

"What do you mean, 'a boy like that'? I would think you'd be pleased that I was going out with a nice Jewish boy," I said in a mocking tone. "Would you rather I dated a gentile?"

"Of course not. But—" Mother paused, biting her bottom lip. "Did you have to choose a hippie?"

Father joined in. "The few times he showed his face around here, he was dressed like a bum—wearing jeans with holes. When I was a boy, we were ashamed to wear torn pants."

"The point is," Mother continued. "We were shocked to get a call from the vice-principal this morning telling us what happened at the prom. You, of all people, Suzy. We never expected it from you."

"Well, sorry if I'm not *perfect*." I said, turning away from them. Under my breath, but loud enough to hear, I muttered, "What do you expect?—Coming from a home like this."

A tense silence filled the room. I didn't dare look up until Father broke in sharply. "So now you're blaming us for your foolishness?"

"It wasn't foolishness," I argued. "It was just a joke. We thought it would be fun if someone wore something different to the prom for a change."

"Well, some fun," Father said. "The vice-principal has informed us that you've been suspended from school for three days. And it will go on your record. Permanently."

"What? Why are they suspending me?"

"For causing a disturbance," Father said. "And that boyfriend of yours is suspended for a week."

Suspended? Both of us? I couldn't believe it. How could we be suspended for something so trivial?

Father loosened his collar and his voice deepened, "Your mother and I have come to a decision: you must stop seeing this boy—Fin, or whatever his name is. He's a bad influence on you."

"What?" I shouted. "That's ridiculous. Fin hasn't influenced me at all. Whatever I do is my own decision."

"Don't be insolent, Suzy. We think that you should cut all ties with that boy and make school your top priority."

"What's Fin got to do with how I do at school? I'm getting good grades."

"Don't you see?" Father said. "You've gotten yourself into the soup. This black mark on your record could nullify your university acceptance. Listen, your final exams are starting next week, and if you study hard and do well, you might be able to redeem yourself."

Black marks; university acceptance; final exams. I hardly heard what my father said. It was all background noise to the main thought pulsing through my brain—the thought of not seeing Fin. I spun around and strode out of the room, shaking with anger. How could they forbid me from seeing Fin? They couldn't do that to me. It was outrageous. Anyway, I wasn't a child anymore. I could do what I wanted. Let them try to stop me. Let them try to prevent me from seeing the only person in the world who made me feel loved.

22

Artur Mandelkorn
London, England
April 1952

Fanny barely had a chance to experience much of English life before she realized that she was expecting another child. The pregnancy was difficult this time and she was given strict doctor's orders to remain in bed. Thankfully, her old friend and maidservant Elsabet came to England and nursed Fanny through the worst of it. We welcomed our second son, Uri, into the world by drinking a toast to both the new Queen of England and the Prime Minister of Israel.

Not long after Uri was born, I received a thin blue envelope from the Jewish Agency. Bracing myself, I tore it open and saw my sister's life condensed into three paltry words—"no record found." How could there still be no trace of her? I crumpled up the letter and shoved it into a drawer under a pile of blankets, not wanting to look at it again.

Of course, I still thought about Manya—more often than I could bear—but whenever her image appeared in my mind, I banished it as soon it entered. It's not that I wanted to forget about my sister. I just wanted to keep her image hidden beneath the surface, set apart from the demands of my daily life. I'd done everything in my power to find her and bring her back to me, I told myself. What more could I do?

Life in England fortunately provided many distractions that took my mind off the past. In addition to immersing myself in my studies at Bartlett, I learned to appreciate rugby and the ritual of afternoon tea. I also discovered that synagogue attendance was a must for all self-respecting English Jews. In Israel, I never felt the need to go to shul. I felt that I had paid my dues in the Haganah and could live an honourable Jewish life just by being a good citizen of the state. But in England, things were different. Without any formal Jewish affiliation—meaning, synagogue attendance—a Jew could get swallowed up by British culture as quick as you can say Jack Robinson. So we joined a congregation and I even began to savour the customs associated with synagogue attendance, such as stopping by a neighbour's house for kiddush as we strolled home from services on Sabbath mornings.

I soon became a regular at what was known as the Docks shul, named for its location near the water, which was headed by an old-world figure named Rabbi Shraga-Feivel Brandes. Despite his long grey beard and black *capote*, Rabbi Brandes was modest about his piety, never making his own observance of Jewish law a subject of display. Mercifully, he also avoided correcting others for their deficiencies. This endeared him to his congregants almost more than his mild eyes and genial handshake. It certainly appealed to my skeptical nature and allowed me to hold my religious doubts at bay as I joined in the Sabbath prayers. All the same, I chose to sit at the back of the shul under the low overhang so that if I occasionally didn't feel like praying, no one would notice. That is why I was so shocked when Rabbi Brandes approached me one day after shul to ask me if anything was wrong.

"No—everything is fine. Perfect," I said, my voice catching slightly.

He patted my shoulder with his purple-veined hand and looked me in the eye. "Please. If I can help. You know where to find me." I flinched, feeling as transparent as glass.

I was restless that night, unable to sleep, so I got out of bed early, craving a walk. Since Fanny was busy preparing breakfast for the boys, I made the excuse that I had left something I needed at the college. I walked several blocks and then somehow found myself standing in front of the rabbi's house. I knocked lightly on his door, somehow hoping he wasn't in. No such luck. The rabbi opened the door and nodded his head several times without saying anything before motioning for me to come into the parlour and take a seat. He pulled up a chair across from me, sat down, and stroked his beard several times before speaking, "So, I guess you do have something to talk about, yes?"

"I—I'm not sure what you want to hear," I said with a shrug. "Everything is fine. I have two healthy children. A devoted wife. A career in the making." My eyes focused on the clock on the wall above the rabbi's head.

"And yet?"

"And—yet," I echoed, surprised to hear the bitterness in my voice. I could feel my throat constricting. I placed my hand over my eyes and tried to regain my composure.

"Steady," he said softly. "No one's rushing you."

I waited for the lump in my throat to dissolve, then breathed deeply. Looking down at my clenched fingers, I leaned forward as the words began pouring out of my mouth. "You have to understand. I promised my sister I'd come back for her. And I did. Just as I said I would. But it was too late—far too late. For years, I've searched everywhere, followed every clue. But they've led nowhere."

"And you believe your sister is still alive?"

"I—I don't know anymore."

"There are some things that only God knows. And you can't force God's hand. If she is alive, you will find her one day. Let it rest for now."

"But whenever I give up searching, I torment myself."

"No one said to stop searching. But you must remember: Judaism teaches that life comes first. Not death."

"Which means?"

"That your first obligation now is to those who are closest to you, u'vasar mibsari."

Seeing my puzzled expression, he explained, "Those who are flesh of your flesh. Your dear Fanny, your kinderlach. They come first."

"And my sister? Should I still have hope?"

"Hope is never lost; it just migrates. Concentrate on your family and their well-being. And—" he paused, drawing in a breath, "Have you ever considered the possibility that if your sister is alive, that it is she who might eventually find you?"

23

Suzy Kohn
Toronto, Ontario
July 1969

Fin and I continued to see each other in secret to avoid the wrath of my parents. It wasn't that I was afraid of them. I just wanted to keep things from getting worse at home. Fin chose an Indian restaurant in the east end as our meeting place since he figured that no one would recognize us there. There was also a secluded park right beside it, perfect for the privacy we sought after eating our fill of curry and naan. Over the savoury Indian food, we talked about music, films, and books, although the conversation always seemed to swing back to Fin's latest passion: political activism.

"Have you heard what those corporate lackeys in government are planning now?" he said, reaching for his glass of cardamom-spiced lassi. "Expanding the Spadina Expressway. Smack through the centre of Toronto. Can you imagine what it would do to the inner city? The poor will be forced out of their homes. And those fat cats will only get richer."

"But what can we do about it?" I asked.

"Take action. I've already joined a peoples' task force. We've planned a demonstration for this Friday morning. You should come."

"If only I could. I started my summer job at Fran's, remember? I'm waitressing from nine to five."

"Oh yeah, I forgot."

"I wish that *I* could forget. It's pretty boring taking orders and clearing tables."

"Think of it this way. You get to meet real working-class people. You can learn all you need to know from folks like that."

Truthfully, I couldn't imagine learning anything from my customers—most of them were tank-top-clad mothers screaming at their children for throwing food on the floor. But if it pleased Fin to think so, that was fine with me.

Final grades were posted and I was relieved to see that mine hadn't dropped as much as I'd feared. Better yet, it turned out that my acceptance to university was not affected at all by my suspension. I wasn't even sure if it was ever in jeopardy. No matter. When the thick brown envelope finally arrived from the University of Toronto with all the registration information inside, my father handed it to me with tears in his eyes.

I assumed that my acceptance to U of T would calm my parents' fears about my future—and perhaps even soften their harsh attitude toward Fin. As they sat reading the newspaper one evening, I took a chance and casually mentioned that I was still seeing Fin. Mother looked at me and said blithely, "We assumed as much. You've become extremely headstrong, Suzy. I only hope you know what you're getting yourself into."

"I can take care of myself," I asserted.

Father sighed, "I guess there's nothing we can do to stop you. As you make your bed, so you must lie in it."

I hated that expression. Why did parents always resort to using it? Nevertheless, I was relieved that the atmosphere at home had finally resumed some semblance of normalcy. It wasn't what I would call happy, but at least it had reached a level of moderate calm.

More than anything, I sensed that my parents were now making an effort to control their anger, which had the effect of making my sisters and me less apt to provoke them. Perhaps it had something to do with the fact that my father seemed to have curtailed his drinking. A few weeks before, I overheard my mother reminding him what the doctor had said, that his blood pressure was dangerously high and he had better "cut back or else." Mother's voice sounded choked, as if she was at the breaking point. It didn't take long for me to understand what "or else" meant, since shortly afterward I noticed that the door to the den was open most of the time and the sour smell of whisky was gone.

I continued to drop in on Bella whenever I could, but saw little change in her appearance or surroundings. The house still looked as if an evil spirit had invaded, rearranging all the contents and setting them askew. One day, however, I walked in to the living room and noticed that Bella's embroidery beads had suddenly reappeared; several bins, arranged according to their shape and hue, were lined up on the coffee table beside a pile of tattered magazines.

I sat down on the sofa and picked out a few vermillion beads from one of the bins. "These would look great on my jeans," I said as I jiggled them in my palm. "Do you think you could embroider them on my back pockets?"

Bella looked away. "I'm sorry," she answered. "I'm not sewing anymore."

"Then why are the beads on the table? I thought—"

"I was just looking at them," she said abruptly. "Nothing more."

"But why stop sewing? You were so good at it. I'm sure your clients will never find anyone even half as talented."

She opened her mouth as if to speak, but instead, she sighed and pressed her lips together.

I wouldn't let it go. "Don't you miss creating all those beautiful designs? You have such a wonderful imagination!"

"Really?" she said dryly. "I'd prefer to have less imagination."

"Why would you say that?"

"I just can't talk about it."

"But—"

Bella cut me off. "I don't want to be pestered, all right?"

I fell back on the sofa as if I'd been slapped. My eyes were stinging as I stood up to leave. Bella followed me and grabbed my elbow. "Suzy, I'm sorry. I don't know why I get this way. Don't leave. Sit down."

"I have to go," I said, grabbing my jacket.

"Listen, we don't need to sit here. We can go for a walk. Like we used to do."

A walk? Bella never went out for walks anymore. She barely left the house. "Maybe another time," I said. "I have an appointment downtown." I hated making excuses, but I had to get out of there. I was tired of Bella's moods. And I didn't want to be the target of her anger anymore.

I returned to Bella's house the following week hoping to smooth things over and was astonished to find her out. When I got home, I asked my mother where she'd gone. "Don't you know? Bella's been going out on walks. Isn't it wonderful?" Mother's tone had an air of lightness to it.

"Really? That's great to hear."

"Yes," she continued, "she's been going out almost every day. Just around the neighbourhood. She's looking healthier already."

After that, I often saw Bella strolling around the area, pausing occasionally to examine a swath of delphiniums or asters as she walked her regular route. From time to time, she stopped and exchanged a few words with some of the neighbours. One morning I joined her on her daily ramble, chatting about trivial things like food and the weather, steering away from anything too personal. Though I tried to put it out of my mind, I hadn't forgotten the cryptic note from Uncle Charles that I'd found in Bella's drawer. I was so tempted to ask her about it and tried to think of ways to subtly work it into the conversation. But I never had the nerve. Besides, I wasn't sure whether Bella was ready to talk about her late husband.

I couldn't help it but that note gave rise to all sorts of speculations, some of them wilder than others. I pondered whether Uncle Charles hadn't really died, but had run off somewhere. Maybe to the "spot by the water." I imagined him working on a ship, or starting a new life close to the shoreline. As a fisherman, or a lighthouse keeper. Maybe he reunited with the girl he used to know, the one he called Manya. But I knew it was absurd. I had been present at the unveiling of his headstone. I saw his name carved into it, in both Hebrew and English. And the years inscribed, 1929–1968. What more proof did I need?

In the second week of August, I was on my way home with Fin late at night when he sprang something on me. It was after I'd been watching him play backup for a music demo at a warehouse on Front Street and we were both feeling particularly mellow. As we nuzzled together on the subway, Fin reached over and pulled a strand of hair from my eyes. Studying my face, he murmured, "You know, I'm taking off for Amsterdam next month. From there, I figure I'll thumb my way through Europe. So, what do you say? Are you coming with me?"

"I—I would love to," I stammered. "But I'm not sure I can. I mean, I've already registered for my courses at U of T."

"What does that matter? You can go to university any time."

"I know, but I've paid my tuition. I can't just take off."

"Suit yourself," Fin answered coldly. He hunched his shoulders and buried his chin in his jacket collar.

"Fin, don't be upset with me. You caught me off guard, that's all. Let me think about it, okay? Maybe I can arrange to go with you."

He shot me a skeptical look that was as much a dare as it was a put-down. As if to say, sure, let's see you prove it.

24

Artur Mandelkorn
London, England
September 1956

Our life in England soon settled into a routine. I worked long hours at school—drafting, designing, and crafting architectural models—while Fanny looked after the household and the boys. Somehow, though, she always made sure that there was time for the two of us. Elsabet was happy to look after the boys at a moment's notice, so we could sometimes even catch a picture at the local movie house or join our neighbours for an evening at the pub.

In recent weeks, however, I started to notice that something was not right with Fanny. She just wasn't herself. She seemed to be distracted all the time, as if something serious was bothering her. Even her attitude toward the children had changed, barely responding when they sought her attention. But whenever I asked her about it, her eyes would widen in genuine surprise, "Really?" she'd say. "I have nothing particular on my mind at all." Nonetheless, she often shut herself up in the bedroom in the evening and played the viola for hours at a time before slipping into bed without even saying goodnight. At first I was afraid that these changes in her might have something to do with her health, that perhaps she never fully recovered from her last pregnancy, which left her temporarily diabetic. I insisted that she undergo a complete physical examination, but when the doctor gave her a clean bill of health, it dawned on me that the problem might not be physical. I remembered Uncle Chaim telling me on that painful Passover night long ago that Fanny had once suffered a severe enough bout of depression that she'd been sent to a rest home. Could she now be experiencing some kind of recurrence?

As it happened, Fanny's former roommate, Etti, was completing her doctorate in psychiatric research at Oxford while we were in London. Since she knew all about Fanny's history, I took the two-hour train ride to Oxford to talk to her about what was happening to Fanny. Etti was understandably hesitant to give a professional assessment without performing her own examination, but she was able to offer some general insights into cases like Fanny's. "You should know, Arthur, that the trauma Fanny experienced as a hidden child was severe. It is not unusual for someone with her background to unconsciously re-enact that trauma. In some cases, people develop certain repetitive behaviours whether they're good for them or not, and sometimes these habits are nearly impossible to break. With hidden children like Fanny, periodic withdrawal from the world is a kind of habit that makes them feel safe and protected."

Etti must have sensed my distress, for she quickly added, "But I wouldn't worry too much at the moment. Artistic people like Fanny have a distinct advantage over most people who have endured similar traumas. You know, creativity can provide a useful outlet for unconscious fears. At the same time, I want to caution you about one thing—too much isolation from the world, even by those who are creative, can be dangerous if it lasts for an excessively long time or if it becomes extreme."

Her assessment hit me like a kidney-punch. My stomach churned and my head felt wooden. But after absorbing Etti's remarks, I thought, why should I be shocked? It made perfect sense.

How foolish *I* had been that I hadn't anticipated something like this. How could I have assumed that Fanny harboured no anger or pain for all that was taken away from her? How could it not overwhelm her one day?

On the train ride back to London, I tried to focus my mind on the view from the window, to take in the beauty of the autumn foliage. But all I could see was my own reflection staring back at me. Looking at it, I recognized a harsh fact about myself—that I had a selfish desire for Fanny to be someone who would make everything fine for *me*. I needed her to be "normal"—uncomplicated, undamaged—so that she could help me heal *my* fractured life. This left me feeling more sadness for our children than for either of us. How could we have been so reckless as to bring children into the world while we were still in need of help ourselves? Would we ever cease being like two invalids trying to steer a lifeboat with no hint of land in sight?

I had no idea how to help Fanny, or even if it was possible. Suggesting a psychiatrist was an obvious route, but I was hesitant to broach the subject with her. I feared that it might arouse panic or distrust in her if I disclosed to her that I was worried about her mental state. So, as with most things, I got used to Fanny's episodes and managed to weather them as best as I could. In my own mind, I came to refer to them as "Fanny's ghosts." Also, my life was so busy with the demands of my professional training—not to mention a recent night job that helped pay the rent—that I was left with little time to fret over Fanny or anything else.

On a rainy Sunday in late November, I heard the buzzer to our flat ringing insistently. By the time I got down the stairs and opened the door, I saw the backside of a woman who had already turned to leave. I called out to her, asking if I could be of any help. When the woman swung around to face me, I realized at once it was my old friend and sponsor, Mrs. Kartash. I must have been struck dumb for several seconds because she said with a slow teasing grin, "Artur, I have just come all the way from Hungary. Are you going to stand there or invite me in?"

On the way up the stairs to our flat, she told me how harrowing her journey had been, that it had taken her more than six weeks to travel from Budapest to London, first on foot and then by train and boat. Of course, I'd heard about the recent uprising in Hungary and about the thousands who had managed to escape. But I had no inkling that Mrs. Kartash would be one of the lucky few who had gotten away and found their way to London.

My correspondence with Mrs. Kartash had become less frequent in recent years, partly because Hungary's Communist government had placed severe restrictions on communication with countries outside the Soviet bloc. But truthfully, much of it was my fault as well—after I had received the terrible news about my parents and Kati, and my search for Manya came to naught, I lost interest in keeping up my connections with the old country. For her part, though, Mrs. Kartash had taken pains to maintain contact with me and—as much as it was permitted—kept me informed of her attempts to locate Manya. In the end, not a single word about my sister had turned up in any of the official documents collected after the war. In fact, little about her life or her death had materialized to prove that she had ever existed.

Seeing Mrs. Kartash in person again came as a shock. She had never been anything but kind to me, even self-sacrificing, but her presence in London unnerved me. Her thick stockings and heavy woollen mantle were reminiscent of the long European winters I had loathed as a child. Even her smell reminded me of the Hungarian forests. As soon as I introduced Mrs. Kartash to Fanny, however, they took to each other immediately and they talked like old, intimate friends. They discovered a mutual love of music and launched into an animated discussion of their favourite composers. They agreed on almost everything—that Brahms' chamber music was undervalued and that Igor Stravinsky's popularity was nothing but a passing fancy. The light-hearted nature of their discussion surprised me since I knew that Mrs. Kartash had shunned anything to do with music after losing her children in the war. How could it be that she was now able to speak about it in such a carefree way?

The answer to that question only became apparent a few months later when Mrs. Kartash tried to convince Fanny to help her set up a small music school for immigrant children. I was opposed to the idea at first, uneasy that it would be too much of a strain on Fanny. Mindful also of the hours that she spent playing her viola alone in the bedroom, I was worried that bringing more music into her life might lead to more seclusion and withdrawal from the world. One evening, despite the fact that I had voiced all these concerns to Mrs. Kartash, she made another attempt to argue her case. "Teaching music to children who have little else in their lives is not only a blessing for them. It is a blessing for you," she said to Fanny. She paused for a moment, then exhaled. "At least, that's the way it was for me. You might say that it saved my life."

I noticed that Fanny had begun to blink nervously as we waited for Mrs. Kartash to continue. "After the war, I suffered from a form of depression that crept up on me, unnoticed and unacknowledged for years. Then, suddenly, there I was, ambushed by it. Unable to function. Not wanting to go on. When I finally forced myself to seek treatment, the doctor prescribed one daily task: picking up my flute. Not playing it. Just touching it. One minute on the first day, two on the next. It wasn't easy. It was one of the hardest things I've ever had to do. But playing the flute? That was another matter. I absolutely refused. Until he had a new idea: instead of just playing the flute, I should teach a child how to do it. For some reason, I was able to endure that. And it worked." She nodded her head slowly. "In retrospect, I think that I was able to return to my music because there were others who needed it more than me."

Persuaded by Mrs. Kartash, Fanny and I agreed that she should give it a try. It didn't take long before Fanny began to thrive in her new role, teaching children as young as five or six to play the violin and viola. Mrs. Kartash taught flute and recorder, while a third teacher taught piano. The children who came for lessons were either from families with little money or were orphans with no family left at all. Mrs. Kartash, with her characteristic zeal, managed to convince some of the immigrant aid societies in London to subsidize the project. The combination of her French inflection and Hungarian charm were impossible for even the most officious bureaucrats to resist. The new venture did not provide a complete cure for what ailed Fanny. All the same, her episodes became a little less frequent. Perhaps it had something to do with bringing beauty into the lives of those who had no other source of it. Clearly, it did not destroy the ghosts that tormented Fanny. But it did seem to placate them.

Every time I came to pick up Fanny from the music school, however, I couldn't help thinking of Manya—of how much she would have loved to study music in a formal setting like this. A hollow ache would settle in my stomach as I looked around and considered all she had missed. For the most part, I had given up searching for my sister, other than renewing my inquiry every year with the Jewish Agency and, more recently, with the Yad Vashem office in Israel. Yet I still thought about her constantly. I even found myself looking for her on the street from time to time. I knew it was irrational. How likely would it be that if she had survived, she'd be in London? But more than once I saw girls who could have been her—at least the way I imagined she'd look as a girl in her twenties. One time, I actually stopped a young woman in Paddington Station and asked if her name was Manya. Her light brown hair and delicate complexion drew me to her like a magnet. But as soon as she turned and looked at me, I knew from her narrow-set eyes and the downward twist of her lips that it couldn't be her. After all these years, how could I still be fooling myself that she was still alive?

The following year sped by like a comet. Fanny continued to teach music with Mrs. Kartash, who assigned more pupils to her now that our own children were both in school. Menachem—or Mark, as he was called in England—was in his second year of grammar school, while little Uri—now called Oliver—was attending the local kindergarten. From their infancy, Mark and Oliver were entirely different personalities: Mark was sensitive and introspective, but displayed a biting sense of humour when he was provoked. Oliver, on the other hand, was mirthful to the point of hilarity, often pulling wild stunts in order to draw attention to himself. Fanny often remarked that Oliver was a showman just like her father, after whom he was named, whose courtroom skills had been celebrated in Germany before the Nazis came to power. On her good days, Fanny was adept at quelling the skirmishes that constantly erupted between the two boys. She was strict without being shrewish, something that was no mean feat. In any event, the boys knew that once calm had been restored in Fanny's household, there were tangible rewards—often in the form of raspberry tarts, eccles cake, or homemade lemon pudding.

I was almost at the end of my studies and was now serving as an apprentice at an architectural firm. Although the hours were long and the work painstaking, it was exhilarating to contribute to the design of buildings that would actually be built in the city. When the time came for me to graduate from Bartlett, I felt I had thoroughly earned my degree. I ascended the podium with the sense that I finally accomplished something that would give me a secure place in the world.

But security, it seemed, was never something I could hold on to for long. At the end of that year, Fanny became physically ill. She took to her bed and refused to eat or drink. Her whole nervous system appeared to have shut down. This was different from anything I had seen before. It got so bad that she had to be taken to hospital and fed through a tube. After a long and complicated series of tests, the doctors broke the devastating news to me: Fanny had a rare blood disorder and was unlikely to live out the year.

I was frantic, enraged, uncomprehending. How could this happen to my beloved Fanny? What had she done to deserve this fate? My grief was so all-encompassing that I longed for my own death. I prayed to God that He would take me instead of her. I was so inconsolable that even the thought of our children gave me no comfort. What use was I to them? Motherless children—what chance did they have for happiness? I shudder to admit this, but I even considered taking my own life and theirs as well. Yet Fanny did not give up so easily. She rallied several times over the next few months, so much so that there were moments when I half-believed that she would overcome her illness and expel the assailants from her weakened veins. During these periods of remission, the nurses were able to remove the feeding tube and Fanny would try to carry on a conversation. One time, as I sat on the side of her bed, she twisted her head toward me and murmured, "I'm going home tomorrow." Slits of light glimmered from her partially opened eyes.

"Yes, yes," I said, knowing that it wasn't true. I took her withered hand in mine and stroked her blue-tinged fingers.

At other times, she was agitated and fixated on the smallest details, such as worrying about whether the boys had proper galoshes for the winter or whether our old oven still needed repair. When I tried to reassure her that everything was fine, she refused to accept it. Perhaps she saw through my facade—everything was not fine and, despite my strenuous efforts to conceal it from her, my entire world had become as dark as the blackest night.

Fanny died the following spring. After slipping into a coma for a number of days, she soundlessly passed away into a world of complete repose. She must have known that it would be easier on me that way—those few days when she lay in a coma allowed me to say goodbye.

At the funeral, Rabbi Brandes opened by quoting from the biblical book of Proverbs, comparing Fanny to a "woman of valour whose worth was beyond jewels." He then spoke about how Fanny had literally sold the jewels that were her inheritance so that she could settle in the land of Israel. His words struck me like a hammer. As soon as I heard them, I knew—I knew in the depths of my being—what I had to do. Through my grief and tears, one thought gripped me like a vise: I had to return to Israel and fulfill Fanny's dream. She had given up her last possessions in order to come to the land of our forefathers and had only left to be by my side. Now it was my turn to repay her. Yes, I would bring the boys back to Israel and raise them the way she would have wanted. Not as Mark and Oliver, but as Menachem and Uri.

The days of shiva provided a small degree of consolation, although many of the people who passed through my door were unknown to me. They were mostly neighbours and friends of neighbours who had heard about my loss and had come to offer comfort. At best, they were a distraction from the loneliness that I knew was waiting to set in. Mrs. Kartash came early every morning and remained until the last visitor had left. She warmed the meals and made sure that the children were properly washed and fed. Elsabet also arrived at dawn each day with the intention of offering her assistance. But her grief over Fanny's death was so great that she was barely able to rise from her chair. Although she was not a Jew, she too tore the corner of her blouse as is the custom of Jews in mourning.

Twice a day, morning and evening, Rabbi Brandes came wordlessly into the house and led the men in prayer. When the seven days of shiva were coming to an end, and it was time for me to rise from my mourning stool, he came over and gazed into my eyes in silent acknowledgement of my suffering.

"Rabbi," I said, anxious to speak.

He waved his hand to stop me. "Sha—sha, words are not necessary."

"Rabbi," I insisted. "I have made up my mind. I am returning to the land of Israel."

"A—ahhh," he mused. "And your children?"

"I am doing it more for them than for me."

He looked at me quizzically. I continued to speak at a desperate pace. "Me? I'll always be a foreigner, no matter where I live. But my children still have a chance. They can be part of a nation that doesn't cringe or cower or pretend to be anything other than what they are. That is what Fanny wanted for them, even if she never put it in so many words."

Unfazed by my bitterness, Rabbi Brandes leaned back and closed his eyes as if he'd suddenly become drowsy. When he opened his eyes, he offered a measured response, "And *parnasah*? Can you make a living there? You cannot sustain the body on ideals alone."

"Israel needs people who are willing to sacrifice personal comfort for the greater good. I'll find work, even if it means performing menial labour."

"Don't try to take on more than you can bear," said the rabbi. "Our ancient sage Rabbi Tarfon understood this dilemma when he cautioned, 'It is not your obligation to complete the task, but neither are you at liberty to desist from it entirely.' Go carefully and may the Almighty grant you strength." I pondered his words as I performed the ritual walk around the block that designated the end of the shiva period. What did Rabbi Tarfon mean when he referred to "the task"? How could his words, spoken nearly two thousand years ago, have anything to do with the unbearable pain I was feeling now? Stricken and skeptical, I dismissed the questions and hurried home to attend to the practical preparations for our impending voyage.

25

Suzy Kohn
Toronto, Ontario
August 1969

As I trudged along the shadow-dappled streets to my house, I mulled over the idea of travelling to Europe with Fin. Should I be daring and take off with him to see the world? Or should I be a "good girl" and continue my education? My parents would be furious if I left home with Fin. But if I didn't go with him, what would happen to our relationship? I didn't want to risk losing him again.

My musings came to a sudden halt the minute I stepped through the door. "Aunt Bella has gone missing!" Julia shouted.

"What do you mean?"

Jan cut in. "She went out for a walk this morning and never came back. She's disappeared!"

"Girls, girls, stop the noise," Mother yelled from the kitchen. "I'm calling the neighbours. I need quiet."

Sweat dripped off my father's forehead as he flipped through the telephone book, looking for more numbers to call.

"Wait, I don't get it. How could she just disappear?" I said. "Are you sure she didn't just stop somewhere? At a coffee shop, or at a friend's house?"

"That's exactly what we're trying to find out," Father answered.

"Yeah, and we even called the police!" Jan exclaimed, jumping up and down, a Band-Aid flapping from her scabby knee.

"The police? Are they out looking for her?" I asked.

Father tried to calm everyone down. "No, no. Not yet. They can't file a missing person's report for twenty-four hours. It's not even midnight yet."

"I've run out of people to call," Mother sighed, coming into the living room where the rest of us were gathered. "Maybe we should get in the car and start looking for her ourselves."

"Good idea," Father declared. "We'll drive around the area. Meanwhile—Julia and Jan—the two of you stay home in case anyone calls. And Suzy—go next door to Bella's and wait there in case she turns up. Here's the key."

I had never gone into Bella's house when she wasn't there. I felt like a thief stealing in under cover of darkness. When I turned on the lights, expecting to see the usual shambles, my jaw dropped—the house was immaculate. It looked almost festive. If I didn't know better, I would think that Bella had been expecting guests. A tall vase of yellow dahlias stood in the middle of the dining room table that was covered with a scalloped lace tablecloth. In the living room, books and magazines had been stacked neatly beside the fireplace, and a footed bowl of grapes rested on the coffee table. A record album, Beethoven's "Piano Concerto, Number 5," lay face up on top of the stereo console as if it was waiting to be played.

The base of my scalp prickled as I wandered through the silent house. I kept hoping that Bella would appear, but after roaming from room to room, I could see that the place was empty. Passing by the bureau where I'd once found that strange note written by Uncle Charles, I couldn't resist opening the drawer where the note had been in order to sneak a second look at it. To my shock, however, the note was gone. The drawer was empty, save for an old pair of reading glasses and a comb. I pulled open all the other drawers, but found nothing but an assortment of silk scarves, gloves, and sewing supplies. What could have happened to it?

I was on my way downstairs when I heard a light tapping on the front door. It was my parents, who had just completed their search of the neighbourhood. Shaking their heads in frustration, they told me that they hadn't been able to find Bella anywhere. Since it was past midnight, they asked if I minded sleeping in Bella's house in case she returned. I was pleased—and a little surprised—that they trusted me with this responsibility. I consented immediately.

First thing the next day a policeman arrived to investigate Bella's disappearance. My parents gave him all the details about her regular routine and habits, the names of people she might know, and the places she might visit. They also told him about her psychological condition, including the fact that she had been in a state of severe depression since her husband died. "I don't want to alarm you," said the officer, "but these cases don't always turn out well."

"What do you mean?" I asked, trying not to panic.

"Nothing specific, miss. I'm just speculating. Let's just hope that she's got her wits about her."

Her wits? I thought, my stomach quaking. This might turn out to be worse than I feared.

26

Artur Mandelkorn
Kibbutz Tivon, Israel
August 1960

My arrival in Israel with two children in tow was nothing like my first encounter with the country. Instead of confusion and mayhem on the shore, the confusion and mayhem were all within me. Israeli life appeared surprisingly orderly as we disembarked in Haifa with our baggage. I carried Uri in my arms since he was frightened by the noise of the docking ships, while Menachem lagged behind, scraping his satchel along the ground behind him. Uncle Chaim was waiting for us, just as he had been waiting for Fanny when she arrived fourteen years before. But this time, there were no cries of joy and recognition from his lips—only sorrowful glances punctured by strained attempts to inject a note of cheer into a dazed and care-worn crew of boys.

"Come, I'll take you to Tel Aviv," Uncle Chaim said as he lifted our bundles into his trunk. "My home is yours. As long as you need."

"Thank you, that's kind of you. But no—I prefer to go directly to Afula. To the kibbutz."

"I understand," he said, nodding pensively. "But let me drive you there. It's the least I can do." We settled into the cramped seats of Uncle Chaim's car, and I watched out the window as he navigated the winding city streets that led to the highway. Everything looked different here. Even the light was different—gold streaked with turquoise, instead of the violet-tinged grey of England. The newness was good. We needed to change our surroundings, even if we could not change our fate.

After travelling for two hours through the Israeli countryside, we finally arrived at the familiar rows of emerald fields that bordered the kibbutz like a gleaming banner. Seeing it once again made me realize how frequently this landscape had wandered in and out of my dreams since I'd left it. The first people I wanted to see were Ruti and Gidon. I had kept in touch with them on a regular basis, especially after Fanny was hospitalized. Once they heard I was returning to Israel with the boys, they encouraged me to come back to the kibbutz. Living in a close-knit community would be the best thing for the children, they argued. I was hesitant at first, remembering how much Fanny had been opposed to the kibbutz policy that required children to live apart from their parents. She felt it was unnatural and even harmful to a child's development. But Ruti and Gidon persisted in their arguments, even citing Fanny's love of nature in order to win me over. Eventually I agreed, albeit reluctantly, to bring the boys to the kibbutz—at least temporarily. I was not going to make a final decision about where we would live until I judged how well the boys adjusted to our new living situation.

Arriving at the kibbutz in the late afternoon, I breathed in the familiar waft of cool air that soothed the sun-stroked fields. After saying our goodbyes to Uncle Chaim, I took Menachem and Uri on a brief tour of the kibbutz. Menachem was particularly excited. Although he was only ten, he was a passionate reader and had already prepared for our move by reading some children's books on the origins of the kibbutz. As we approached the chicken house, I spied Ruti driving a tractor in a nearby field. When she saw us, she leapt down, and sprinted toward us, throwing her arms around my neck with such a deafening cry that I couldn't tell if she was laughing or crying. It was soon obvious that she was weeping over the loss of Fanny—seeing me in person had brought the tragedy back to her in full force. I too must have shed some tears, for she pulled a long rag from her pocket and began to wipe my face as well as her own.

Ruti's tears subsided only momentarily, for the moment that she noticed the boys standing awkwardly behind me, her ululations began all over again. Within seconds, she descended upon the boys, hugging them with such fierceness that I thought she might crush them. Yet when they emerged from beneath her hefty brown arms, I immediately saw that they were unscathed. From their blushing smiles, I could see that they were more than slightly dazzled by Ruti's unabashed show of affection. Ruti next scooped them up and placed them on top of the tractor, then climbed aboard and squeezed her body tightly between the two of them. Before long she was driving the tractor across an open field at full speed. The sight of Menachem and Uri giggling and waving to me from their perch on top of the tractor convinced me that I had made the right decision. The air, the sun, the fields. It was all here. And I glimpsed that there was some joy left in the world.

27

Suzy Kohn
Toronto, Ontario
August 1969

Once the police departed in order to start their search for Bella, my parents decided to broaden their own hunt for her in the neighbourhood. I was told to remain at Bella's house to "hold the fort," while my sisters manned the phones at home.

Unsure what to do with myself at Bella's place for so many hours, I called Fin and asked him to come over and keep me company. He said he'd be there by noon. I passed the time by flipping through old issues of *Life* magazine and half-watching a series of noisy game shows on television. All of a sudden, I realized how late it had become—it was already well past noon and there was no word from anyone. Not a single call from the police. Or from my parents. And where was Fin? Why hadn't he shown up?

It was almost one p.m. when I heard a loud knock at the door. I rushed to open it, but instead of Fin, two hulking police officers stood before me. Between them was Bella, hunched over, her face buried in her hands. I shrieked with joy when I saw her, though she barely acknowledged me. She was struggling to disentangle herself from the cops, who maintained a tight grip on her upper arms. She kept repeating that she was fine and that they should leave immediately. But the officers were in no hurry to go. I asked one of them where they had found her.

"She was dozing on a bench. In Scarborough."

"Scarborough?"

"Yes, miss. Near the bluffs."

The Scarborough bluffs? What was Bella doing there? She couldn't have just wandered there by accident. Even by subway, it was more than an hour away. It was way east of the city. Right on the lake. The officers led Bella to the sofa, where she flopped down on it as if her limbs were made of rubber. Her face was patchy and red, burnt from the August sun. One of the officers brought her a glass of water and insisted that she drink it to avoid dehydration. In the meantime, the other cop lingered in the kitchen filling out forms and radioing messages to the station. They were both waiting to speak to my parents.

I sat down beside Bella and rubbed her shoulders, telling her how relieved I was that she was safe. I asked her how she was feeling.

"Satisfied," she said matter-of-factly.

"I guess it feels good to be home."

"Home? Why would I want to be home? I was happier there."

"There? Where's there?"

"You know, by the water."

My mind darted from one thought to the next. By the water? Wasn't that what Uncle Charles had written in his note? "You mean," I prodded, "the place that Uncle Charles loved so much?" I knew I was taking a chance, but I had to ask.

Bella stared straight ahead and smiled, as if she was remembering something pleasurable. She nodded slowly, saying, "Yes, that's the place."

Oh my God. Could I have been right? Was Uncle Charles still alive, living near the water? Somewhere on the bluffs? No, that was absurd. There must be some other explanation. Just then, Bella said that she was tired and wanted to rest. I helped her to the bedroom and covered her with a blanket as she lay on the bed. After making sure she was comfortable, I went to the kitchen and thanked the officers for bringing Bella home safely.

"I'm so happy you found my aunt," I said. "How did you think of looking near the beach?"

"It was actually your mother's idea," explained one of them. "She called us a few hours ago and suggested some new places to search. Apparently she suddenly remembered that yesterday would have been your aunt and uncle's anniversary, and something clicked. It dawned on her that your aunt might have gone to visit her husband's gravesite—which we checked first but came up empty. Or, that she might have gone to the bluffs."

"But—why the bluffs?"

"Well, I'm sure you know. That's apparently where your uncle—took his life."

"What? Are you telling me that—that he—committed suicide?"

"I'm so sorry. I suppose I shouldn't have said anything. But I figured you knew."

28

Artur Mandelkorn
Kibbutz Tivon, Israel
September 1962

When I first returned to the kibbutz, I kept telling myself that it was only temporary. That we might be leaving at any time, that I would look for work in the city. But as six months grew into a year, the thought of uprooting Menachem and Uri filled me with apprehension. They were robust, boisterous, and overflowing with youthful energy, traits that seemed to emerge naturally in this environment that was tailor-made for boys. Right before my eyes, they became young *kibbutzniks*—brash, sweet for a moment, then brash, and brash again. Life here was good for them. What more could I ask for?

In the meantime, the kibbutz executive was prodding me to make a decision about applying for formal membership. If I didn't apply soon, we would be asked to leave. The thought of actually leaving the kibbutz forced me to think about what was truly important in my life. I suppose that I must have known the answer all along: I submitted my application for official status and before long we were welcomed into the kibbutz as full-fledged members—with little ceremony other than a quick announcement in the dining hall between servings of barley soup and minced beef kabob.

Now that we were settled there permanently, I gave up my aspirations of becoming a practicing architect, figuring that the last thing any kibbutz needed was an expert in urban design. Of course, I often thought about my aborted career and how I'd wasted all those years becoming proficient in my trade. But when I watched my motherless boys growing up closely connected to the other kibbutz families—some of whom fussed over Menachem and Uri almost more than me—I knew that I'd made the right decision

As a full-fledged member of the kibbutz, I did whatever work I was assigned, no matter how tedious. Yet, whether I was picking bananas or collecting eggs from the *lul*, the repetitive work left my brain feeling stunted by the end of the day. I struggled to take the philosophical view that being part of a cooperative enterprise was like having a higher calling—that the larger goal was greater than the sum of its parts. In fact, I must have said to my children more than once, perhaps a little too adamantly, "Contentment only comes from being useful." Still, I wasn't sure how long I would be able to live by that maxim myself.

Our time on the kibbutz stretched from months to years and before I knew it, Menachem was approaching his thirteenth year. Along with all the other boys in his class, the time had come for him to prepare for his bar mitzvah. I knew that the socialist leaders of the kibbutz had long gotten rid of the religious rituals involved in this rite of passage. But I still expected at least some vestiges of these practices to somehow resurface, to spurt up like a forgotten underground spring. How could there not be any chanting from the ancient parchment scrolls or binding one's arms in leathery *tefilin*? It wasn't that I didn't appreciate the excitement that came from making the bar mitzvah a communal affair. Certainly every May I had clapped and stamped my feet with the rest of the kibbutz members as I watched that year's bar mitzvah boys display their common class project before joining them all at the outdoor banquet around a festive bonfire. I was pleased that the class project of Menachem's year was devoted to Joseph Trumpeldor, the hero of the Battle of Tel Chai. He was a figure I had long admired. When Menachem's teacher asked me to be their design consultant in constructing a model of Trumpeldor's final battlefield, I gladly consented. It gave me an excuse to stop by often and watch the boys working on their project—researching Trumpeldor's biography, painting a wall-sized mural, and staging a re-enactment of the final battle where he lost his life.

Yet despite all of that, the fact that my son's bar mitzvah was not going to take place in a synagogue continued to gnaw at me. Not that I was religious, at least not in the conventional sense. But I couldn't help feeling that Menachem would be missing out on a vital aspect of what it meant to be a Jew. I could almost feel my father's eyes rebuking me for allowing my son to become disconnected from his religious tradition. Would my boys never know what it felt like to hold a siddur in their hands or to kiss the crown-embellished scrolls as they were carried from the sacred ark? Was I to be the final link in this ancient chain of religious tradition that my family struggled so hard to preserve? Would it all end with me?

Unable to dispel these thoughts, I began to hatch a plan. I determined that I would take Menachem to a synagogue in Jerusalem so that, at the very least, he would be able to experience a religious service. When we'd lived in London, the boys had occasionally come with me to shul, but they had seldom joined me in the sanctuary to pray. Instead, they had spent their time racing through the outer corridors, playing games of hide-and-seek or trading sweets with the other children. Now that Menachem was almost thirteen, I felt that it was time for him to be introduced to the inside of a synagogue. I knew that I would have to do it surreptitiously because the other members of the kibbutz would certainly scorn the idea if they found out.

The only person who might know how to find a synagogue that

would appeal to a boy Menachem's age was Dudu. Now working as a photographer in Jerusalem while studying philosophy on the side, he occasionally mentioned that he enjoyed exploring the motley array of synagogues scattered throughout the city. Of course, he always made sure to explain that his interest stemmed from historical curiosity rather than any religious motivation. When I called him with my question, he responded with his usual wry humour, "You mean you're willing to expose your boy to how Jews lived before they embraced the god of socialism?"

"I know it's daring," I quipped, "but I'll take that risk."

"Well, if you want to give Menachem a glimpse of the exotic, I know of a one-room shul that allows the women to only view the service through a tiny peephole. After all, you said you want a place that's interesting—"

"Not *that* interesting, Dudu. And less medieval, please."

"Hmm. I might know just the place you're looking for. It's a little shul near Agrippas Street, not far from the open-air market. It's a hovel on the outside, but dripping with charm inside—burnished wood, colourful walls, gas lamps, and a whiff of schnapps in the air. You get the idea. Why don't you bring Menachem there after he's turned thirteen? He can even be called up to the Torah and say the blessings. You'll give him a synagogue experience and a bar mitzvah in one fell swoop."

After Menachem's thirteenth birthday at the end of November, I asked him what he thought of the idea of having his bar mitzvah in a synagogue. "In a synagogue?" he exclaimed. "I thought we weren't religious."

"You know, there are many ways of being religious," I replied.

Menachem looked puzzled, so I did my best to explain. "Listen, I know we live on a *chiloni*, secular, kibbutz. But that doesn't mean that we can't have our own private feelings about religion."

Menachem was silent for a moment, his eyes pensive. "So you believe in God?" he asked bluntly.

"I—I'm not sure," I answered. "I'm certainly open to the possibility that God exists. And as far as I can tell, no one has ever proven that He doesn't."

Menachem rocked his head gently as he pondered what I'd said. He then looked up and gave me his answer. "Sure. Why not? A synagogue bar mitzvah might be kind of interesting. Are there any books on the subject? I might want to start reading."

Our trip to Jerusalem was scheduled to take place during the Chanukah break at the boys' school. When some people on the kibbutz asked about our planned visit to Jerusalem, I just said that we were going to visit my old friend Dudu. I didn't tell a soul that we would be going to a synagogue so that Menachem could have a bar mitzvah in accord with Jewish tradition. At first, the boys thought it strange to keep it a secret, but soon embraced it as a kind of clandestine operation.

Early that Saturday morning in Jerusalem, Dudu led us through a maze of hilly streets to the tiny shul off of Agrippas Street. It was so early that the Arab vendors at the nearby market hadn't even unpacked their wares. The door to the shul was still locked when we arrived, but a young man with a stringy black beard soon appeared carrying a large ring of keys. Once inside, we marvelled at the dizzying array of images that covered the walls and ceiling— paintings of animals, plants, stars, and planets were colourfully rendered in one continuous fresco. Dudu grinned and raised an eyebrow as if to say, "See what I mean?"

Menachem pointed at the paintings of oxen and camels. "Those animals look so realistic. I wish we could paint something like that for our Trumpeldor mural."

Tilting his head back, Uri studied the height of the ceiling. "How can anyone get up so high?" he asked. "Do they make ladders that tall?"

We all sat down on the long wooden benches that formed a

square around the central *bimah*. Within minutes, a steady stream of men filed into the room. Before taking their seats, some of them wrapped their shoulders in white prayer shawls, while others placed the shawls on their heads like keffiyehs. A sprinkling of women looked down on us from a raised balcony, peering at the men like mother birds safeguarding their young.

I had already given Menachem a few lessons on how to chant the Torah blessings and when his turn came, he leapt out of his seat and strode confidently up to the *bimah*. Wrapped in a prayer shawl provided by the *gabai*, he sang the ancient words in a voice that was both sweet and full. My heart fluttered in my chest. When had Menachem acquired this ability to sing? Why had I never noticed it before? But my reaction was more than just surprise. I knew that sound from somewhere else. Indeed, it was unmistakable—my son's voice was just like Manya's. Watching Menachem standing on the *bimah*, his smooth face bent down to the Torah scroll, I was suddenly aware that he was almost the same age that my sister had been when I last saw her.

As Menachem descended the *bimah* and walked back toward his seat, every man he passed grabbed his hand and shook it, wishing him a *yasher koach* for a job well done. His eyes crinkled as he thanked them and I couldn't help thinking how self-possessed he was. How I wished Fanny could be here to see this. Just this. I would glance up to her in the balcony and she would wave to her son. Gently. Never wanting to draw undue attention to herself.

When the service was over, we followed the crowd into an adjoining room for kiddush and refreshments. As I sipped some grape juice, a few people approached me, welcoming me to their shul. One broad-chested man with a shock of white hair grabbed my shoulder and told me that he'd been coming to this shul every day since he arrived in 1956. He leaned in closer to me until his nose was practically grazing mine, the stench of vodka filling my nostrils. "Wanna know the truth?" he pronounced. "Being religious is the key to our survival. Why can't most Jews understand that?"

"It's not so simple," I retorted, trying to curb the edge in my voice. "What about all those young men in the army? They're sacrificing their lives for the Jewish state. Most of them aren't religious."

"Ach, what do they know about Judaism? For them, Shabbos is just an excuse for a day at the beach."

I bit my tongue and for a split second, I wondered if I'd been right to bring Menachem to a synagogue. Pulling away from the man, I muttered something about needing to find my boys. Scanning the room I found them filling up on rolls of cream-filled sponge cake. When I said that it was time to go, they looked disappointed for a moment, but soon acquiesced.

After finding Dudu in the crowd, we strolled back to his apartment in the blush of the late morning sun. Reaching the top of a hill and looking out over the glistening stone walls of Jerusalem, my mind was heavy but my heart was light. No, in the end I had no regrets about bringing my son here. Not really. Yet like all weary travellers, I knew that no matter how fine the journey, it's always good to be home.

29

Suzy Kohn
Toronto, Ontario
August 1969

I felt knocked down, flattened, as if the police officer had slapped me with his pistol. It was hard to breathe, hard to think. My sweet, gentle Uncle Charles. How could he have taken his own life? How could he have done that to Bella? To our family? To me?

No. The officer must've gotten it wrong. My uncle died of a heart attack. Didn't my parents say he'd been sick? That he'd been ill for a long time? And yet—maybe they were lying about it. Maybe that's what their evasiveness was all about. Their anger. And silence.

When my parents showed up and heard that Bella had been found, their ecstatic shouts reverberated through the house. They then insisted that the two police officers tell them every detail of Bella's rescue. But I couldn't stand hearing the sound of their voices so I retreated into the den to call Fin. I desperately needed to talk to him. To hear his soothing voice. To tell him everything about Uncle Charles. About my shock and confusion. Then I remembered—Fin was supposed to have been here hours ago. Where was he? Why hadn't he come? I dialled Fin's number and no one answered.

I kept trying, dialling over and over again, letting the phone ring, but no one picked up. My hands were shaking, making it difficult to dial. I needed someone to talk to. But who?

I decided to try Lynne. Despite our differences, we were still close. I called her number, though no one answered at her house either. Where was everyone? I suddenly thought of calling Lynne's friend, Margot. Maybe Lynne was at her place. And if not, maybe Margot would know where to find her. To my relief, Margot answered the phone. "Hi, Margot. This is Suzy. Suzy Kohn. Do you know where Lynne is? I've been trying to call her, but no one's answering. It's important."

After a brief silence, Margot replied, "So—I guess you don't know."

"Know? Know what?"

"Well, I hate to be the one to tell you this, but I guess you'll find out anyway. Lynne left this morning. To go to some rock concert across the border. Somewhere in New York State. She—went with Fin."

"With Fin? What are you talking about? I just spoke to him this morning. He was supposed to come see me."

"Well, all I know is what Lynne told me. They got a ride with someone at the last minute. To some place called Woodstock."

"I don't believe it. Why would he take Lynne?"

Again, there was silence on the other end. Only this time, Margot took longer to answer. "I—um—suppose you might as well know the truth. Fin has been hanging out with Lynne. Going out with her behind your back. It's been a few months."

"What? I don't believe you. You're making it up."

"Why would I make up something like that? Anyway, don't blame *me* for it. You're the one who's been blind."

I was frozen, struck dumb. I couldn't even cry. After a numbing silence, I finally heard myself ask in a small quivering voice, "So has she been sleeping with him?"

"What do *you* think?" She answered dryly. "Fin always gets what he wants."

30

Artur Mandelkorn
Kibbutz Tivon, Israel
November 1963

Now that my boys were older and involved in their own activities, I was getting increasingly restless on the kibbutz. Nights were particularly hard—I had too much time on my hands, too much time to think. To fill the evening hours, I turned to reading, and soon found myself combing the kibbutz library for volumes of interest. More than any other subject, I was drawn to stories about the ancient history of Israel—the troubled monarchy of Saul; David's battles to unify the kingdom; the cultural aspirations of Solomon; and the tragic split between the kingdoms of Israel and Judah. It sometimes seemed to me that the struggles of those ancient monarchs weren't that different from those faced by the political leaders of our day.

Although I had never paid much attention to the assorted day trips organized by the kibbutz—visits to museums or cultural exhibits—when I heard that a series of field trips to Israel's historical sites was being offered, I signed up at once. I was ashamed to say that I'd lived in the country for years without learning much about many of its landmarks and antiquities. Our first trip was to the mountaintop fortress of Masada, where the ancient Jews held out against the Romans, eventually choosing to die by their own hand rather than being taken captive. Hiking with the others to the top of the mountain, I stopped momentarily to scan the view. My chest ached at the sight of such beauty—the golden hills of the Negev rising and falling like shadow-swept waves as the desert *wadis* pooled beneath them. When we finally reached the summit, sweat-soaked and breathless, I expected to be overcome with emotion on seeing the remains of this legendary enclave. Yet as I wandered through what was left of the ancient ruins—the roofless stone buildings and broken implements—it seemed to me I could smell the stench of despair still lingering in the shattered vessels. Was it really courageous for those Jews to have taken their own lives rather than be enslaved by the Romans? Wasn't life always to be preferred over death? Wasn't that the Jewish way? As I descended the mountain, I was left with an uneasy sense that Masada was nothing more than a shrine to the dead. A tribute to the triumph of death over hope.

I decided not to sign up for the next excursion, a field trip to Tiberius, where the second-century remains of the martyred Rabbi Akiva lay buried. I had seen too many graves in my lifetime and had no desire to see more. I was ready to wash my hands of all future outings until I heard about a trip to Safed, the centre of Jewish mysticism and Kabbalah. I knew that Safed had been a haven for mystics since the sixteenth century and was considered to be one of Judaism's Four Holy Cities. Curious to experience its "magic," I signed up for the trip—despite my instinctive wariness about mysticism and its claim to possess the secrets of existence.

As our tour bus zigzagged up the steep hilly rise, I immediately understood why both mystics and artists were drawn to this spot—secluded on the top of a mountain between clouds and sloping forests, the mist-covered city of Safed appeared to be suspended between heaven and earth. We got off the bus at the centre of town and were soon walking through a labyrinth of narrow cobble-stoned streets lined with low crouching buildings.

Our first destination was a centuries-old synagogue named after one of the masters of Jewish mysticism, Isaac Luria, also know as the Ha'Ari. Just as our group leader was about to escort us inside, we were accosted by a white-bearded man in a frayed jacket and multi-coloured cap who asked if any of us were Jewish males over the age of thirteen. When he heard some of us mumble yes, he asked if we would help him form a *minyan*, a quorum of ten men, the requisite number to properly conduct a Jewish prayer service. I was too embarrassed to say no and stepped forward with several other men in the group. We went into the synagogue and took our seats on the long wooden benches as the prayer leader began chanting the short afternoon service. Unfamiliar with his Middle-Eastern melodies and the unusual order of the liturgy, I gaped at my prayer book, barely able to follow along. As the service wound to an end, the prayer leader suddenly banged on the lectern and called out, "Kaddish! Kaddish! Any mourners here for Kaddish?"

I wasn't sure what to do. It had been three years since Fanny died and according to Jewish law, I was supposed to have said the kaddish prayer for thirty days after her passing. But I never did. Once the funeral and shiva were over, I never wanted to hear the prayer again. Now, for some strange reason, I found myself jumping to my feet, striding to the *bimah*, and identifying myself as a mourner. With prayer book in hand, I joined two other men in mourning, both of them hunched with age, and together we repeated the ancient words offering praise to the Almighty. When I finished, I hurried back to my seat, not sure why I went up there in the first place. The words confused me as much as ever. I doubted I even believed in them. It was as if a tiny voice was whispering in my ear: Why praise God after losing a loved one? After losing so many? After millions of Jews had been gassed and burned?

I found the rest of our kibbutz group lingering in the vestibule, ready to begin their official tour of the synagogue. But by then I was drenched in sweat and chose to wait for them outside where I could inhale the cool Safed air. I paced in front of the shul, but as the minutes passed and there was no sign of them, I decided to wander through some of the nearby streets on my own. Around the corner from the shul, at the end of a dim laneway, I noticed that a cluster of artists had set up their easels in the refracted light of the alley. The luminous colours on one of the canvases drew me toward it and, coming closer, I stopped and watched as the grizzled painter brushed the canvas with his pasty oils. And it struck me that he was able to create the shimmering colours because the rest of the painting was covered in darkness. Moving from one easel to the next, I could feel my imagination expanding, like dough rising in an oven, as I watched each artist remake the world according to his own vision. And more than just admiring them, I thought about what it must be like to be one of them. Still, I couldn't help wondering: after all the darkness I'd seen in my life, was it really possible to rescue the light before all its radiance is sucked out of it?

I rejoined my group, but decided that I would skip the scheduled hike through the bordering mountain paths to explore more of Safed. As I continued my tour of the streets, I came upon a narrow sliver of a store wedged between two houses, its front window packed chock-a-block with religious trinkets. I felt compelled to go inside, though I had no interest in buying any of the gaudy wares on display.

As soon as I stepped inside, my heart stopped. I instantly recognized the proprietor of the shop. It was the man to whom I owed my life—Ferko. On seeing me, his mouth dropped open and his eyes grew wide as saucers. "Artur!" he yelped. "My boy, Artur!" We fell into each other's arms, embracing one other like long-lost brothers.

"I don't believe it! I don't believe it!" I kept repeating, half-wondering whether the mystical air of Safed had tricked me into seeing ghosts. But he was no apparition. Ferko was as real as anyone I'd ever known. And here he was. Standing in front of me. In the middle of a shop in Safed. I had assumed that he was dead, killed like so many others in the war, and had never imagined that I would see him again. He didn't look much different from the way I remembered him, except that his thick neck and shoulders had caved inward and were engulfed by a belly of mountainous proportion. But the thing that stunned me the most was seeing him here in Israel of all places. What was he doing here?

Instead of answering my questions right away, Ferko begged me to sit down behind the counter and join him in a cup of Turkish coffee. He was wheezing and wiping his forehead as he placed the steaming cups on a brass tray. Sitting down on a wide stool across from me, he leaned forward and said, "Do you really mean to tell me, Artur, that you didn't know that I am a Jew?" It took me a moment to understand what he was saying. Ferko—a Jew? I never dreamed that he was anything but a Christian. A lapsed Catholic, maybe. But a Jew?

"And your wife, Ana? Was she Jewish, too?"

That made Ferko roar with laughter, interspersed by coughing fits that made his entire body jiggle. "Ana? Oh my heavens, no! My late wife, may she rest in peace, was a true Christian from the top of her head to the tip of her toes. She didn't even know that *I* am a Jew!"

Ferko's story soon poured out of him like a river overflowing its banks. "I didn't always know I was Jewish," he began, "but I suspected it for as long as I can remember. My mother died in childbirth and my father remarried when I was still in diapers. Can you imagine me in diapers?" He started laughing again so hard that the floorboards shook beneath my feet.

"My father was born into a good Catholic family, but he never had any use for religion. My stepmother was the opposite—she always had her nose buried in a Bible. She often said that Jews were akin to the devil. She'd take me to church and tell me to repeat the catechism extra times so the prayers would 'clean out my rotten blood.' I didn't understand what I'd done wrong, so I started to think that I must have been born evil or was the son of a whore.

"One day an elderly woman came to our house and sat at the kitchen table talking to my father for quite some time. When I came in, she called me over to her, using a foreign name—Velvl. She stroked my cheek and told me I was a fine boy. My father told me later that she was a distant relative of my late mother. When I told him that I'd like to see her again, he pounded his fist on the table and said she was örült—crazy. So that was the end of that. Yet I always knew I was somehow different and the name Velvl had something to do with it. I didn't discover the truth until I was about twelve years old. A small band of musicians had arrived in our village to perform at the local fair and—lo and behold—one of them was named Velvl! Until then, I thought Velvl might be a nickname like 'scamp' or 'good-for-nothing.' But I had to find out for sure. So I waited until the end of the show and approached this fellow, Velvl, and asked him what his name meant. And what do you know—he glared at me as if I was trying to pick a fight with him. I had quite a time convincing him that I meant no harm. Finally he snapped, 'Listen, it's just a name. I don't know what it means. It's an ordinary Jewish name. That's all.'

"I felt as if a bomb had gone off in my head. What? A Jewish name? How was it possible? But then, like a dark curtain lifting before my eyes, everything began to make sense. Yes, of course. My mother had been a Jew and that is why I had 'bad blood'!

"The idea that I was a Jew made me crazy. I was sure that people in the village knew about my mother and looked at me as a dirty little Jew-boy. I tried asking my father about my mother's background but he refused to say anything. When I finally blurted out that I knew she was a Jew, he turned white with rage and hollered,

'I never want to hear you say that again! Once she married me, she gave up being a Jew!' After that, I never spoke to him about it again.

"Years later, when I married Ana, we moved to a far-off village and started a whole new life. No one knew me there and I was happier that way. Life was simple, uncomplicated—at least until the Nazis started spreading their hatred like a disease. For the longest time, I tried to convince myself that it had nothing to do with me. It was only when you arrived, Artur—you and your sister Manya—that I felt my Jewish soul rise up inside of me. I had to help you, even if it meant putting myself at risk. Maybe I felt I owed it to my mother, or to my mother's family.

"Do you remember the day we were caught? The Germans beat me so badly that blood ran from my ears for days. But I was young and strong as an ox, so I managed to survive. The Germans never found out that I was a Jew. I wasn't circumcised, so they never suspected. I spent the rest of the war in a camp doing hard labour, being practically starved to death. When the war was over, I ended up in a DP camp with all the other living skeletons. Most of them were Jews, except for a few oddballs like me. I didn't know who I was or where I belonged. With the Jews, I felt like a goy, and with the Christians I felt like a Jew. The moment of truth came when I had an opportunity to go to back to Hungary. I realized that I could never live there again. The bit of family that I had left meant nothing to me. I felt closer to these human shells in the DP camp than I did to my own kin.

"Why did I finally decide to go to Palestine? Probably because of the Zionists I met in the DP camp. They talked a lot about the new country and what it meant for the Jews to have their own land. Of course, there were many who hated the Zionists—even there in the camp. Some of them were old communists or Bundists who still believed that the Jews should stay in Europe and fight for the proletariat. Bah! What did those fools know about workers? Most of them didn't know a hammer from a pitchfork! When I arrived in Palestine, I had to declare my religion. For the first time in my life, I said the words, 'I am a Jew.' That was a big moment for me. But I still had one problem: Was I really a Jew if I had never been circumcised? I found out pretty fast that I had no choice about going through with the operation on my 'you-know-what.' So I did it. There was even a special *mohel* at the hospital who said a blessing. I also had to learn to read. You can't be a real Jew unless you read from a siddur once in a while. I think I must be the only Jew in the world who grew up without knowing his letters. But, you know, I'm not bad at it now. I guess I'm using my *Yiddishe kop!*"

Hearing Ferko speak Yiddish sounded so comical to me. What made it even funnier was that he used the Yiddish expression "Yiddishe kop"—Jewish "smarts"—in a literal way. I knew that native Yiddish speakers usually use it ironically. But I tried to conceal my smile, and let him continue.

"Anyway, I decided to settle in Safed because I liked the clean air and the simple way of life. I also found myself a good Jewish wife and before long she presented me with twins: a boy and a girl, Natan and Dalia. Can you believe it? Me—a father at my age!"

My eyes watered as I listened to Ferko's story. I didn't know which part moved me more—the revelation that he was a Jew, or his determination to restart his life in Israel. At the same time, learning that it was a Jew who saved my life rather than a gentile left a trace of bitterness in my mouth. For years I clung to the image of Ferko as my model of a righteous gentile. It was my proof that humanity was not rotten to the core. And yet—as I looked at my dear friend and saw the joyful slant of his eyes as he smiled back at me, I was able to quickly bury these thoughts. Finding Ferko was like retrieving a part of myself. After all, he knew me as a child, and that was something few living people could claim after the war.

Now that he'd finished his story, Ferko leaned over and clutched my arm, "Tell me, Artur, you haven't said a word about your sister Manya. Is she—?"

I shook my head, struggling to explain. The words burned in my throat like acid. "I—I tried to find her, but nothing—nothing turned up."

Ferko gripped my arm tighter and closed his eyes as he hung his head. Lifting his face, he asked softly, "And you, Artur? Is there a wife? Children?"

"I have two boys—thirteen and ten," I responded. "My wife—she died a few years ago. From a rare illness. There was nothing the doctors could do."

After several minutes of silence, Ferko announced that he was closing his shop early so that he could take me home to meet his family. We walked to their tiny apartment that was lodged behind a bakeshop, and when we arrived he led me into the kitchen to meet his wife, Tsipora. She was a plump Moroccan-Jewish woman with dumpling cheeks and a gold tooth in the centre of her mouth that sparkled when she smiled. She was probably no more than forty, but looked older because of her thick waddling hips and fleshy arms. She insisted that I stay for lunch and before I could respond, she slapped a pile of oil-soaked burekas down in front of me. The twins soon darted in and out of the room, curious to catch a glimpse of the stranger in their home. Round-faced with burnished olive skin, Natan and Dalia were the image of their mother—except for their eyes which were all Ferko's, clear and blue as the Magyar sky.

My time with Ferko and Tsipora passed swiftly and I soon realized that the tour group would be wondering what happened to me. Yet I couldn't manage to tear myself away. It seemed that no matter how much we talked, we never ran out of things to say. I finally forced myself to leave, and promised that not only would I return to Safed soon, but I would also bring my boys along with me.

On the bus back to the kibbutz, my head was light, almost floating. Meeting Ferko seemed unreal, like a dream you thought could never come true. But it wasn't a dream. It happened. It felt almost miraculous. And then—little by little—a new thought fluttered into my consciousness, like a tiny moth seeking a flame: if I was able to find Ferko, who knows what other miracles might happen? If Ferko was able to survive, why not others? Why not Manya too?

31

Suzy Kohn
Toronto, Ontario
September 1969

It was so liberating to be finally finished high school. No more petty gossip. Or striving to be cool. No more fear of being labelled a loser or a browner. It was a new world. And I embraced it.

When I went down to register at the University of Toronto, one of the first things I had to do was choose a college affiliation. Since U of T was divided into individual colleges, all incoming students had to make that choice. I immediately picked Victoria College as my home base, knowing that most of my high school friends were choosing other colleges like UC, New College, or Innis. I figured that I wouldn't know anyone at Vic and I preferred it that way. Of course, once classes started, I did occasionally see someone on campus that I recognized from high school. But I always tried to avoid making eye contact. I wanted to forget everything to do with high school. Especially anyone who had anything to do with Fin.

Most of all, I was trying to forget the last conversation that I'd had with Fin. When he got back from Woodstock, he had the gall to call me and act as though nothing had happened—defending himself after I told him I knew all about him and Lynne. (What a horrible irony: even their names rhymed.) He even tried to make it seem as if it was *me* who was at fault.

"Whooaa! What's come over you?" He asked, feigning surprise. "You're acting so—possessive."

"It has nothing to do with possessiveness. I thought you cared for me."

"I do care for you."

"You sure have an odd way of showing it," I said, trying to control the sarcasm in my voice.

Fin's tone suddenly became shrill. "You just don't get it, do you? Yes, I care for you. I care for many people. In fact, I have tons of love in me. What's wrong with sharing my love with more than one woman? I don't believe in monogamy," he sneered, "and all that bourgeois stuff."

"Well, then," I said, my voice shaking. "It seems we have no more to say to each other." Choking back tears rising in my throat, I added, "But I *will* say this—I have no intention of becoming another member of your free-love harem." With that, I hung up the phone. Hard and firm. Cutting off Fin. Cutting him off for good.

Before that conversation, I'd been seething with anger toward Fin. His lies. And betrayal. With my closest friend, no less. He couldn't have picked a crueller way to hurt me. But after hearing all his excuses and justifications, something clicked inside me. Like a key turning a lock. It wasn't that my anger had become any less intense. It was something else. I finally realized how unbelievably stupid I had been. How could I have expected anything different from someone like him? Right from the start, he'd made it clear that he didn't believe in commitment. "It's totally unnatural," he said often. "Like being bound in chains." So why hadn't I listened? Why hadn't I taken him at his word?

Hating Fin was easy. Understanding *myself* was much harder. I began by staying away from people, searching for wisdom in books instead. Not the kind of books that Fin had given me, but classics and works of philosophy. Taking courses in world literature, I read selections from Plato, Locke, and Rousseau; thick Russian novels; and the collected Greek tragedies. I wasn't sure whether these books would give me any answers. It just felt good to have some kind of purpose. Like the satisfaction one gets from practicing scales. Or aiming darts at a target. I figured that if I persisted at it, perhaps I would see some results.

I didn't mind the loneliness at first. I was still living at home and commuting almost an hour each way to campus, which left me little time for anything but my studies. I ate lunch alone in the cafeteria and wandered from class to class hardly speaking to a soul. Between classes I sometimes stopped for a smoke and watched the clusters of students streaming by me—talking and laughing, throwing their heads back carelessly—and I wondered how it would feel to be like them.

One afternoon in mid-October, I saw a flyer on a campus bulletin board announcing auditions for the Vic Choral Society. The tryouts were happening that evening and on impulse I decided to give it a shot. A few hours later, I found myself queuing up for an audition along with fifty or so other hopeful singers. Directly ahead of me in line was a slender young man with smooth brown hair parted on the side and a checkered shirt tucked firmly into slim-cut chinos. He looked over his shoulder at me and quipped, "Want to get accepted? Let me share a piece of advice. Sing your heart out, but don't let it show."

"Why do you say that?" I asked, tilting my head to one side.

"Trust me. They're looking for singers who can keep their cool."

"I'll keep that in mind," I answered smoothly.

He turned around to face me and extended his hand. "By the way, my name is Tom. Tom Fletcher."

"Nice to meet you, Tom," I said, shaking his hand. It was cool to the touch but sturdy, with nails filed short and even.

"And your name?"

"It's Suzy."

"Suzy what?"

"Just—Suzy."

"I get it. I have to get to know you better before you'll tell me more."

"Hmm—how did you guess?"

32

Artur Mandelkorn
Kibbutz Tivon, Israel
May 1964

Ever since the day we found each other, Ferko and I made a habit of getting our families together at least once a month. Whenever I took the boys with me to Safed, Ferko would offer us an adventure, often leading us on foot through the historic alleyways to see the secret enclaves hidden within the city, such as the remains of the Magrab synagogue or the Cave of Shem and Ever. At the end of each tour, we went back to his place to feast on his wife's traditional delicacies such as Moroccan fried eggplant or chicken tagine. When Ferko and his family came to spend the day with us on the kibbutz, we'd picnic in the fields while my boys played soccer with Ferko's twins. Tsipora always supplied plenty of homemade wine and anise bread, while I provided olives, cheese, and melons. In time, the twins became like cousins to the boys. Other than Ruti and Gidon, they were the closest thing to family we had.

Meanwhile, my old buddy Dudu decided to move back to the kibbutz. Newly married and tired of urban life, he and his wife, Amalia, returned on the condition that he could continue to pursue photography in his spare time. The kibbutz allowed him to set up a darkroom in an abandoned tool shed and I soon found myself joining him there in the evenings, watching him transform his stark photos into works of art. While we waited for his pictures to develop, we'd share a cup of tea in the darkness sitting on wooden crates that doubled as chairs. After one of my recent visits to Safed, Dudu was anxious to hear all the details about Ferko, so I told him the entire story from start to finish.

"You know something?" said Dudu after I finished. "I would like to photograph you and Ferko the next time he comes to visit. I'll write it up and submit it to the papers. Can't you just see the headline? 'Jewish man reunites with his gentile rescuer—only to discover he's also a Jew.'"

"Ha! That would be something. Do you think the papers would be interested?"

"Are you kidding?" said Dudu. "They love these kinds of stories. It makes people feel good. Gives them hope."

"As a matter of fact—" I said slowly, "I have to confess that finding Ferko has revived *my* hopes."

Dudu was clearly baffled. "Hopes?"

"You know—that I might still find Manya."

I could hear the scraping of Dudu's crate on the floor as it shifted beneath him, "I don't know, Muki. After all these years. And no word—"

"I thought that if there was anyone who believed in miracles, it was you," I muttered with some bitterness.

"Listen," Dudu said gently. "I don't mean to be callous. It's just that I would hate to see you get your hopes up and be hurt again."

"But my hopes are all I have left," I said weakly. Silence filled the room—all I could hear was the sound of Dudu's breathing in the darkness. Finally, he coughed several times and walked over to his drying rack. In the shadows, I could just make out his hands moving photos from one tray to another.

"Of course," Dudu conceded. "There's always a chance. As a matter of fact, I just read a story about a husband and wife from Poland who each thought that the other one had been killed. It turned out that they'd both survived. And years later, they discovered that they lived only a few blocks away from each other in New York. What are the odds of that happening?"

"That's my point," I said. "You hear stories like that all the time."

"Hope is generally a good thing. But don't torture yourself in the process. Remember—wherever your sister is, she would want you to be happy. I'm sure that she would hate to see you ruining your life because you want so much to find her."

"But I can't just turn it off, like—the lights in this darkroom."

"Perhaps not. But you can decide how much to let it control your life. Look at these pictures," he said waving a bunch of photos in the air. "Without my manipulation of the images, they would be nothing but blank paper. People are no different—they have the capacity to beautify or destroy their own lives."

"I suppose you're right. But—I'm not sure that I like being compared to a blank sheet of paper," I mused, a smile breaching my lips.

"Really?" Dudu answered. "I can't think of anything more hopeful."

In the middle of that summer, I received a letter in the mail bearing the formal stamp of a Tel Aviv law firm, Frisch, Bar-Lev & Weitzman. Brief and to the point, the letter stated that the firm was seeking individuals who had been interned in forced labour camps during the years 1944–1945 in order to gather evidence for a war crimes investigation. The letter offered no further details, but requested my presence at the law office on Ahad Ha'am Street, Tel Aviv, on August 17 at 10 a.m. It was signed Ephraim Bar-Lev, Attorney at Law. I had no idea how they had gotten my name—not to mention my whereabouts—and I wasn't at all sure about going. Nor did I know if I had much information to give them. After giving it some thought, I planned to write a polite letter to Mr. Ephraim Bar-Lev declining the invitation.

Sitting with Dudu in his darkroom that evening, I told him about my decision. "How can you not go?" he said sharply. "If you can do anything to put even one of those monsters in jail, it would be worth every second of your time."

"That's not the issue," I responded. "I hardly remember what any of them looked like. It was so long ago and I was just a kid."

"But surely you remember *some* details."

"Only bits and pieces. Insignificant things."

Dudu would not let up. "Let *them* decide what's significant and what's not. Even the smallest thing—the colour of a button, the shape of a bootstrap—might make all the difference in a trial."

"I suppose so," I said. "I just don't think I remember enough to be of use to the prosecutors."

"Who knows what might come back to you," Dudu persisted, "once they start asking questions."

I bit down hard on my lip. "I guess that's what I'm afraid of."

Dudu was silent for a moment. "It's what we're *all* afraid of," he said quietly, shaking his head slowly as he stared down at the floor.

On the morning of August 17, I set out early to catch the bus to Tel Aviv; I wanted to make sure to be on time for the ten o'clock meeting at the attorney's office. Arriving in the city at nine, I stopped for breakfast at a café before heading over to the offices of Frisch, Bar-Lev, and Weitzman. I was greeted by an impeccably groomed secretary whose hair was teased high into a beehive hairdo. She affirmed that Mr. Bar-Lev was expecting me and led me into his teak-clad office. Rising slowly from his chair behind a massive desk strewn with papers, Bar-Lev shook my hand and offered me a seat.

Despite his full head of grey hair, I was surprised to see how young he was—he looked no more than forty. Tall and gaunt, with deep-set eyes, he had the sallow appearance of someone whose entire life had been spent sitting in dim libraries pouring over legal tomes. He buttoned up his collar before beginning to speak. "Thank you very much for coming," he said. "We realize that asking people to talk about their past experiences related to the war can be a sensitive matter."

I nodded my head and waited for him to continue.

"However," he said, now drawing out his words, "I must admit that I had—another reason for inviting you here." He stopped and looked down at his fingers, which were tapping nervously on his desk. Tiny beads of sweat glistened on his upper lip as he cleared his throat once and then a second time. "Let me get to the point," he said at last, rising slowly from his chair. "The truth is—I am Emil Lenzner."

"What?" I said, jumping up out of my seat. "I—I—don't understand." My head was reeling. What kind of game was this man playing? This must be a hoax. Or some kind of test. Was he trying to shake me up? To see if I could hold up under interrogation?

"I'm sorry," he said quietly. "Let's sit down." He made a light patting motion in the air as if to calm me with his hands. "I assumed my name would still mean something to you, even though it was a long time ago—fifteen years at least. You wrote a letter to me in Cyprus. About your sister."

I sank back into my seat and rubbed my head. "But—I thought you were a lawyer. That you were asking for my testimony. What does any of this have to do with my sister?"

"This must be a great shock to you," he continued. "I understand. I really do. Yes, I *am* a lawyer, and my legal name is Ephraim Bar-Lev. But I was born Emil Lenzner. You see, I changed my name when I came to Israel—my Hebrew name was Ephraim, so I dropped Emil. As for Bar-Lev, well—I chose it because my father's name was Lev. At the time, I considered it preferable to Lenzner—more Israeli."

"But wait, if you *are* Emil Lenzner—and I'm still not sure if I believe you—why did you wait so long to contact me?" I was still struggling to absorb what I was hearing. "You say that my letter reached you in Cyprus. Why didn't you contact me then?"

Bar-Lev looked away as if he were avoiding my question. After that, he began to speak so softly that I had to strain to hear him. "I couldn't respond to your letter. Not then. You have to understand," he said turning to face me directly, "I tried to forget the war and everything associated with it. Even when I was in Cyprus, I had already decided to bury the past. What was the use of dwelling on it? When I got your letter, I was at a low point in my life. I read the letter and then burned it with a match. I had already given testimony in Europe. What more could I say? Talking about it wasn't going to bring back the dead."

I felt a surge of anger rising in my chest. But I didn't say a word. I couldn't. His story seemed to suck the air from my lungs.

His voice grew louder as he went on, stopping and starting with increasing speed. "When I got to Israel, I wanted to start fresh. I went to school, studied law, married, joined the firm. I achieved what I wanted—order, contentment, recognition. But four years ago, everything changed. My past snuck up on me, waiting to pounce. You see, I had been a rising star in the firm, unexpectedly handed a plum assignment. We want you to prepare some briefs, they said. It's a historic moment. For Israel and for the world. The lord-master of murder, Adolph Eichmann, was on trial. Right here in the Jewish homeland. How could I possibly say no?" Bar-Lev's eyes narrowed, "Do you have any idea what that did to me? Can you even fathom it? My entire being was turned inside out. Working on the trial was gruelling enough, but the nightmares that followed were unbearable. They say that memories can haunt you. *My* ghosts returned bearing knives."

He got up from his chair and started pacing the room. "After the trial was over and Eichmann was sent to the gallows, my life appeared to return to normal. But I was not the same man. I saw who I was and there was no use denying it—I was still Emil Len-zner, the frightened boy who'd been sent to hell and back, and somehow—somehow—survived." His thin lips curled into a twist-ed smile. "From that point on, I asked to be assigned to the most heinous murder cases, criminal trials, tribunals. In fact, I craved them."

"I—I still don't get it," I sputtered. "What about the letter you sent me about investigating war crimes? Did you invent that just to get me here?"

"That's the strange part of it," Bar-Lev replied. "No, I didn't fab-ricate the case. My firm *is* involved in an investigation into Nazi labour camps during the war. In fact, several European jurisdic-tions have asked for our cooperation. The thing is—when I saw that article in the newspaper about you and the man who saved you—Ferko, was it?—and it mentioned that you'd been in a labour camp, well, the coincidence cried out to me. It was like a sign. You see," he said, lowering his tone, "I remembered the letter you'd sent me—and I had to find you. To tell you I'm sorry that I never wrote back. To finally tell you everything I know."

I squeezed my eyes shut, bracing myself for what I was about to hear. Yes, I would listen to what he had to say. Then I would be equipped to challenge his story. Perhaps I'd learn something about what really happened to Manya. If, in fact, he knew anything at all.

Returning to his seat, Bar-Lev folded his hands in front of him. "I guess I should begin by telling you how I first met the girl I knew as Manya," he continued softly. "I first noticed her in the line-up on the railway platform before we were herded onto the trains bound for Poland. She was holding the hand of a little boy who was no more than two or three years old—I thought that he must be her brother."

With a little boy? I thought. That proves it! It couldn't have been my sister.

"Something about her stood out," he went on. "The way she carried herself with such composure made me think that she was unlike other children. When the German soldiers shoved us into a stinking cattle car, I found myself not far from her, squeezed into a spot on the floor. What caught my attention was the way she tended to that little boy. He was clearly ill, coughing up blood. The girl took off her own jacket and used it to wipe up his bloody sputum. Some of the people around her started to shriek that they would all be infected and insisted that the boy be moved into a corner where he would be isolated from the rest. Finally, a man stood up and shouted at them all to be quiet. It turned out that he was a doctor. He made his way over to them and examined the boy. Whatever he said, a rumour soon spread that the boy had consumption and might not last the night. Someone also whispered that the boy was not the girl's brother but a stray child whose parents had been murdered."

My stomach dropped. Oh, no, I thought. Maybe it was my Manya after all. It was just like her to care for a child in need.

"After a few hours, the train came to a halt. The doors were unlatched and more people were loaded into our car, which was already crammed far beyond capacity. There was no longer any room to sit, so we were all forced to stand, pressed up against each other like a wall of hanging carcasses. But when the train came to another stop, something unbelievable happened—as the guards unbolted the doors to shove in more people, all of us suddenly burst out of the cattle car in one enormous surge. Once it gained momentum, it was like a stampede, with people running in every direction. The Germans started screaming and shooting wildly. But they were totally unprepared for the tidal wave of human desperation. Many were killed or wounded on the spot, while there were some like me who managed to get away."

He paused briefly, looking up at the ceiling and inhaling deeply before going on. "I was one of the lucky few who avoided being shot or captured. I fled into the forest next to the tracks and ran through the brush for what seemed like hours. Eventually, I came upon a small encampment of others who also managed to escape the train—five in total—including the young girl I'd seen earlier. It was there that I learned her name was Manya and that she was barely thirteen. Apparently, she was from a town in Hungary— Szeged or Szegda, I can't remember which."

When I heard the name Szegda, my heart began to pound. No— no. It couldn't be Szegda. Ours was just a small town. It must have been Szeged. Thousands of Jews lived there—surely there'd been hundreds of Jewish girls named Manya in Szeged.

Lenzner didn't seem to notice the rising panic in my eyes; he re- sumed his account with barely a pause. "I saw Manya sitting cross- legged quietly on her own with her head down. The others talked about her in hushed tones. The poor boy she'd been looking after had been shot while he was in the arms of the doctor who carried him off the train. The doctor was also killed—shot in the back by a German guard.

"Knowing that the Germans would be combing the area for the escapees, we quickly devised a plan. Since I was young and quick, I volunteered to scout the forest for partisan encampments where we might find aid and shelter. While I was gone, we agreed that the others would wait there for one full day. If I hadn't returned by then, they should assume that I'd been captured or killed. I spent the entire day moving cautiously through the heavily wooded area, making sure to mark my path so I could find my way back to the others. But I never found any evidence of human activity.

"I made my way back to the group, hoping they would be suf- ficiently rested to go further into the forest in search of food. But when I got there, I found—" His voice broke, forcing him to stop. He covered his face with his hands as his shoulders heaved. He then went on, speaking haltingly, his voice muffled behind his fin- gers. "Everyone—all the people at the site had been—shot. Their bodies just left on the ground—covered—in their own—blood."

He slowly removed his hands from his face, now heavily creased and drawn.

Swallowing several times, his began to speak again, this time only slightly more composed. "I saw Manya's body on the ground, apart from the others. Her shoes were beside her, unusual ones for a girl her age—heavy and brown, with dark red laces. She had obviously taken them off before lying down to rest. I remember thinking, it's a mercy she was shot before she'd even woken." Looking at me directly, he quietly said, "If it's any comfort to you, I believe that Manya died without suffering. She'd been shot through the heart. You should know that her body was not defiled—her clothes were bloody but her face was pure."

My mind was racing and I could no longer think straight. Until he'd reached the end of his story I had firmly rejected the idea that the girl he'd seen was my sister. But the shoes—what hit me were the shoes. Manya had always worn heavy brown oxfords with red laces. They'd been made especially for her, to straighten one foot that turned inward when she walked. Because of those terrible shoes, I knew—I knew that I had to face the truth that I'd been trying so hard to deny. Manya was not coming back. Manya was dead.

My entire body went cold except for my head, which was hot, so hot, that it felt like it was on fire. They say the truth hurts. It doesn't just hurt, it burns. And the more it burns, the less you feel—until you are no longer sure who you are and what you were before. "It's over." I murmured, pulling myself up, my knees trembling beneath me.

Emil jumped up and took hold of my arm. "Please. Stay a while. You—you don't know how sorry I am." His face was etched in shadow.

"I don't blame you for what happened," I said. "Truly, I don't. But I—I must—go. There's nothing more to say here." Steeling myself, I walked out of his office, past the secretary with her towering hairdo, and made my way to the stairwell. Back on the sidewalk,

I was assaulted by the glaring sun that momentarily blinded me. I needed to get away. Anywhere. Anywhere was better than here.

I found myself roaming through the streets of Tel Aviv, oblivious to where I was going and why. It no longer mattered. Nothing did. I just had to keep moving. It was the heat of the day and the roads were deserted. Shops were closing, rolling down their grates. In an open market, an Arab vendor beckoned, offering me halvah and tea spiced with mint. His smile was friendly. I could have accepted. But I couldn't stop, no. Keep moving, I muttered. I wandered for hours, soaked through with sweat that leached from my pores. My tongue was like plaster; I could barely swallow. But I couldn't stop, no. Not even a second. The sun was fierce, burning a hole in my skull, burrowing like an animal into my brain. All I knew was that I had to keep moving. Forward. Forward. One foot, the other. Until the sidewalk was swimming. My knees were folding. I was strewn on the pavement. Weightless and torn. Like a dead branch. Snapped from a tree.

No more feeling. No more pain.

Only sirens. A distant screech. Louder. Louder. Grinding in my ears.

33

Suzy Kohn
Toronto, Ontario
November 1969

I was sprawled across my bed, wading through sections of Plato's *Republic* for an upcoming exam when the phone rang. On the other end I heard an all-too-familiar voice. "Hi Suzy, what's happening?" I almost dropped the receiver. It was Fin.

"I—I thought you were in Europe," I stammered.

"Yeah, I was," he said. "Hitched through Holland, Spain, Italy. Ended up in Portugal. Now *that* was a trip. I crashed with some dudes who'd never even heard of Toronto."

"So—um—what brought you back?"

"I ran out of money—had to get back here to make some bread. I'm hoping to cut a record. If not, I'll look for a job in construction or something." I was silent, not sure why he was calling me. "So—," Fin continued, "How about we get together? I still have some great weed I copped in Amsterdam. Pure stuff. You can't get anything close to it here."

"I—don't think so. I'm busy. Anyway, I—don't think we should see each other."

"Why not? Still *mad* at me?" he said with a snigger.

"No, actually I'm not. I just don't think we have anything in common anymore."

"Well, you wouldn't have said that six months ago."

"I guess I've changed."

"You mean, now that you're a *college girl*?"

"Yes," I said, trying to ignore his sarcasm. "As a matter of fact, I enjoy university. Studying philosophy, literature, classics."

There was silence for a few seconds. "Hmmm," he said finally. "They've really sucked you in, haven't they?"

"What is that supposed to mean?"

"You sound so—middle class. What's next? Are you going to marry a lawyer and move to the suburbs?"

"You obviously missed my point."

Fin gave an exaggerated sigh. "All I can say is, if you want to be part of the boring establishment, well, that's your choice."

"You're right." I said, my voice now sounding strained. "Whatever I choose to do with my life will be my choice. No one else's. Just mine."

Banging down the phone, I lunged for a cigarette, but didn't light it. My hands were shaking so hard that I couldn't even strike the match.

A few weeks after my audition for the Vic Choral Society, I got word that I'd been accepted and started going to the weekly practices. I was a bit late for the very first meeting and the guy I'd met at the audition, Tom Fletcher, caught my eye from his spot among the baritones. He shook his head, warning me not to be tardy again. He was right. Derek, the choirmaster, was a stickler for punctuality—his watchword was "lateness equals laziness." Being late was grounds for dismissal.

We practiced in the Vic Chapel, a stone-covered building with arched wooden beams and stained glass windows. I was a little uneasy at first about singing in a church, but, thankfully, our repertoire had nothing to do with religion. As it turned out, Derek was a fanatic for show tunes, preferring *Oklahoma* and *Carousel* to Handel's *Messiah*. During our breaks, Tom often came over to chat and after a few such exchanges, he asked me out for a beer after rehearsal. On the walk over to the campus pub, Tom told me that he was a pre-law student and had grown up in Rosedale, not far from the university. "I'm a local boy, born and bred," he joked. "Like my father. And his father before him."

"Three generations. That's amazing."

"You think so?" he said, surprised. "What's your story?"

"I'm the first generation born in Canada."

"Really? Where's your family from?"

"Um—Hungary."

"That's different," Tom said. "You don't look Hungarian." He leaned back and squinted at me, scrutinizing my face. "I'd say you look—Italian or, maybe—Spanish." I froze, waiting for him to say the word that I knew he was thinking. But he didn't say it. It was as if it had never crossed his mind. Maybe he'd never even met a Jew and didn't know what to look for. I didn't offer to fill in the blanks.

Tom and I began getting together often on campus—for lunch, coffee, or a pint of beer after class. It took a while for him to tell me much about himself, which was fine with me—I was in no rush to disclose the details of my own life. He talked a lot about sports, especially about his weekly pick-up hockey games with an old group of school buddies. He was also a jazz buff with an extensive record collection, proudly admitting that he would stand in line for hours whenever a new album by Dave Brubeck or Dizzy Gillespie was released. One day, after several beers, he confessed that although he planned to go to law school, he dreaded the idea of being a lawyer. I asked him why on earth he would study law when his heart wasn't in it. He winced slightly, then said, "My dad's an attorney and I'm his oldest son. It's expected of me."

"Why don't you just tell him that you want to choose your own career?"

"I can't go against my father's wishes," he said as he looked down at his sturdy fingers. "I've accepted the fact that I'll go to law school, get my degree, and then try to find some branch of law that I can tolerate."

I gasped lightly, unable to understand how he could be so blasé about his future.

"And what about you?" Tom asked. "Do you always do whatever you want?"

"Of course not," I said, a playful smile curling on my lips. "But I always try."

34

Artur Mandelkorn
Tel Aviv, Israel
September 1964

I woke up in a dull green room, bound to a bed, unable to speak. White-clad figures swung in and out, prodding my body with needles. Words flitted by me. Concussion. Laceration. Subdural hematoma. Drifting in and out of focus, I glimpsed faces I knew. Menachem and Uri. Dudu. Ferko. Perhaps apparitions. Only with sound. I was assaulted by dreams, more so at night. My parents sinking in a boat on a river. Manya tearing the collar of her dress. I tried to run to them, but I couldn't lift my legs. I woke up gasping and a woman appeared. "Manya?" I cried.

"No, I'm the nurse. Get some sleep. You need your rest."

Weeks passed before my body started healing. Bandages were removed. Stitches extracted. My voice returned fully and my limbs began moving. Yet I didn't feel better—almost worse than before. Nausea and panic soon filled me with tremors. My thoughts turned bleak and my life seemed futile. Gazing into my future, I saw a deep, dark hole. No wife. No sister. No hope. Just emptiness.

Menachem and Uri visited me in the hospital whenever they could take a break from school, but it was Dudu who was always by my side. Granted an extended leave from the kibbutz, he came and sat with me every day. Sometimes he slept all night in a chair beside my bed. He never appeared to mind that I had no interest in conversation. He talked and I merely pretended to listen, for my own dark thoughts had me sealed behind an impermeable barrier. Dudu tried bringing me books to read, hoping that they would lift me out of myself. But I was only able to read a line or two before the words started scrambling on the page. He also brought me sheets of drafting paper and encouraged me to try doing some sketches similar to the sort I did in architecture school. But I told him that I had no interest in drawing buildings that no one would ever build. Undaunted, he suggested that I try sketching other subjects, or even attempt painting with watercolours or oils. He offered to pick up some paint and brushes, but I pooh-poohed the idea. I had no talent for it, I argued. Before long, he took back the paper and pencils he'd brought, seeing that I'd never touched them.

The only thing that caught my interest was a massive jigsaw puzzle that Dudu had found among his old possessions. I spent hours fitting the pieces together, then taking the whole thing apart again, only to begin anew. One would think that it would be tiresome to do the same puzzle over and over again, but somehow, I found it soothing.

My return to health was so gradual that I wouldn't have noticed it if the doctor hadn't insisted it was true. It began with a desire for particular foods. The first thing I craved, of all things, was a bowl of borsht with a boiled potato, the kind my mother used to make me as a child. Dudu searched the area near the hospital until he found some beet borsht at a Russian-style eatery and brought it to me in an old army thermos. It didn't look at all appetizing at first. When he poured the soup into a bowl and I saw the insipid white chunks swimming in the deep pink liquid, I wasn't sure I wanted it anymore. But when I tasted it, it was just the way I remembered it. I ended up devouring every drop of it, even scraping the bottom of the bowl.

I also started taking an interest in watching the birds outside my hospital window. Soon feeding them became a daily ritual. It got to the point where the nurses began calling me "the bird talker" because I spoke to them as I fed them crumbs from my meals. I invented names for some of the birds and fancied that they understood our conversations. I'm sure that they were mainly interested in their daily morsels, but I liked to think that they valued my company as much as I did theirs.

Encouraged by my progress, Dudu convinced me to start taking short strolls with him in the hospital courtyard. As it turned out, walking put me at ease and made me feel like talking. I suddenly wanted to know all about what was happening at the kibbutz. Which crops were flourishing? Had the henhouse been modernized? Had the sheep been taken to be shorn yet this season? The one thing I had no desire to hear about was the people. Other than my boys. I had no interest in anyone else there. Every time that Dudu referred to one of the kibbutz members, I changed the subject, interrupting him mid-sentence. I knew I was doing it, but couldn't stop myself. Finally, Dudu's jaw grew taut and his eyes narrowed. "I don't get it," he said. "Why don't you have any interest in your friends?"

"Friends?" I snorted. "I have no friends. And even if I did, they wouldn't want to be friends with me anymore."

"Why would you say that? What could you possibly have done to lose their friendship?"

"Can't you see?" I said, raising my voice, "I'm a disappointment to everyone."

"Why? Because you've had troubles? And shown some weakness?"

I was unable to answer. My stomach seized up and I felt nauseous. "Yes," I whispered. I looked down at my lap and mouthed the words, "I am so ashamed."

Dudu waited for a few moments before he began to speak, "Do

you think that there is anyone who has not felt helpless at some point in their lives? People are not born strong. It's something they acquire—like whiskers or strong biceps," he added with a mild grin.

"That may be true for others. But not for me," I insisted. "I feel like I've failed everyone around me."

"Look at this country," said Dudu. "It's filled with people like you and me. The weak. The forlorn. The broken. We all live with loss. That's why we're such good builders. We have no choice but to start from the bare foundations."

"But how, Dudu? How do you start?"

"You start by doing. Even a rascal like me remembers the phrase from the Torah, 'Naaseh ve-nishma'—we'll do and then we'll believe. The ancient Israelites must have known something about human weakness. If they had waited until they believed in themselves, they would have been waiting forever."

"But I've lost the desire to start," I said bleakly. "What's the point of someone like me trying to build a life for myself? I would probably let everyone down in the end. Like always."

"I don't understand. Who have you let down?"

My head was throbbing and I could not speak. All I could see was my sister Manya's face, searing my brain like hot oil. I just shook my head and murmured, "No one. Just forget I ever brought it up."

Dudu peered at me through squinted eyes. "But are *you* able to forget it?"

How well Dudu knew me. I felt as transparent as glass. Slowly my body felt light, as if a cool consoling breeze had swept through the courtyard. I lowered my head and from some unknown place, I heard myself saying, "You're right, Dudu. I must take action. I will try. Yes—I promise. I will try."

35

Suzy Kohn
Toronto, Ontario
December 1969

Though Tom and I often held hands as we strolled across the quad and kissed when we said goodnight, I still had trouble thinking of him as more than just a friend. In fact, whenever Tom and I were together, I couldn't help comparing him to Fin. A mere smile from Fin used to make my knees tremble—not to mention his kisses which had me soaring to the moon. Much as I tried to fight it, the more time I spent with Tom, the more I missed Fin. Of course, I knew that Tom was much better for me than Fin—he was courteous, reliable, and considerate to a fault. Yet something was missing, and I couldn't figure out what. It wasn't the "Jewish thing" for I'd told Tom that I was Jewish on our third date. He seemed perfectly fine about it, saying that he respected the Jewish people and admired their spirit. He even asked about my family history, though I said I had little to tell since most of my relatives had been killed by the Nazis. He didn't know what to say. His eyes grew wide as if someone like me was beyond his comprehension.

One evening when I was visiting Bella, I brought up the subject of Tom. Bella was easier to talk to these days. It likely had to do with the fact that she was now in group therapy. Twice a week, she attended sessions at a community centre in North York where she was linked up with other European Jews who were still suffering from the psychological after-shocks of the war. I noticed that she was wearing makeup again and pinning up her hair. The dishes in her sink were scraped clean and the garbage put out at the curb. But the biggest change was that Bella started talking. Not as much as she used to, but she was getting there.

While we were drinking tea at her kitchen table, I mentioned casually that I'd met someone new. I didn't say anything about his name or his religion. Not that Bella would have cared that Tom wasn't Jewish. She was much more worldly and open-minded than my parents.

"Hmm," she said. "It's good that you're dating. It's better than being alone."

"It's more than that. He happens to be a great guy. With all the qualities I could ask for—he's intelligent and funny and attractive. But—" I paused, not knowing what to say next.

"But, what?"

"There's no—connection," I said bluntly.

"Ahhh," said Bella, putting down her teacup. She pursed her lips and nodded.

"But there should be, right?" I asked. "It doesn't make any sense."

"It will never make any sense," Bella responded.

"What do you mean?"

"Exactly what I said. Love is a mystery. It's not supposed to make sense. If it did, we could manufacture it."

"And so?"

"All you can do is trust your instincts." Bella rubbed her eyes and sighed. "When the magic is there, you'll know it."

When Tom and I met for dinner after choral practice the next evening, I could tell that he had something on his mind. We were sitting in a crowded bistro not far from campus and he wouldn't stop drumming his fingers on the table. He didn't look me in the eye, focusing instead on the people walking by our table.

"Tom," I said, stubbing out my cigarette, "There's something—"

"I know," he said, facing me straight on. "You don't need to say it. I could feel it coming for weeks now."

"I—I'm sorry. I really like you. It's just—"

"Let me guess—you just want to be friends."

"Well—yes."

"Is it because I'm not Jewish?"

I was relieved that he didn't ask me if there was someone else. How could I explain that I was still hung up on Fin? "No, no. That's not it at all," I said, trying to control the quiver in my voice.

"Well, either you're not telling me the truth or you're lying to yourself."

"I don't understand—"

"Listen, Suzy, we could be great together. I knew it the moment I met you. But you always seem so distracted when we're together. Like there's this barrier. I couldn't care less that you're Jewish and I'm Christian. But you do. Admit it."

I hardly heard what he said; I was thinking about how foolish I was to still be dwelling on Fin. I had truly believed that I'd tossed Fin out of my life like a fruit that had gone bad. How could I still be thinking about him? Besides, I'd recently heard that Fin was living with a woman now—probably some groupie from his precious music scene.

My insides felt hollow as Tom waited for me to respond. "I'm sorry, Tom." I said weakly. "It seems that I don't know anything about myself anymore." I covered my face with my hands and prayed that he wouldn't pursue the matter further.

36

Artur Mandelkorn
Kibbutz Tivon, Israel
March 1965

Coming home from the hospital was less traumatic than I'd feared. I had imagined that the kibbutz members would give me pitying looks and treat me like one of those stray cats that scratches at the rear door of the dining hall on sweltering evenings. Yet for the most part, everyone just went about their usual business and paid little attention to me—except friends like Ruti and Gidon who tried to conceal their worry with exaggerated good humour.

The same was not true of Menachem and Uri. Every day after school they dropped by to see me with anxiety-filled eyes, and insisted on staying with me for the entire evening. I finally had to inform them, albeit gently, that I didn't need a nursemaid, that if they had other things to do, they shouldn't feel obliged to stay. But try telling that to boys who were worried about their father's sanity. They ignored all my protestations and sat with me until it got so late that they had to race back to their residences to make it there before curfew.

One night Menachem stayed behind later than usual, saying that he had something important to discuss. At fifteen, he was almost as tall as me, but it wasn't only his height that made him seem older than his years. It was his eyes—wide and deep, like two cavernous wells, reflecting a sensitive soul immersed in contemplation. Sitting on a chair across from me, his feet curled around its wooden legs, Menachem coughed a few times before he spoke. "Abba, I've been thinking—maybe we should leave the kibbutz. Move somewhere else."

"Leave? Is anything the matter? Are you unhappy here?"

"No, no. It's not about me. It's you. I thought that maybe you might want a fresh start. A change of scenery. You know—to begin again."

"Listen, Menachem," I answered. "I know you have good intentions. But one thing I've learned is that running away never solves anything."

"Are you sure about that?"

"Absolutely sure," I said firmly. "Unless you have some other reason for wanting to leave."

"Who, me? Not on your life. I love the kibbutz. It's my home. I just thought—if *you* wanted to, I would go along with it for your sake."

"No, no. I can't imagine living anywhere but here," I insisted.

Menachem was silent and tugged on his fingers.

"Please, son. Don't worry about me," I said, blinking away a wayward tear. "In fact, it's past your curfew. You better get back to your quarters. If not, you'll be tossed off the kibbutz anyway, whether you want to leave or not."

Almost worse than being an object of pity was being a man without a wife in a close-knit community. When I first moved back to the kibbutz after Fanny died, my status as a widower was the least of my worries. All I could think about was how hard it would be to raise my boys without a mother. I never thought about looking for a new wife. The idea was as foreign to me as dying my hair red or changing my religion. But now, my loneliness was like a rash concealed beneath my shirt—I was constantly aware of it, though ashamed to let it show. It was not that I lacked for company. Aside from my boys, there were occasional friends who dropped by in the late afternoon, when the heat subsided and everyone rose from their midday naps. And yet—I was lonely in ways that were tough to conceal. There was a hole in my life that was hard to fill with friends alone.

For this reason, I'm sure, I nearly allowed myself to get entangled with several unsuitable women. Married women were regularly introducing me to their unmarried sisters and cousins, but in the end, they were often just trying to find out if I found *them* more attractive than my intended match. It was not as if I was such a desirable catch. I had acquired some odd habits since Fanny died that would make most women recoil—such as having to fall asleep with the radio on loudly so that I could hear it throughout the night. Nonetheless, there were quite a few women who somehow imagined that I would be a better husband than the one they had at home.

One exception was Nira, a pert black-eyed beauty with a mop of curls to match, who had recently divorced her husband of ten years. I knew that she'd been an actress before she came to live on the kibbutz, and now directed most of the plays performed here. We were chatting about set design one day in the dining hall when she surprised me by inviting herself over to my place for tea the following afternoon. She arrived on schedule the next day and immediately settled herself down on the sofa, her bare feet pulled up under her. Just as I was placing our cups of tea on the coffee table, Nira spied some of my playful doodles on top of a pile of books. "Muki!" she gasped. "You're an artist."

"Hardly. I just enjoy drawing in my spare time. It's nothing."

"Oh, I disagree. You have talent. Do you paint as well?"

"No, I'm loyal to my trusty pencil," I said wryly.

We conversed for an hour or so and then Nira got up to go. In the doorway, she stood on her tiptoes and kissed me lightly on the lips, promising to return again soon.

A week later in the early evening, there was a knock on my door and someone called out, "I have a surprise for you." Nira walked in carrying a large wooden easel along with a canvas, a palette, and some tubes of paint. "I want you to paint my portrait," she declared, setting everything down on the floor.

"Hold on a minute. I don't know a thing about—" I stopped, distracted by Nira's strange attire. She was wearing an embroidered Russian-style blouse with a rope tied around the waist, like those worn by peasants at the turn of the century. "Say," I asked. "Are you coming from a rehearsal?"

"No, silly. I want you to paint me as an early Zionist pioneer. We can hang some sheaves of barley in the background for effect."

"You're kidding, aren't you?"

"I'm perfectly serious. C'mon, Muki. Do it for me." Pushing out her bottom lip, she gazed up at me through thick lashes.

"Alright." I shrugged. "Whatever you say." Since she went to so much trouble, it was hard to say no. I set up the easel and squeezed some paints onto the palette, while Nira positioned herself on a tall stool, placing one hand behind her head and the other loosely on her hip. After mixing some colours to achieve the right hue, I put my brush to the canvas like a blind man groping for direction. I soon discovered that the paint was more forgiving than I expected, allowing me to cover my mistakes by adding gradual layers on top of one another. As I glanced from canvas to subject and back again, I saw that my creation was becoming more abstract than realistic, depicting the feeling of the scene rather than its literal appearance. Finally, when I finished painting and set down my brush, I looked around and realized that the sun had set and the room had grown dim. Many hours had passed. It was like waking from a dream.

"You're a natural," said Nira, standing back and studying the results.

"You think so?"

"Yes. You've really managed to capture my essence. That's no easy feat." She reached up and grazed my cheek with her fingers. Her black eyes, shot with sparks of gold, drew me in and without thinking I put my hands around her waist and pulled her toward me. "You know, Muki," she murmured, resting her head on my chest. "I'm always the one who comes to visit you. Why don't you come to my place tomorrow night? You can bring me the painting. And stay as late as you wish."

The following evening was raining and I arrived at Nira's house a little late, carrying the painting wrapped in an old bed sheet. I tapped lightly on the door and waited a few minutes, but no one answered. I was about to leave when the door opened a crack and Nira poked her head out. "Muki!" she whispered. "I'm so sorry. So much has been happening here—I completely forgot I invited you. It's pouring. I guess you better come in." As soon as I entered, I saw a man sitting at the kitchen table, his back toward me. Nira led me around a corner to the tiny living room, and said in a hushed tone, "I don't know how to say this, but—Yoram has come back. He showed up this morning, begging my forgiveness, promising that he'll be faithful. He says he can't go on without me. What could I do? We were married for ten years. I guess I still love the guy."

Studying the floor, I put my hands in my pockets, not knowing how to respond.

"You should know, Muki, that I never meant to hurt you."

I nodded, still focused on the hexagonal pattern of the floor tile. "Well, I guess that's that." I shrugged and turned to leave.

Nira touched my elbow. "By the way," she said, "perhaps you should keep the painting. I think it would be better for all of us."

Despite the incident with Nira, I soon realized that once I caught the art bug, I was hooked. Painting seemed to soothe my mood, especially on those days when I was feeling particularly low. Sometimes the pain was so intense that I was tempted to bang my head against something hard just to make it stop. But once I discovered painting, the pain became less severe—perhaps because I was focused on something other than my own misery. It didn't work all the time, but it offered me some relief. Now, the main thing I thought about while working in the fields and orchards all day was getting home in the evening to my paint and canvas. I mainly practiced doing portraits—since that's where I'd first started—using my sons or anyone else who was willing to sit for me.

After a while, I branched out into landscapes and still life and began to get a bit of a reputation as an artist. I was pretty much using all my free time to paint, so when I was invited to join an artists' club on a neighbouring kibbutz, I accepted eagerly, even though I wasn't sure what was involved. The artists in the club were an idiosyncratic bunch, but we got along well enough to go on monthly sketching trips together without much contention. Most of these early morning outings were visits to nearby sites such as the ruins of Megido or the fragrant hills of Givat HaMoreh. When we got there, we would unfold our stools and begin to sketch the landscape from different angles, studying the play of light and shadow so that we could reproduce it later on canvas.

Our first major excursion that spring was a full-day outing to Caesarea where we planned to sketch the ancient Roman amphitheatre perched on the Mediterranean shore. When we got there, however, we encountered several busloads of tourists who were already swarming the ruins as if it were an amusement park. As I pushed through the crowd, I suddenly felt a hand grab my forearm and a voice exclaimed in English, "Charles! How are you? What brings you to Israel?" I swung my head around and saw a middle-aged man in a madras shirt with a camera dangling from his neck. "I'm sorry," I said. "You must be mistaken. My name is not Charles." The man immediately apologized, explaining that I was the spitting image of someone he used to work with in Toronto, a man named Charles Mandelkorn.

"Mandelkorn? But my name is Mandelkorn."

"How strange," replied the man. "Do you have any relatives in Canada? A cousin perhaps? The Charles I knew was a bit shorter than you, but other than that, the resemblance is uncanny!"

My mind was racing. Thinking quickly, I said, "I might be interested in looking up this fellow. Are you in touch with him? Do you have an address? Or a telephone number?"

"Me? No. I haven't seen him in at least five years. Not since he left the firm. He was a hard worker and moved up the ladder—got a job at an insurance company. Don't know which one. I also switched jobs not long after, so I never heard what became of him. I'm sorry to say that I didn't get to know him very well. Nice fellow. Very genteel, if you know what I mean. I think he was Hungarian."

The word "Hungarian" hit me like a lightning bolt. A Hungarian by the name Charles Mandelkorn? Who looked just like me? I knew that the names Charles and Karl are often interchangeable. And that Karl was often changed to Charles in English-speaking countries.

God in heaven—could it be possible? Was my brother Karl alive?

37

Suzy Kohn
Toronto, Ontario
December 1969

After that painful conversation at the bistro, Tom and I stopped seeing each other. We still saw one another at choral practice, but we never exchanged more than a perfunctory smile or nod. For the most part, I was relieved. Still, I felt a slight twinge when I noticed Tom taking an interest in Patricia Mills, a chirpy redhead who sang soprano in the choir. It wasn't that I wanted him back. It just hurt to be replaced so quickly. Every once and a while after that conversation, I thought about the accusation that Tom had hurled at me—that I'd kept him at a distance because he wasn't Jewish. Of course, I knew that it wasn't true. Being Jewish meant little to me. If I liked someone enough, religion wouldn't matter. Besides, I suspected that Tom was using it as an excuse. He didn't want to admit that I didn't like him as much as he liked me.

Near the end of that semester, Bella had been invited to our house for Friday night dinner, but as usual, she was late. While everyone else was upstairs or in the kitchen, I was idly looking out the living room window. The street was coated in the dull grey mixture of snow and rain that was so typical of a Toronto December. Only the colourful strings of lights hanging from the eaves and porch railings of our neighbours' houses did anything to dispel the gloom. I watched Bella arrive at last with a bouquet of red flowers in her arms. "Sorry about the colour. It was the only thing I could get at the florist this time of year. I'm so tired of red and green."

"Not me," I countered. "I like Christmas colours—especially the lights. I wish we had some on our house."

"I would never hang up Christmas decorations," Bella stated.

"Why not? Some Jews do. We're certainly not religious."

"It has nothing to do with religion," Bella cut in. "It's a matter of loyalty."

At that moment, Mother joined us in the living room. "What are you two nattering about?" she said.

I took my stand. "Whether or not Jews should hang up Christmas lights. I say there's nothing wrong with it. Christmas is just a holiday—like Thanksgiving. But Aunt Bella disagrees."

Mother pressed her lips together. "Well, you know—we do have our own lights, Suzy. Today is, after all, the eighth day of Chanukah. I know we don't make a habit of it, but we could light the menorah for a change." She sighed. "Every year we bring it up from the basement and then we forget to light it."

"So, why don't you go get it and we can light it already?" said Bella.

"Well—I suppose we could," Mother said haltingly. "All right. Let's do it." The tall brass menorah, shaped like a tree with branches stretching upward, stood on the teacart in the corner of the dining room. Mother pulled a package of slender multi-coloured candles out of a drawer and put a different colour in each of the menorah's branches. Just as she was about to call my father and sisters to join us for the lighting, Bella interrupted. "One minute," she said. "When we were children, our grandfather put the menorah in the front window so people could see it when they went by. He said it was an ancient tradition."

I'd never heard that before. "Why don't we do it, too?" I asked. Without waiting for an answer, I scooped up the candle-laden menorah and carried it over to the round mahogany table in front of the living room window. After the others were called in, my father was given the honour of lighting the candles. We gathered around him as he lit the centre candle first and then used it to light all the rest. My jaw dropped when I saw that Father knew how to recite the prayer so easily, chanting it in the same minor-key tune that I vaguely remembered from Hebrew school. After the benediction, we all pulled up chairs around the menorah and watched as the rainbow of colours blazed in front of the window. Bella turned to me and said, "So there, you have your lights. Aren't they prettier than red and green?"

I felt my shoulders tighten. Since when did Bella care about Jewish things? Did it have something to do with those group therapy sessions she was going to? Were they changing her view of the world, making Jewish things suddenly seem more important? I watched as the thin candles melted rapidly, their colours blending into streams of multihued wax. Yes, they had a certain quiet beauty. But no matter how pretty they were, I still wasn't convinced. These short-lived candles couldn't compete with the dazzling array of lights outside. How could anyone pretend otherwise?

Ever since I found out about Uncle Charles' suicide, I'd become obsessed with looking for the truth. I needed some frank answers from my parents, rather than the dodging and evasiveness I received in the past. One evening in late December, while we were reading the newspaper in the den after dinner, I just came straight out and asked them about it. My mother shot a glance at my father, her eyebrows raised. Father shook his head slowly. "What's the use in hiding it?" he said. "She'll find out eventually." He took a deep breath before starting to speak. "As you know, the police were the ones who found Charles. At the bluffs. He was in his car.

Apparently he died of asphyxiation. In fact, we now know," he sighed, "that he had planned it out meticulously."

"I—don't understand," I said, my voice catching.

Father turned his head away. "He attached a piece of garden hose to the tailpipe of his car. Then fed it through to the interior. Once he turned on the engine, the gas did its work."

I gasped and put my hands over my mouth. Mother reached over and placed her hand on my arm. "You should know," she said gently, "that as far as we can tell, he died peacefully. There was evidence from the post mortem that he'd taken a sleeping pill not long before starting the car. And, if it's any consolation," she continued, "he likely died with strains of music in his ears. Music was found in the car's tape deck—Beethoven's 'Piano Concerto'—one of his favourite pieces." When I heard those words, my thoughts flashed back to the record album I'd seen on top of Bella's stereo the day she disappeared. I now understood why her house had been so spotless and festive that day. Despite the fact that Charles was gone, she was celebrating their wedding anniversary.

Father cleared his throat. "More than anything," he said quietly, "I pity Bella. She had no idea that Charles was suicidal. He kept it from her completely. She didn't even know he was depressed. She blamed herself for not detecting it." No wonder Bella had said that Charles had hidden something from her, I thought. He hid his pain. He hid it from us all.

One detail still puzzled me, though. "Why the bluffs?" I asked, searching my parents' faces. "Charles always loved the water," Mother said. "He particularly enjoyed going to the bluffs and observing the water from the heights. He used to take Bella there when they were first courting." So that explained what he meant in the note when he wrote that he had "always loved this spot by the water." The letter I'd found in Bella's drawer was his suicide note.

Although I now had all the basic information, I still wasn't satisfied. These were just the bare facts, the outer shell. The underlying truth was floating around somewhere, missing. I leaned forward, straining to make sense of it. "But *why?*" I asked, "Why did Uncle Charles do it?" My parents looked away in opposite directions. Father chewed on his lip while Mother blinked rapidly.

"That's the part we don't understand," Father said finally, shaking his head again. I knew he was speaking the truth—I could see it in his furrowed cheeks, the hollows of his eyes. My mother reached over and put her arms around me. I curled my head into her chest and listened to her heart pulsing fitfully against my cheek. I wasn't sure if any of us would ever find the answers to our questions. But I knew that we couldn't stop trying. Even if we would regret it in the end. We had to know. We had to find out *why.*

38

Artur Mandelkorn
Kibbutz Tivon, Israel
March 1967

The moment I heard the name Charles Mandelkorn, I knew that I couldn't let the tourist board his bus without getting his name and address. The bus driver was already shouting for him to hurry up, so I dug through my pockets and pulled out a scrap of paper. He hastily scribbled down his name—Louis Nevsky—and a Toronto address. Wishing me luck, he scrambled onto his bus.

I assumed it would not take much effort to trace the whereabouts of Charles Mandelkorn. I began by calling the long distance operator in Toronto and asking for a phone number for Mandelkorn, Charles or Mandelkorn, C. But there was no such listing. I then asked for the phone numbers of anyone with the last name Mandelkorn, figuring that perhaps Charles might be listed under his wife's name. I got contact information for two Mandelkorns to call, but in the end neither of them had any connection to my family.

I next decided to write a letter to Louis Nevsky, asking him to please forward me the name and address of the firm where he and Charles once worked. Since Charles had switched firms, there might be some forwarding information there. Mr. Nevsky responded promptly, enclosing details about the company.

I wrote a letter to the firm explaining that I was trying to trace the whereabouts of their former employee Charles Mandelkorn. I tried to impress on them how important it was for me to find him; I believed, I told them, that this man might be my brother whom I thought had perished in Europe. If this was indeed my brother, I added, he was the only living relative I had, the only one to have survived the war. I received a response—if you can call it that—fairly quickly. All they sent was a form letter notifying me that all information about employees, both past and present, was strictly confidential.

I'd clearly hit a brick wall. Was this how people behaved in Canada? Even the most officious Israeli bureaucrat had more compassion than that. Nevertheless, I was not going to give up so easily. I called the firm directly, hoping that I might find a sympathetic employee who was willing to bend the rules. But I had no such luck—each person I talked to acted as if I was requesting top-level state secrets. I was simply unable to persuade anyone to perform this small act of human kindness.

Almost three months had passed since I'd met Louis Nevsky, and I'd made no progress at all in finding my brother, Karl. At this point, I was almost ready to jump on a plane and head to Toronto myself. I entertained thoughts of storming into the firm and demanding an audience with the company president. But then I had an idea that was far more practical—I would ask Mrs. Kartash to help. She had once known all the important people at agencies like the Joint Distribution Committee and the Immigrant Aid Society. Maybe she could still pull some strings.

I never did get the chance to call Mrs. Kartash that summer to ask for help in locating Charles Mandelkorn. In June 1967, we suddenly found ourselves at war once more, surrounded by Arab armies on all sides. Fear was palpable in every corner of the country. No one wanted to say out loud the thoughts that were on everyone's minds. Would the State of Israel be destroyed? Would the Jews once again be slaughtered, the remnants of our people scattered through the world like dust? Yet along with the fear was a fierce determination to overcome that fear. If the Israeli army could succeed in 1948, they could do it again—despite the fact that their odds of survival seemed tinier than a grain of sand.

But within six days, Israel's victory was so swift and complete that it was likened to David defeating Goliath. Almost overnight, the handsome faces of Israeli generals were spread across the covers of international magazines. For a brief moment in history, Jews were respected for being victors rather than pitied as victims. The word "miracle" was tossed around like confetti at a wedding. Some Christian groups even declared Israel's victory to be a sign of the Second Coming.

Although I would like to say that I played a vital role in the war, my own part was negligible. I did, however, experience something that I would never forget. While I was waiting to be called up as a reservist, I volunteered to replace soldiers in a local unit who had been sent into battle. I was stationed close to my kibbutz to do night patrol. As Israeli warplanes soared overhead in sharp alignment, I saw a peculiar orange-blue light hovering high above them in the night sky. I radioed the security station to report my finding, only to be told that they were fully apprised of it. I never found out what the light actually was or whether it was even significant. Perhaps it was merely a plane that was flying off course. But to this day, I like to think that it was some divine light guiding our boys in their mission to save the nation from annihilation.

With all the upheaval and euphoria following the successful conclusion of the war, I didn't contact Mrs. Kartash until many months later. Somehow, my personal struggles seemed insignificant in relation to the historic changes that were taking place in Israel. How could I worry about my individual concerns, when Jerusalem was finally reunited and Jews could at last worship at the remains of their ancient Temple? It was a dizzying time and I was caught up in the frenzy as much as anyone.

When I did finally telephone Mrs. Kartash in London and told her about the possibility of Karl's survival, she was silent at first. "You should know, Artur, that most of these cases prove to be dead ends," she said, her voice stretched thin. She told me about several former clients who had thought that they'd found a missing relative, only to discover that it was a false lead. "The disappointment can prove to be a major setback. You've succeeded in building a new life for yourself, far from the pain of Europe. Are you sure you want to take the chance of reawakening all the old grief?"

Though I could feel my pulse throbbing inside my ears, I insisted that I was psychologically prepared for any disappointment that might come my way. After all, I had long given up hope that anyone in my family had survived. I had assumed that Karl was dead, even though there had never been any real proof of it other than an unconfirmed report that he died of typhus in 1945. No news had surfaced about him since, so why would I expect to find him alive? All the same, I had to follow this lead—just *in case* there was even the slightest possibility that this Charles Mandelkorn in Toronto would turn out to be Karl.

In the end, I talked Mrs. Kartash into helping me. But she only agreed on one condition—that I would not ask her to reveal her sources. That was no problem for me, as I had little interest in knowing how she obtained her information. Nevertheless, I could sense from her strained tone that the entire venture was putting her on edge. I wondered if she had gotten too old for this kind of task. Or had those years of living under Communist rule caused her to lose her nerve? The most I could hope for was that she would be more effective than I had been in tracking down Charles Mandelkorn, the man who, despite my declarations of doubt, I secretly believed was my brother, Karl.

Months went by without Mrs. Kartash turning up anything concrete. After more than a year of searching, however, she finally called me with some promising news. As we had agreed, she couldn't tell me how she'd managed to get the information, but she had uncovered one very significant fact. The reason that we'd both had so much difficulty trying to trace this man was that, when he came to Canada, he changed his last name from Mandelkorn to Mond. Mrs. Kartash also discovered that, for some unknown reason, he went back to using the name Mandelkorn in the early 1960s. She suspected that it might have had something to do with the fact that he began to work for a Jewish firm. Perhaps he felt as though he could finally use his real name without fear of prejudice. However, she continued, he never bothered to legally change his name back to Mandelkorn. He continued to be Charles Mond on all formal documents, bank statements, and, of course, telephone listings.

Mrs. Kartash saved her most crucial disclosure for last. Her contact in America had unearthed a document showing that Charles Mandelkorn of Toronto was from Szegda, Hungary. That was the one piece of information, she admitted, that finally convinced her that Charles Mandelkorn and my brother were one and the same.

When I first heard the news, I was barely able to contain my joy—my head was spinning and my feet were ready to dance a jig. Karl—my only brother—*alive*. A torrent of questions flooded my brain: What did he look like as a grown man? Was he married? Were there children? Had he achieved success in his career?

But soon some worries began to coil themselves around me like a snake. How had Karl managed to survive? Did he know that our parents and sisters were dead? Did he try to search for me after the war? And for me, the hardest question of all: Would he be happy to see me after all these years?

Mrs. Kartash didn't have any more details about his private life, although she expected to hear more in the coming weeks. In the interim, I was filled with uncertainty about how to approach him. I couldn't just pick up the telephone and call him. He might collapse from shock or think it was a cruel prank. No—a letter would be a better means of communication. But how could I prove to him that I was really his brother and not an imposter? Then it dawned on me—I still had the toy hurdy-gurdy. It had belonged to Karl before he had given it to Manya. That was it. I would send it to him as proof of my identity.

I started digging through all the old things I kept in storage, things I hadn't looked at in years. I found a bundle of letters that I'd written to Fanny, held together by a velvet hair ribbon she used to wear. There were photographs of Menachem and Uri as babies and some mementos from our years in England, including an English bobby's cap that I'd once worn on Purim. And then I found it—the toy hurdy-gurdy, wedged inside a shoebox like a cardboard coffin. It was much smaller than I remembered, and more fragile. I was afraid to even turn the handle in case it crumbled. I carefully lifted it out of the box and cradled it in my hands. Seeing the little organ again was not as bad as I'd feared. I thought it would distress me, but it had little effect on me now. In fact, I knew that I could bear to part with it. It was only a toy, after all. Holding onto it would not bring back my sister, or my family, or my old life. No, let it be put to better use. Release it and let it be returned to its original owner. Maybe Karl would benefit from seeing it again. It would let him know that something from his childhood remained.

39

Suzy Kohn
Toronto, Ontario
January 1970

Bella burst into our house, her cheeks flushed and damp, carrying
a bulky package bound with what looked like two worn bootlaces
knotted in the centre. She didn't seem to notice that we were in
the middle of dinner and plunked the parcel down on the table,
right beside the plates of cutlet and cabbage. Before we could say
anything, words started tumbling out of her mouth in short breathless phrases. "The strangest thing just happened! Something woke
me up from my nap—a noise from downstairs—and I ran down
to see what caused it. I opened the front door, and there it was
on my doorstep—this huge package—not for me—for Charles."
She paused and swallowed, patting her chest rapidly. "And that's
not all," she exclaimed. "You see right here? It's addressed to *Karl*
Mandelkorn. Not Charles. Who could possibly have known that his
name used to be Karl?"

"Doesn't it say on the package who sent it?" Mother asked.

"That's the point!" Bella said. "There *is* no return address. But
the handwriting! It's the same as Charles'—"

Uh oh, I muttered to myself, sharing a tense smile with my

sister Julia. I'd thought that Bella was getting back to normal. Did she somehow imagine that this package was sent by her husband? Express from the grave? Bella stood up and began walking around the dinner table, poking the unopened package at each of us in turn. "Look, look at the writing! It's the same signature, written in the same hand!"

"But, Aunt Bella," my youngest sister Jan asked with a smirk. "Why would Uncle Charles have addressed the package to himself?" Bella rolled her eyes at Jan, revealing that she was in full control of her faculties. In fact, Bella immediately went on to ignore the query, likely blaming it on what she called "the inborn nosiness of children."

My mother led Bella to the sofa, for she was panting as if she had run a mile. Meanwhile the package was left on the dining room table along with our plates of half-eaten food. Julia and Jan were already huddled in the kitchen, discreetly shaving the sides off an orange cake with their dinner knives, then sliding them into their mouths. Father paced—or rather stomped, stopped, and heaved at regular intervals—annoyed at having his meal disturbed, his wife distracted, and his latest dinner-table story interrupted. I stayed behind in the dining room to take a closer look at the package, wondering why Bella hadn't bothered to open it. Picking it up, I was surprised by how light it was for its size. I then carried it over to Bella on the sofa. She gurgled something that sounded like, "You open it, Suzy," but Mother's sudden stiff expression cautioned me not to.

Mother snatched the package from my hands and dropped it into Bella's lap like a winning basket shot. "No, Bella," she said. "You should be the one to open it." As if summoned by Mother's firm tone, Bella immediately began tearing open the parcel with an uncanny vigour. Ripping through several layers of crumpled newspapers, she finally lifted the long-awaited contents out of the package. We were all puzzled by what we saw, for none of us knew exactly what it was. Until Bella cried out, "Why, it's a hurdy-gurdy. You know. What organ-grinders play."

And that's precisely what it was—a small hurdy-gurdy or bellow organ, a toy one, really—with a half-broken crank, chipped rims, and tattered red-and-gold bellows. We each took turns cranking the handle, but it didn't make a sound. It was entirely mute.

Bella dug deeper into the package and found a note tucked into a corner. She carefully unfolded it and read its contents aloud.

My dear Karl,

It has been many years since we have seen each other, my dearest brother, and I hope that I have found you at last. I am sending you this little organ because it is yours. Do you remember when Papa brought it back for you from Czernowitz as a present for starting school? I have kept it all these years—or maybe I should say it has kept me. But I shall explain all of this to you when we meet. I hope the organ will also be proof to you that it is really me who is writing to you, and not some tricky player looking for a free handout, as they say.

How can I begin telling you all that there is to say? Likewise, there is so much about you I want to know. I will be waiting every day to hear from you.

Faithfully yours,

Artur (Arthur Mandelkorn)

Kibbutz Tivon, Israel

I held my breath, waiting for Bella's reaction. A brother of Charles. Alive. What must she be feeling? Was she happy to hear from this brother-in-law whom she never knew existed? Or would it bring back all the pain of losing Charles and make her feel even more alone? I was so afraid that she wasn't strong enough yet to deal with this new situation. How could she tell this perfect stranger that his brother had survived the war, but had so recently died? That he had missed finding him by only eighteen months?

All of this passed through my mind as Mother and I exchanged raised eyebrows of wonder and doubt. Why was Bella so silent? She just sat and stared, grasping the letter, and mumbling to herself in what sounded half like Hungarian and half like Yiddish. Although she and my father had been children when they escaped from Europe before the war, Bella still reverted to her native tongue whenever she was under strain. All of a sudden, she leapt to her feet and declared, "I think I'll wear my red tweed when he comes. Red always suited my complexion. Do you think a necklace would do?"

That evening Bella went home and composed a letter to Arthur Mandelkorn. By early the next morning, it was on its way to him, special delivery. None of us actually saw the letter, for Bella had recently become secretive about her newly discovered relation. The letter was followed by frequent telephone conversations between the two of them over the next few months. Before long, Bella broke the news: Arthur was planning a visit to Toronto that coming spring.

40

Suzy Kohn
Toronto, Ontario
April 1970

For days before Arthur arrived, Bella began to prepare my sisters and me for his visit by insisting that we call him *Uncle* Arthur. Father wasn't thrilled. I overheard a snippet of his conversation with Mother in the kitchen as I paused above them in the upstairs hallway. "My sister has always been childish, but this takes the cake! She's living in a dream world, that woman. She's acting as if this Arthur of hers were Charles' ghost, magically returned from the grave. We have to disillusion her."

"Maybe she's happier this way," Mother responded smoothly.

Father was speechless for a few moments and then I heard his chair scrape the floor as he stood up to go. Before leaving the room he paused and said, "Anyway, if he *is* a ghost, why has he got such big feet?" My mother's sudden laugh reverberated from below. I understood the joke. Bella had told Mother that Arthur wears a size fourteen shoe, a fact he revealed during one of their recent phone conversations.

The day that Arthur Mandelkorn was scheduled to arrive was cold but brilliantly sunny. Mother insisted on having him stay at our house so he could meet the entire family. While we were waiting for him, I was in my room trying to finish an essay on Milton's *Paradise Lost* for my course in Late Renaissance Literature. But I was finding it hard to concentrate on writing, knowing that our mystery guest would be arriving soon. I had various ideas about what I expected Arthur to look like. Sometimes I imagined him to be short and round with painfully large feet and hands, like a sad penguin that can't find its balance. More often I saw him as a taller version of Uncle Charles himself, fastidiously dressed and zealously European. I was also curious to know more about the toy hurdy-gurdy that Arthur had sent in the mail. How had he managed to hold onto it during the war? And why, of all things, did he choose to save that odd little plaything?

My parents were mainly concerned about what exactly Bella had told her newfound brother-in-law about how Charles had died. Had she told him the truth about his brother's suicide? Mother had tried to ask Bella whether "the situation," as she called it, had been fully explained. But Bella only shook her head and replied, "I don't see how I could tell him everything when he already knows." Whatever Bella meant by that, Mother was not reassured. I wasn't worried, though. My aunt seemed more and more like her old self again. Granted, the change in her had been gradual. Like snow melting on a mild winter day. Yet the process had started. Drip by drip.

Arthur finally arrived at our house and I was shocked at first by his appearance, which was different from anything I'd imagined. He was tall indeed—so tall that he had to bend his neck to avoid hitting his head on our stooped archway. His raincoat and hat were creased and worn, and looked as if they had come out of a bus station locker. His eyes were what took me most by surprise, for they nearly jumped out at me with playful indignation. They were light green and yellow eyes, and they showed no hint of sadness or suffering.

He entered the hallway to meet the family, though Bella was yet to arrive. His face was streaked with red from the cold and under his coat he wore a heavy looped sweater of orange and gold. Mother and Father introduced themselves and welcomed him to our home, but I preferred to stand to one side in order to get a better look at him. I had never heard of someone turning up out of nowhere before—except in kids' books or tabloid articles. To me it seemed as if he had somehow gotten lost in the war and had never emerged until now, almost like an orphan who had grown old only on the outside.

My parents showed Arthur into the living room, offering him a seat and some cold refreshments. As they chatted, Arthur nodded his head a great deal when responding to questions with mostly one-word answers and short lingering phrases. His was the kind of English I knew so well—deep, sonorous, rounded syllables—a European tongue caressing the flatlands of our plain Canadian speech. When Bella finally arrived, she paused briefly in the doorway of the living room before entering. She was smiling, really smiling— without that recent habit of stretching her lips into a horizontal line. With her hair swept off her forehead, Bella's pale blue eyes caught the light, causing flickers of turquoise to peek through her lashes. It was at that moment that I caught a brief glimpse of the rare beauty that Bella was known to have possessed in her youth.

Arthur jumped up from his chair, rushed across the room and grabbed hold of Bella's hands without letting go. I don't remember exactly what they said to one another, perhaps because they hardly finished the phrases they'd begun. I was mainly struck by how much they seemed to know about each other. "So this is the house near the ravine," Arthur said. "You were right. There are more trees here than I gave you credit for."

Bella flushed and threw back the taunt, "What do you take me for, a teller of tall tales?" They both laughed giddily, although I wasn't sure why it was funny. What was even more surprising was seeing a man behave with such chivalry. He insisted on giving Bella his seat and searched around for extra cushions to make sure that she was comfortable. Ordinarily I would have viewed such gentlemanly behaviour as passé, even insulting, to a modern-day woman. But in Arthur, I had to admit, it seemed quaint, almost charming.

Mother had tea and pastry waiting in the dining room, so we all took seats at the table, except for my sisters who dashed back upstairs to finish their homework. From the clinking of cups and the buzz of light conversation, it seemed that everyone was relieved to be distracted by the food and drink. I soon noticed however that Arthur began shifting about in his seat as if he couldn't find a comfortable spot on it. After some last sips of tea, he put down his cup and began a short speech that went straight to the point. "I just want to say," he said, looking around the table, "that I am grateful for your kind and generous invitation. As you may know, I've been searching for my brother, Karl—er, Charles—for a very long time. But the moment I heard Bella's voice on the telephone just a few months ago, I realized that my brother was dead. Don't ask me how I knew—I just did."

After pausing for a moment to look at Bella, he continued. "It was not as bad as you might think. Hearing that Charles had survived the war and married—that he'd *lived*—this gave me joy, great joy. Of course, I know about Charles' pain—Bella told me all about that. He was not able to speak about the war, about his family. I know. I was like that too for a while. I am only sad that he never managed to get over that. Are you aware that we had two sisters?" he asked. "The youngest, Kati, was just a baby when the war broke out. And our sister Manya was two years younger than me."

Manya—she was their *sister*! The news hit me like an electric jolt. For years I'd felt as if I had a twin on the other side of the ocean. But wait, it's not like we were blood relatives. How could Manya be so similar to me?

Arthur took a deep breath and tensed his lips, as if he was trying to think of how to phrase his next statement. "You should know, my situation was entirely different from that of Charles. I was never in a concentration camp. In fact, I have only just learned about what Charles went through at Auschwitz. The files were discovered recently by Mrs. Kartash, my dear friend who helped me track down my brother's whereabouts. While doing so, she unearthed a document showing that Charles was part of a forced labour crew at the camp—one of the *Sonderkommandos* who worked in the crematoria. Most people aren't aware of it, but the SS forced Jews, not Germans or Poles, to perform the most gruesome tasks in the camp. Under threat of death, of course. Can you imagine? My brother was all of fifteen when he was compelled to do the worst job imaginable—to cart the dead bodies from the gas chambers to the crematoria." Arthur paused, his jaw tight. "No one, not a single living person, could lead a normal life after that."

On hearing this, a pain shot through me, burning like iodine on a wound.

Arthur glanced briefly at Bella again and then back at us. "As soon as I learned of this, I called Bella. I knew that it would help her understand why Charles had never shared any of his past with her, why he had kept it locked inside him. And why he eventually—gave up on life." The silence that filled the room was now dense as fog. No one knew what to say, or how to say it. What Charles had suffered was too terrible to imagine. It was beyond thinking, beyond comprehension.

Finally my mother turned to Arthur and gently shifted the subject of conversation away from Charles, asking Arthur how he had spent the war years. Arthur rocked slightly in his chair. His eyes were half-closed and a faint shadow of pain brushed across his pale lips. But when he began to speak, he did so without a shred of affectation or self-pity.

He told us that he and Manya had fled on their own after the Nazis invaded their town. He explained how they were sheltered temporarily, then captured and separated when he was sent to a labour camp. But he never gave up searching for Manya. Even when the war was over and he made his way to Palestine, he continued to look for her, convinced that she was still alive. "All I had left," he said, "was the toy hurdy-gurdy that she had left behind." He stopped and swallowed several times. Finally, in a voice that was choked and hoarse, he managed to say, "I eventually found out that Manya had been killed. You can't imagine what that did to me."

So Manya had never made it through the war. Why did I feel such an ache in my chest? Arthur looked down at his cup, his finger scraping the edge of the gold-rimmed saucer. The rest of us sat motionless, except for Bella, who covered her eyes with one hand. Arthur took another deep breath and continued his story, telling us about his marriage to Fanny and the birth of their sons. But when we heard that Fanny eventually grew sick and died, leaving him alone with the two children, the walls in the room seemed to shudder with the sound of our sighs. In fact the air around us was so charged with Arthur's story that it seemed it could ignite with the tiniest spark. How much suffering could this man bear?

Arthur shifted in his seat and began to rub the back of his neck. After a few minutes, he composed himself and continued to speak in the same slow steady voice. He described how he'd learned that Charles was living in Canada and how fruitless his early attempts to contact him were. And the pain he'd felt when he learned that, by the time he actually found him, his brother was dead. "If such a thing hadn't happened to me, I would say that this whole story was implausible—or a cruel joke. Yet I refuse to feel sorry for myself, or even for Charles." He looked around the table, gauging our reaction, while a meditative smile settled on his lips. "As I said earlier, I am pleased—no, happy—that my brother survived. No one will ever know how he managed to make it through to the end of the war. The files revealed that when the camp was finally liberated, he was suffering from an acute case of typhus. Yet Bella tells me that he never mentioned any of it. He took everything with him to the grave. But, looking at all of you, there is one thing I do know. He had *some* good fortune in his life—because he had a kind and loving family. Even before I arrived here today, I understood that.

"Through all of my telephone conversations with Bella, I've gotten to know you all very well. Don't be embarrassed. She only told me good things, I assure you. I assume you know that Bella and I spoke on the telephone every day. I have limited access to a phone on the kibbutz, but I made sure to be at the designated spot each day to receive her calls. They became the high point of my day. After a few months of these daily exchanges, I finally told Bella that I wanted to come to Toronto for a short visit. My sons, Menachem and Uri, are big boys now—young men, really—so I had no qualms about leaving them. Menachem is already serving in the army and was just accepted into the tank corps. And Uri, never to be outdone, is dreaming of becoming a paratrooper once his turn comes. They are fine boys despite the loss they've endured. Fanny would be proud of them, I'm sure. And the boys encouraged me to come to North America. They know how much it means to me to get to know my brother's family."

He stopped and looked down at his cup again, then drew a quick breath. "But there's another reason for my coming as well." He shot a quick look at Bella and continued. "You see, although I am not religious in any conventional sense, I still feel obligated to fulfill my duty according to Jewish law. I must release Bella from the obligation to marry me." We all stared at Arthur as if he were speaking in a foreign language. Marry him? What could he possibly mean?

Seeing our confusion, Arthur smiled. "Yes," he said, his voice wavering slightly as if he were trying to suppress a nervous laugh. "You heard me correctly. Judaism holds a man responsible for his brother's widow, requiring him to marry her in the event of his brother's death. The only way out of this obligation is to perform the ancient ritual of *halitzah*. It's a fairly simple procedure, though it sounds slightly outlandish these days. It entails removing the shoe from my foot and throwing it on the ground to indicate that I have given Bella the freedom to marry another man. Of course, the ritual would have to be performed in the presence of rabbis, but I am sure that it could be arranged without too much difficulty. What do you think, Bella? Would you like to be released?" There was total silence in the room. Bella looked at Arthur, stared down at her plate, and then looked at Arthur again. Her face was as red as a pomegranate and tears welled in her eyes.

Finally Arthur broke the silence. He jumped off his chair, got down on one knee and whispered gently to her, "If you say no, you will make me a very happy man." As soon as Bella's no left her lips, shouts of "Mazal tov!" burst from ours. The room pulsed with cries of joy and disbelief. Arthur made a toast to Bella, calling her his beloved. Bella called Arthur her prince.

How did this happen? *When* did this happen? It seemed that their courtship was taking place right before our eyes.

Yet in reality it was quite the opposite. It had developed over the past few months, in private, on the telephone. Somehow Arthur and Bella knew they were right for each other even at a distance. It was destined, or *bashert*, as they put it, using a familiar Yiddish phrase. As implausible as it sounded to my ears, they clearly believed that their coming together was all part of a divine plan: designed, arranged, and sealed in a realm that was high above them.

41

Suzy Kohn
Toronto, Ontario
August 1970

Arthur and Bella's wedding was scheduled to take place in Israel at the end of the month. Bella had already flown back to Israel with Arthur to plan the event and to get to know his sons, Menachem and Uri. Naturally, I longed to go to the wedding, but the university semester was starting early this year and my parents didn't want me to miss classes. Not only that, but the cost of plane tickets was steep and I couldn't expect my parents to cover it. Meanwhile, my mother decided that she wouldn't be attending the wedding either because she needed to help my sisters prepare for the coming school year. My father, it seemed, would be the only one available to represent our family.

One afternoon in early August, as I was lounging on our front porch reading a book, Father pulled up a chair beside me. "Zsu-zsu," he started. "I've been thinking. Would you be interested in joining me on this trip to Israel?" It had been such a long time since anyone had called me Zsu-zsu that my shock at hearing it made me almost miss what my father was saying. "I realize," he continued, "that it's the beginning of the semester. You'd have to miss a few classes. But your grades have been stellar—I'm sure that you'll be able to catch up easily. And there's a sale on airfare. I can pay your way without breaking the bank."

"Of course I'll come," I said, banging my book shut. "I can't think of anything more exciting."

As soon as I could, I went downtown to apply for a passport at one of the government offices. It required a long wait in a dimly lit reception room crammed with people dozing, coughing, or pacing in frustration. Seated next to me was a silver-haired woman who turned to me and asked, "How long have you been waiting? I've been here an hour and they've only called up two people."

"Same with me," I replied. "Maybe they're all on coffee break."

She snickered, "It wouldn't surprise me. These government workers have it good. At *our* expense." Lowering her voice, she added, "When I lived in Europe, there weren't any line-ups. The bureaucrats were forced to be efficient." I nodded in agreement, though her words left an odd taste in my mouth. Eyeing me up and down, she changed the subject. "Is this your first passport? You must be going on a big trip."

"Yes—um—I am," I said quietly. "I'm going to the Middle East."

She gave me a sidelong glance and I could tell that she was about to say something more. But at that moment her number was called and I was spared further questions. What a relief. I knew that if I'd said Israel, the word Jew would have been stamped on my forehead. Why bother? It was easier to keep quiet and fit in. Waiting my turn, though, I couldn't help thinking about that little act of evasion. I began to realize that keeping quiet about being Jewish was something I'd gotten quite skilled at. It was a habit I'd acquired a long time ago. I was twelve and my best friend was Gina Monetti, an Italian girl in my seventh-grade class. For some reason, I never told Gina that I was Jewish. She just assumed that I was Christian like most of the other kids at my elementary school. And since my family wasn't overtly Jewish, at least not enough to give me away, I never corrected her mistake.

I loved spending time at Gina's since her place was always hopping. By comparison, my home seemed so restrained, as if a tight rubber band was wound permanently around its middle. Not so at Gina's—every weekend, her mother warmed up a huge pot of homemade tomato sauce in preparation for the horde of aunts, uncles, and cousins who would appear on their doorstep. This was a whole new experience for me—other than my immediate family, including Uncle Charles and Aunt Bella, I had no relatives to speak of. But Gina was not as taken with her relatives as I was, and even her parents sometimes got fed up with the ruckus. One evening, the crowd stayed so late that Gina's father climbed up onto a chair, removed his trousers, and wearing only a vest and boxer shorts, announced that he was going to bed. Insulted, the relatives marched off, cursing under their breath. Yet, that didn't stop them from returning the next week as if the entire incident never happened.

Until Gina's family moved away to another neighbourhood, her place was like my second home. One Christmas eve, her family even took me to midnight mass with them—although I didn't dare tell my parents about it. Even years later, long after I'd lost touch with Gina, I still never told them about that visit to a church. Somehow I knew that my parents would get that disappointed look on their faces: their lips pursed and eyebrows lifted into stiff round question marks. Much more than their raised voices, it was that look that made me want to keep things to myself.

I was pulled back to the present when my number was called; after that, it took only minutes for my passport to be stamped and processed. As I was leaving the office and walking down the corridor, I heard someone call my name. "Is that you, Suzy Kohn?" Spinning around, I saw it was Fin. As he strode toward me, I noticed straight away how much his appearance had changed—his hair was shorter (although his curls still grazed the tips of his ears), his shirt was tucked in, and he wore high-top sneakers rather than his trademark Birkenstocks. I could feel the blood rushing to my cheeks as Fin stood before me, gazing down at me with his sapphire eyes. "You're looking good, Suzy. You must really be getting your act together."

"I suppose so. How are things with you?"

"Everything's freakin' great. I have a manager. And my own band. You've probably heard of it—Yellow Dwarf. Cool name, right? We're playing the El Mocambo next week."

"That's terrific."

"And we're up for some European gigs," Fin continued. "That's why I'm here. I need to renew my passport."

"Well," I said. "I won't hold you up then."

"No, no, wait—I wish we could hang out longer. Listen, I have my own pad now. On Dupont. Just down from Casa Loma." As he said the word "pad," he slid the edge of his fingers up my arm, causing shivers to shoot straight up to my scalp. "So," he said, leaning closer and murmuring into my ear. "Why don't you drop by my place tomorrow afternoon?"

My heart was beating wildly. "Maybe," I said, gulping some air. "But—wait—aren't you living with someone now?"

"Yeah," he said casually. "She's really cool. Works as a script assistant at the CBC."

"But—"

"Don't worry," Fin laughed. "She works during the day. We'll have the place all to ourselves." I could swear that he winked when he said that. But even if he didn't, I got his drift. All he wanted was to seduce me. To rack up another score. To finally conquer the girl who said no.

My stomach started to heave, as if I'd seen something foul that I hadn't seen before. But no, I *had* seen it before. I just hadn't been willing to let go of the Fin that I'd held onto so tightly. The fantasy Fin. The one who never really existed. Except in my mind.

"No, Fin," I said firmly. "I can't come to your place. Not tomorrow—not ever." I felt as though a thick film had been wiped from my eyes, leaving me with perfect vision.

Fin's mouth dropped open as though he was about to protest. But before he could say anything further, I quickly interjected. "Let's just say goodbye like two old friends. With no bad feelings. No words we'll later regret." My voice was steady and clear.

Fin was silent for several seconds. Then pressing his hands together, an ironic smile crept onto his face. "Sure. I'm cool with that."

I looked straight into his eyes, which now seemed less blue than I remembered them. "It was good to see you Fin," I said, this time almost meaning it. Little did he know what a favour he'd just done me.

"Good to see you too, Suzy. Have a good life."

"You, too, Fin. You, too."

While packing my bag for the trip to Israel, I instinctively reached into my pocket for some cigarettes to throw into the suitcase. But that was just a reflex. I had actually quit smoking—I'd given it up the day after I'd seen Fin at the passport office. When I'd woken up that next morning, I'd gathered up all my packs of cigarettes and thrown them in the trash. Just like that. It may have been a minor gesture. But getting rid of my smokes made me feel free, like I was starting my life over in a way that was honest and pure.

My father and I boarded our flight with carry-on bags stuffed with as many guide books as they could hold. But once I was on the plane, I barely looked at any of them. As Father dozed beside me, I was happy to just stare out the window and think about the coming adventure. Before I'd met Arthur, I hadn't given much thought to Israel as a real place. Though as a child I'd been a diligent student at Hebrew school, everything I'd learned about Israel—war, struggle, self-sacrifice—was alien to my life in Canada. Certainly when I looked at myself in the mirror, my image did not cast Israel into the background setting.

Soon sleep overpowered me and I ended up dozing right through the morning meal. I was having a strangely pleasurable dream. I was swimming in a backyard pool and discovered plant life growing at the pool's bottom. The colours of the plants were brilliant, almost luminous, and I desperately wanted to dive down to see them close up. But just as I was about to plumb the depths of the pool, I was jolted awake by a sudden blare of piped-in music that filled the cabin as the airplane began its descent. I recognized the tune immediately—it was the familiar Hebrew folk-song "Haveinu Shalom Aleichem." As the plane hit the runway in Israel, the song swelled to a crescendo from the overhead speakers. Spontaneously, the passengers began clapping to the rhythm of the song and some even sang along. I couldn't believe what I was seeing—grown people clapping and singing as if they were at a child's birthday party. My face grew hot, flaming. I wasn't sure if it was from embarrassment. Or a surge of unexpected joy.

42

Suzy Kohn
Kfar Yonah, Israel
September 1970

After stumbling our way through airport security and finally exiting the terminal, the first things I noticed were the billboards. All in Hebrew, of course. Seeing them for the first time, I thought, How could the familiar letters from my Hebrew-school prayer book be advertising soft drinks and magazines?

At first I didn't recognize the two people waving to us, a man with one arm draped lazily around the shoulders of a woman with large sunglasses stuck casually on top of her loose-flowing hair. They were both wearing baggy white shirts belted at the waist. My father, however, knew them right away. "It's Arthur and Bella!" he exclaimed. I blinked several times and squinted. Really? Was he sure it was them? But as we got closer, I realized that Father was right. It *was* them—looking suntanned and carefree as if they'd just come from an ocean cruise. Although they were both close to forty, at that moment they didn't look much older than teenagers. They welcomed us with kisses on both cheeks (Arthur let Bella go first), and after inquiring about our trip, they asked how it felt to be in Israel for the first time. I didn't know what to say. The newness of it all had my mind turning somersaults. Bella leaned in close to me and whispered in my ear, "Don't worry," she said in her throaty voice. "You'll get used to the hubbub. The main thing is— you're here. It means so much to me."

Arthur and Bella led us toward a clunky taxicab that was waiting for us at the side of the road. The sullen-looking driver was sitting on the curb smoking a cigarette while simultaneously cleaning his fingernails with the edge of a matchbook. When he saw us approaching, he stretched and slowly got up. Then, with the cigarette still dangling from his lips, he grabbed our suitcases, hurled them on top of the cab, and tied them to the roof with a long rope.

Arthur gave him instructions to take us straight to our destination, a place called Kfar Yonah. No sooner had we climbed into our seats than we were off, the cab careening down the road as if we were on a speedway. As the driver zigzagged around obstacles at high speed, I gripped my seat so tightly that my knuckles turned white, worried that our suitcases would fly off the roof of the cab. Arthur and Bella, however, seemed completely unperturbed, chatting about the growth of the country while pointing out sites along the road. They made it seem as though seeing Israel from the back of a speeding cab was all part of some tribal initiation rite.

I eventually loosened my grip as the cab slowed down and pulled into the village of Kfar Yonah. And what a sight it was—its miniature houses and curving roads made it look like something out of a storybook. With a dove serving as the municipal emblem, pictures of the bird were displayed on signs throughout the town. Arthur explained that the founder of the village named the town after his father whose name was Yonah. But since that word also happens to mean dove in Hebrew, the bird was adopted as the symbol of the town.

Arthur and Bella had arranged for us all to stay at the guesthouse where the wedding would be taking place the following evening. The inn itself was a simple frame building, but its setting was magnificent. Situated on a hill, it looked down on masses of orange trees, heavily laden with golden fruit. Facing west, I glimpsed a brilliant strip of turquoise on the horizon—the Mediterranean Sea.

After we settled into our rooms, Father declared that he was ready for a nap. But I was perfectly awake, having already slept so much on the plane. I wandered outside into the yard and saw Arthur standing on a rocky ridge at the edge of the garden, gazing into the valley below. Not wanting to disturb him, I was about to reverse my steps, when he turned and caught sight of me. "Suzy, come quickly," he called out. "There's something you should see."

I hesitated, suddenly shy about being on my own with him. What could I possibly talk about that would be of interest to him? After all he'd seen in life, how could he not see me as a child who'd never experienced much of anything? I was already planning an excuse for making a quick escape, when he waved me closer.

His voice was animated as he pointed to something in the distance. "See that spot of light bouncing off the pine trees? It looks as though it's dancing. That's caused by the sun. It only happens once a day when the sun is at this exact angle. There it goes. It's fading now. Gone." He turned to me. "When I studied architecture, I learned a great deal about light. I still find it fascinating."

"Don't you ever miss being an architect?" I blurted out. I didn't realize that I might be touching a raw nerve until I noticed him rubbing the back of his neck.

"Y—es," he answered slowly. "I suppose I do miss it. But I look at it as a kind of—sacrifice. And what would a sacrifice be if it were not something that's painful to give up?"

"But why do you need to sacrifice?"

"Well," Arthur said. "I came to the conclusion long ago that one can't have everything in life. And some things are more important than others. My boys, for instance. When their mother died, I had to make a choice. To do what pleased me or to do what was best for them. I chose them. That's it. Pretty simple, wouldn't you say?"

"You make it sound so easy."

"Easy?" Arthur gasped and then laughed wryly. "Nothing has been easy for me. In fact, I take everything very hard. I can torture myself with indecision. But once I decide, it's final. I can live with it." I must have looked perplexed because Arthur tilted his head as if to analyze my expression. "Now I can see that I have thoroughly confused you," he said.

"No—not confused," I said, searching for the right words. "I'm just amazed. You seem so—how can I put it?—happy. I don't get how you can be that way. To have overcome all the things that have happened to you, all the people you've lost—your parents, your wife—Manya. But, maybe I shouldn't be saying any of this."

"No, please. Tell me what's on your mind."

"Well, would you be bothered if I asked you something about Manya?" I said. "I mean, is it all right to talk about her?"

"Please. Go ahead." He blinked rapidly, his eyes darting to one side.

"Uncle Charles once told me, when I was younger, that I—reminded him of her. I'm curious. Is there anything to it?"

"I can understand why he'd say that," Arthur mused. "Of course, there's no physical resemblance. It's—something else. A similar temperament, perhaps. She was a quiet girl, with a hint of melancholy. Yet she was generous to a fault. And tough when she needed to be. Most importantly," he added, "she loved to sing."

"Hmm. I also sing."

A smile played on his lips. He drew back a bit and studied me again. "Yes. The way you hold yourself is like her. Actually, I would say it's quite uncanny."

"It's so strange," I said. "Ever since Uncle Charles made that remark, I have felt a kind of—connection to her. I know it's ridiculous. She died long before I was born."

Arthur looked down at his hands. "Even though you didn't know her, I'm glad you think about her. Believe it or not, it brings some measure of comfort to me. Perhaps it will help when I'm feeling low."

"I don't understand. You seem so—normal most of the time. I think it's remarkable."

"I'm gratified to hear that I strike you as normal," he chuckled dryly. "But you shouldn't be amazed by me. I'm not extraordinary in the least. In fact, I consider myself to be a fairly typical example of a Jew—industrious, a bit creative, with a good dose of tenacity thrown in. That's the magic ingredient, you know."

"Tenacity?"

"Oh, yes."

I was silent, unsure of what to make of that word, as if it held some power that I couldn't quite grasp.

Arthur paused, peering down into the valley below. "I once came across a poem that captured it perfectly," he said. "It was written in Yiddish by a poet named H. Leivick. I'll never forget the way he put it. Even if every last Jew were erased from the face of the earth, he wrote, one thing would remain: 'a stiff neck and nothing more.' I was haunted by that image. A stiff neck that is so strong that it outlasts the body. How incredible!"

"But—I always thought that being a 'stiff-necked people' was a curse. Wasn't that what God called the Jews when they made the golden calf? At least, that's what they taught us in Hebrew school."

"Ah," said Arthur. "I can see that you were an attentive pupil. But that is what is so startling about Leivick's poem. He saw that our weakness can also be our strength. Our stubbornness can be put to bad use, but it can also be used for good. I sometimes wonder if that's what being 'chosen' means—being loyal to a goal that all others have abandoned. Just think about it. To cling to a nation that is half-dead takes stubborn determination, beyond all sense and reason. How else can you explain Jewish survival after thousands of years of dispersion?"

He grew quiet, almost pensive. "Soon after the war ended, I

often thought—why not give up and blend in? Be like everybody else. But I eventually looked around and realized that there is no such thing as 'everybody else.' It's a delusion. Everyone belongs to a group, a tribe, a family. I can live a relatively 'normal' life, as you call it, because I know where I belong. I don't just live among people but *with* people. We share a common goal. Even when I'm plagued with morbid thoughts and nightmares—which, I assure you, happens often enough—people soon lift me out of it. It's not anything they say that does it. It's just being together—working, striving, building something out of nothing. I sometimes think that if I didn't live on a kibbutz, I would have to invent one."

Grinning playfully, he added, "Mind you, finding someone to love doesn't hurt. As long as they love you back, that is. But you needn't concern yourself with such things now. That's something you will surely have plenty of time to worry about." He turned and gazed distractedly toward the guesthouse, then sighed in an exaggerated sort of way, "Now where has your aunt Bella disappeared to? I'd better go remind her that she's getting married tomorrow."

Menachem and Uri arrived just as the sun was about to set, having caught the last bus of the day to Kfar Yonah. I was surprised to see how grownup they were. For some reason, I had an image of them in my mind as little boys. But they were nothing of the sort. At twenty, Menachem was as tall and lanky as his father. But unlike Arthur, he had shiny black hair and eyes to match. His face had a slightly mournful look, though his deep-set eyes transformed into glistening half-moons when he laughed. Uri, two and a half years younger, was almost as tall as his brother. He was the spitting image of his father—except for his red hair, which was as fiery as hot ginger. It didn't take me long to realize why everyone called him "Gingie."

At dinner that night, Arthur thanked us all for coming and said how appreciative he was that my father and I had come all the way from Canada. His voice then turned grave. "I should let you know that Menachem almost didn't make it here tonight. There was an emergency call-up this morning after a terrorist planted a bomb near the entrance to Menachem's army base. I'm proud to say that my son refused to leave his group of soldiers until they had swept the entire area for explosives and made sure everyone was out of danger."

Blushing, Menachem shrugged his shoulders. "It wasn't anything so dangerous," he said. "My commander gave me permission to leave, knowing I had my father's wedding to attend. But I couldn't just abandon my comrades. They trust me and I couldn't let them down. Luckily, no one was injured. We finished the operation in no time. It was no big deal. So, as you can see, here I am."

I was struck by Menachem's remark about trust. I certainly hadn't heard that word taken seriously by my contemporaries lately. As I looked at him, he caught my eye and smiled shyly. I felt a tingle of embarrassment creep up my neck and spread behind my ears. Before my relationship with Fin, I'm not sure if I would have been drawn to someone like Menachem. But I'd changed so much since then.

After dinner, Arthur approached me and asked if I would mind helping his boys set up chairs for the wedding the next day. The ceremony was to take place on the patio behind the guesthouse, where an amethyst-coloured rock garden sloped down toward the orange groves below. Eager to help, I went over to where Menachem and Uri had already started carrying in chairs from the storage shed, lining them up in rows for the guests who were expected to arrive in the morning. The boys soon began competing with each other over who could carry more chairs at one time. They stacked their piles so high that I couldn't make out which of them was behind his individual tower. Suddenly, one of the piles began to teeter and almost came falling to the ground. It was Uri's. "Oy vey, oy vey!" he cried, swivelling his body around to save the chairs from crashing to the ground at the last minute. Uri obviously dramatized the event to make it even funnier, and we all laughed at his antics.

"That was so funny!" I exclaimed. "Especially the way you imitated an old grandfather, with your 'Oy veys.' It was hilarious!"

Uri looked confused. "A grandfather? What grandfather? I don't get it."

"I didn't mean that you *are* a grandfather," I quickly explained. "I just meant, you know, that *oy vey* is something an old Jewish *bubby* or *zaidy* would say. I've never heard young people like us say it."

"No? Here, we say it all the time. I never think about it."

I swallowed several times. I wouldn't have been caught dead using an expression like that, especially among my friends. But I hadn't meant any offense. I just thought he was using the expression as a joke.

"Listen—you shouldn't feel bad," said Menachem softly. "You're from *galut*. That's what Jews from there are used to. You can't help it. In Israel, we don't worry about what the gentiles think. In fact," he smiled, "you should try saying *oy vey* sometime. It isn't so bad."

"Yes, try saying it now," Uri piped in. "It will feel good, I bet you."

"Of course I can *say* the words," I answered. "But I can't promise I'll be comfortable doing it."

"We'll teach you!" Uri cried. "Come on. Let's all of us run down that hill and scream it fifty times. We'll do it with you. Let's go!" And so we began to run and as we picked up speed, we began to chant, "OY VEY! OY VEY!" over and over again. And as we ran, we screamed it louder, until my voice was hoarse, my head was whirling, and my heart was pounding from laughter and exhilaration.

Guests began to arrive for the wedding at seven the next morning. Most of them were carrying trays of food wrapped in long white dishcloths. It seemed that almost every guest had cooked or baked something for the wedding meal. Ruti and Gidon were the first to arrive. They were exactly the way I pictured them. Ruti—large and motherly, commanding the room like a general; Gidon—quiet but obstinate, relying on short quips and ironic shrugs to make his presence known. Following them came Arthur's friend Dudu, who arrived with his camera and tripod. I was assigned the task of showing each new arrival to the kitchen and finding a place for them to put their heaping trays. Menachem and Uri were busy helping their father greet the guests, while Bella was upstairs dressing for the occasion.

The excitement increased when Ferko arrived with Tsipora. Arthur rushed over to embrace him and soon there were tears streaming down both men's cheeks. I couldn't believe that this was the man who was responsible for saving Arthur's life. He didn't look in the least brave or heroic. In fact, he had a kind of childlike quality that was almost impish. With his pocked nose and large belly, he made me think of the seven dwarves from the story of Snow White.

Since neither Ferko nor Tsipora knew much English—and my spoken Hebrew wasn't much better—I could only exchange a few words with them. Finally, Menachem came to my rescue and acted as a translator. I asked him to tell Ferko and Tsipora that I was Bella's niece and was delighted to meet them. Tsipora clasped her hands to her bosom and rattled off something in Hebrew that sounded to me like one continuous phrase. Menachem hesitated at first, but then translated what she'd said. "Tsipora says that you must promise to come back to Israel very soon—that you are a true daughter of Abraham, Isaac, and Jacob." He paused, cleared his throat, then sped up as if determined to get through the rest as quickly as possible. "She wishes that God may send you a bridegroom, so that together you'll be privileged to build a lasting home in Israel, speedily and in our days. Amen."

By the time he finished, Menachem's face was so flushed that shiny beads of sweat were rolling down his forehead. Luckily, before he could see my own face turning red, he rushed off, mumbling something about being needed outside. Now that I was left alone with Ferko and Tsipora, I babbled a response. "That is— very kind of you," I stammered. "I appreciate your good wishes. But, you know, I've only just turned nineteen. I'm certainly not ready to settle down. I'm not even thinking about marriage." I knew that Tsipora didn't understand a word I said, yet she nodded her head meaningfully. And all the while she flashed a gold-toothed smile at me that seemed to say, all in good time, my dear, all in good time.

The wedding canopy had been set up on the patio in the shade of an ancient olive tree whose thick, gnarled trunk looked as though it had witnessed thousands of such ceremonies. Along the periphery of the garden were towering tropical ferns and bushes covered with magenta-hued blossoms. A violin player stood off to one side, tuning his instrument. Several guests arrived just before the ceremony was about to begin. One of them was an elegantly attired woman with short-cropped grey hair and tiny spectacles hanging from a gold chain around her neck. She looked around, not knowing where to sit, so I offered her an empty chair beside me. "Merci beaucoup," she said with an appreciative smile.

"Excuse me," I asked. "Would you, by any chance, be Mrs. Kartash?"

"Indeed I am," she replied. "Have we met before?"

I introduced myself and we chatted for several minutes. She then opened her handbag and took out a yellowed photo of a boy, asking me if I recognized him. I knew him immediately—it was Arthur. He appeared to be about sixteen or seventeen in the picture and bore an expression of deep sadness on his face. I was taken aback by the realization that when the war ended, he hadn't been much younger than I was now. How different my life had been from his—and from that entire generation of Jews. And all because of when and where I was born.

Before I could think about it any further, the violinist launched into a vigorous medley of Hebrew tunes, signalling that the ceremony was about to begin. A hush fell over the crowd and everyone craned their necks to watch the wedding procession come into the hall. Menachem and Uri entered first, dressed identically in crisp chinos and light blue shirts. Dudu took their pictures as they sauntered casually down the aisle, smiling to everyone and gesturing giddily to some of their friends. Next came Arthur, walking with a long boyish stride, making me briefly wonder how he could be the father of those two young men. Dressed in an ivory linen suit that was mellow as a bowl of cream, Arthur was the model of a love-struck groom hurrying to greet his bride. For a split second, I believe I was half in love with him myself.

At last, it was Bella's turn. The violinist changed to a more solemn tune and those who weren't already standing rose to their feet. Bella's entrance was like a burst of springtime. Her hair, pulled high on her head, tumbled down her neck and forehead in loose coils, and was covered by the sheerest of veils. She was wearing a lilac-coloured gown, the bodice trimmed with tiny rosebuds composed of seed pearls and shimmering stones. I recognized the embroidery immediately—it was unmistakably the work of Bella's own hand. At her side was my father who, as her older brother, had been given the honour of escorting her to the *chupah*.

Arthur and Bella stood under the wedding canopy, flanked by Menachem and Uri on one side and my father on the other. As is the custom, the rabbi in charge of the proceedings began the ceremony by filling a silver beaker with sacramental wine. He first handed the cup to Arthur, who took a small sip to fulfill the initial part of the wedding ritual. But just as Arthur was about to pass the cup to Bella so that she could also partake of the wine, the rabbi called for a pause in the ceremony. A hasty muffled discussion ensued between the rabbi and the bride and groom.

What could be wrong? I thought. Why was the rabbi stopping the ceremony?

The rabbi stepped forward to make an announcement. He explained that since Bella had neglected to appoint a young lady to be her *shomeret*, or her maid of honour, there was no one to lift her veil so that she could drink from the ritual cup of wine. He went on to say that after consulting with the bride, it was decided that her niece Suzy Kohn would be the appropriate person to fulfil this honour. I jumped to my feet, my heart thumping like a kettledrum. Just as I was about to leave my spot, Mrs. Kartash caught my hand and pressed it hard, as if giving me her consent.

I hastily squeezed my way through the seats and moved toward the wedding canopy. Going beneath it, I felt like Cinderella arriving at the ball. The wine, the ring, the sacred oaths, the *ketubah*—it was like entering an enchanted world. The rabbi then delivered a short speech about the joyousness of the occasion. He spoke personally about Arthur and Bella, alluding to some of the fateful events that led to their meeting. By request of the bride and groom, he said, he would name some of their loved ones who were no longer alive. He explained that just as the groom breaks the glass beneath his foot in order to remember the destruction of the Holy Temple in Jerusalem, so too is it appropriate to recall our sadness even in our moments of greatest joy. He began to recite the list of names, beginning with Arthur's and Bella's respective parents and ended with Arthur's beloved sister Manya. I glanced at Arthur—a shadow of that expression in the photograph flickered across his face, but was quickly suppressed.

After the rabbi finished the recitation of names, he turned to the bride and groom and blessed them with the following words: "You should have the privilege of building a lasting home in Israel, speedily and in our days, Amen." Did I hear him correctly? Those were the very same words that Tsipora had said to me that morning. And now I was hearing them again, this time to bless Arthur and Bella as they started their life together. Standing under the *chupah* with my father beside me, and Menachem and Uri facing us, my body began to feel weightless and I grabbed my father's elbow for support. He put his arm around my shoulder and drew me close.

All of a sudden, I could feel Menachem's eyes focused intensely on me. His gaze seemed to be summoning me, drawing me toward him like a magnet. But I was afraid to look up. I kept my head bowed, as if in prayer. What was happening? I felt as though Tsipora had cast a spell on me. Was she some kind of magician, or conjurer?

The rabbi started to chant the Seven Blessings that would conclude the wedding ceremony. By the sixth blessing, everyone in the crowd began to clap and sing along. Then Arthur stepped on the glass. There was a loud bang, and everyone shouted, "Mazel tov!"

I finally raised my head and saw Menachem's half-moon eyes crinkled and glowing as he clapped and sang along. Returning his gaze, I suddenly had an irrepressible desire to kiss those eyes. But of course I didn't do it. Instead, I just imagined myself doing so. And I knew at that moment that I would continue to imagine it for the entire duration of the year. That is, until I could return to Israel the following summer with the hope of making it a reality.

ACKNOWLEDGEMENTS

I would first like to extend my sincere thanks to my publishers at the New Jewish Press, Malcolm Lester and Andrea Fochs Knight, whose faith in *Come Back for Me* has been unwavering. I am truly honoured that they chose my novel as the NJP's inaugural fiction offering. I also had the added pleasure of working closely with Andrea as my manuscript editor. Her sharp eye, keen attention to detail, and wise advice were invaluable in making the novel ready to greet the world.

In addition, I would like to thank two other members of the NJP staff: associate publisher Robin Roger and publicist Geneva Bokowski, who both worked hard at laying the groundwork for the book's public debut.

I don't even know how to begin to thank my agent, Amaryah Orenstein. Her encouragement, expertise, and unflagging determination to make things right for me helped get me through each step of the publication process. I'm not sure I could have done it without her.

I would also like to pay tribute to Nora Gold, whose esteemed journal *jewishfiction.net* has made such an enormous contribution to the advancement of Jewish literature. A special thank you goes to Nora for recently publishing an excerpt from *Come Back for Me* in a stand-alone issue of the journal. I am deeply grateful for the honoured place she's given my work.

There are many friends and family members who deserve my thanks, but they are too numerous to mention by name. However, I must make mention of two friends who, at an early stage of writing this novel, kindly offered to critique a first draft of the manuscript: Judy Shaviv (z"l) and Evelyne Michaels. I will always be grateful for their incisive comments; they helped shape the novel at a point when it needed all the help it could get!

I also received support from several individuals in the publishing industry who believed in this manuscript and worked hard at helping me along the way: Marly Rusoff and Laura Gross. I hope they know how much I appreciate their help.

I would also like to thank several other publishing professionals who played a role in helping me rethink some key elements of the novel: Gail Hochman, Kevin Hanson, and Stephen Barbara.

A special thank you is reserved for my dear friend and critique partner, Suri Rosen. Suri's enormous skill as an editor is only surpassed by her talent as a writer. Without her, I am certain that the novel would not be in the shape it is in today.

Most of all, my deepest thanks goes to my best reader of all: my husband, Ken. He read every word in this novel, many times over, and then some. He was at my side during each stage of the writing and publishing process, comforting me in my moments of despair and cheering me on when everything finally fell into place. I am so grateful for his patience, wisdom, and especially his love. He made me feel that I could succeed even when I doubted it the most. With him by my side, I can almost believe it.

Sharon Hart-Green received her PhD in Judaic Studies from Brandeis University and has taught Hebrew and Yiddish literature at the University of Toronto. She is the author of two scholarly works, *Not A Simple Story*, a study of the work of Hebrew novelist S. Y. Agnon, and *Bridging the Divide*, a compilation of her translations of the Hebrew poems of Hava Pinhas-Cohen. Her short stories, poems, translations, and reviews have appeared in a number of publications, including *The Jewish Quarterly* and *The Jewish Review of Books*. *Come Back for Me* is her first novel.

17 18 19 20 21 · 5 4 3 2 1